SHADOW TRADES

A BARRY ROSEN NOVEL

MITCH STERN

Copyright © 2025 by Mitchell I. Stern, LLC.

All rights reserved.

No part of this book may be reproduced in any form or by any electronic or mechanical means, including information storage and retrieval systems, without written permission from the author, except for the use of brief quotations in a book review.

Ten Hut Media
tenhutmedia.com

This is a work of fiction. Names, characters, businesses, places, events and incidents are either the products of the author's imagination or used in a fictitious manner. Any resemblance to actual persons, living or dead, or actual events is purely coincidental.

ISBN: 978-1-96400-716-8 (Paperback)

ALSO BY MITCH STERN

The Barry Rosen Series

Shadow Trades

Shadow's Children

Standalone Thriller

The Resident Agent

Non-fiction

A Prosecutor's Guide to Radiological and Nuclear Crimes (ed. & contributor, UNICRI 2024)

To find out more about Mitch's books, visit:

severnriverbooks.com/collections/mitch-stern

For Linda: a scholar and teacher, librarian and advocate, and fine sister-in-law who holds thirteen votes for "World's Greatest Aunt."

Then came Amalek, who fought Israel in Rephidim. And Moses said to Joshua: "Choose men, and fight with Amalek..." [a]nd Joshua discomfited Amalek and his people with the edge of the sword....And [Moses] said: "... the Lord will have war with Amalek from generation to generation."

    Exodus 17:8-16

PROLOGUE

Newark, New Jersey, 1939

The door of the hideout slammed open, helped along by a gust of autumn wind, letting in the rain and the gray and the cold.

"Lads, no need to stand up—I'll be in the area all day!" A mountain of a man dwarfed the doorway, his barrel-chested torso crowned by a large head. He doffed his brown fedora with a swing of his arm, spraying collected rainwater high and wide. A gaggle of complaints took flight from a group of men playing bridge in their shirtsleeves at one end of a battered dining room table.

"At ease lads, a little rain won't hurt you!" Big Meyer, the walking mountain, bellowed. "In the Great War, it rained on us all the time and we still smashed the sour-krauts. And it wasn't this wonderful American rain. No, it was that stinking European rain—"

The players put down their cards and joined in with Big Meyer, shouting in unison: "Cold even in summer!"

"Amusing, lads, very amusing!" Big Meyer replied with a smile.

"Shut the door!" Little Meyer shouted as he pan-fried pork chops over a hot plate. "Will you shut the damn door?!"

Teenaged Bernie Rosenbaum staggered into the hideout, struggling under the weight of a Thompson submachine gun, a Browning Automatic Rifle, and a Springfield 1903 bolt-action rifle, all of which he carried cradled in his arms. An olive drab duffle bag, faded almost to khaki, dragged down his right shoulder where it swung on a wide canvas strap. He managed to close the door with his foot before lurching across the room. The clunk of stock butts hitting the floor echoed around the room in the momentary silence as Bernie propped up the rifles with their barrels on the end of the table, opposite the card players.

He removed his slouch cap and hung it on a chair, combing his thick, mouse-brown hair with stiff fingers. Intelligent dark brown eyes absorbed the world over defined cheekbones. He wiped snot from under his nose, which was otherwise conventional but for a bump on the downward slope. The boy needed to grow into his ears, but a strong chin already anchored his face.

The hideout made Bernie happy. Little Meyer and his gang operated out of the unimproved rear section of Reb Shenkler's bookstore. The moldy smell of religious tomes seeped in from the front and mingled with the delicious odor of fatty frying meat. The men in this room were his world. He ran errands for them. Cleaned their weapons. Cherished their banter. The most important part of Bernie's life took place over the bare concrete floor of the shop's back room.

"Boys," Little Meyer announced, "we'll be eating soon. Meyer, some pork chops?"

"No *treyf*, you *shaygets*," Big Meyer boomed, using the Yiddish words for unfitness and unbeliever, before lowering his voice. "I need to talk to you about Bernie."

Bernie's ears perked up.

"You're too religious, Big. It's 1939, for Pete's sake," Little said.

"I'm too religious? You're the one who won't eat with the Eye-talians. If you're so modern that you left our religion behind, why ain't we eating with them? They invited us to eat over at Spatola's. You got us meeting them in a garage. Why are you slaving over a hot plate?"

"I may eat *treyf*, but I'll be damned if I eat it in front of them dago bastards. Leave that to Longy. By the way, I got you some chicken. It's in the icebox. What about the kid?"

Abe piped up from the card game. "Longy Zwillman, traitor extraordinaire. He pays his *tzedakah* to the Pope, like the Vatican even needs charity."

"I don't think you get it." Big Meyer leaning in. "The kid's a natural. We been at Anselm's farm all day. He can hit anything with those rifles. He makes the Thompson dance—dance I tell you! Them pistols, too. Even hand-to-hand. He drives like he was born to it."

"He was. His pop drives," Little said. "I mean, what's he eatin'?"

"Oh yeah, his pop drives," Big sneered. "Smell the coffee. The kid does a good job around here. We can take him on."

"Look, this racket ain't for a smart guy like him. He needs to finish school. Your boys are in school; Jerry is gonna graduate this year. Hell, Abe's kid is down in Trenton at the State Teachers College."

"That's my Jerry and Abe's son. You think Bernie's pop is paying for Princeton University, maybe? If we don't take him on, I don't know what he'll do." Big Meyer stood up straight, put a neutral expression on his face, and gazed down at his fingernails. "He could go with Longy."

"He ain't goin' with that *gonif*!" Little yelled, throwing his fork. It hit the frying pan and bounced onto the floor.

Bernie popped out of his chair and ran to pick it up. Masterstroke, he thought. Little Meyer hated Longy Zwillman, a Jewish goodfella who had taken up with the La Cosa Nostra, the all-American mob dominated, run, and controlled by Italians.

Bernie handed the fork to Little Meyer and tried to look innocent. The leader of the gang glared severely at the boy.

Then his face softened. He took the fork and slapped Bernie hard enough for the slap to be heard but not hard enough to hurt. Little, struggling against his own face, cracked a thin smile.

"You want some pork chops?" Little asked him.

Bernie glanced up at Big, who shook his head slightly.

"No sir," Bernie said, although the wonderful smell triggered rumbling in his teenage stomach.

"Oh, great, just what we need. Another shooter who don't do jobs on *Shabbos*," Little Meyer moved the frying meat with the fork. "You been palling with Big too much. You be careful or he'll get you circumcised again. You know what's going on tonight?"

"A little."

"We're gonna sign a treaty with Richie the Boot. We're gonna keep the Third Ward and they'll get the rest of Newark. We don't need to get in bed with them dagos like Longy. The Third Ward is Jewish, and we're the Jewish gang who's going to keep it right. They mind their business, and we'll mind ours."

"Dutch tried to be independent," Abe murmured, squinting at his cards. "They shot him and his boys dead, you know."

"Oh, very funny," Little replied. "Dutch was crazy. I ain't bugs. By the way, Abe, you think you can lead this gang better? Like by a business executive? Maybe you want to take over? Well?"

"No Boss, I was just making an observation."

"Well, observe your cards." Little inspected Bernie with a critical eye. "You join up with us, you're going to need something to wear." Little Meyer pulled a thick wad of rolled bills out of his pocket. He thumbed past larger denominations until he came to the twenties. He stripped off three and held them out. "Quick run over to Gosdorfer's and tell the little guy with the loose teeth I sent you. Tell him you want a suit, two shirts, two pair ah trousers, two ties and a decent hat, and I said you better get it like yesterday. Meet us back here later. This is a loaner; you gotta start earning, *farshteyn*?"

"Yes, sir. I understand."

"Good. Get over there before they close. Go on, get outta here."

Big grinned, winked, and nodded in the direction of the door. Bernie snatched the money and started running. Laughter and shouts of congratulations chased him outside.

Bernie sprinted through crowds of people surging through the wet gloom—the rain had stopped! What a great night, he thought as he ran. He could not believe he was in Little Meyer's gang. He was somebody! He rounded a corner and smacked so hard into three boys his own age that they all tumbled to the ground.

Bernie jumped up, ready to fight, and got a good look at his potential adversaries. They wore dark suits and white shirts, their Sabbath best. Clearly, they were religious schoolboys from the *yeshiva*.

It was Friday. The crowds were at peak high tide. As people finished their shopping, they would recede home for the candle lighting marking the start of the Sabbath and then walk to Synagogue. With sunset imminent, the shops would close and the streets would empty momentarily. Bernie remembered his *cheder* and his religious schoolteacher's exhortation to always keep the Sabbath and the *mitzvot*.

"You fellas ought to watch where you're going," he counseled, feeling magnanimous toward them since he was one of Little Meyer's guys now and kind of in charge.

Then he dashed away.

Bernie forced his way into Gosdorfer's as the tide of people surged out. Up on the second floor, he tried to engage the tailors in conversation, minding his manners, but they ignored him. All at once, he had had enough.

"You," Bernie called out sharply, pointing to the old guy with loose teeth, "Little Meyer sent me. Let's get crackin'. Stop holding me up, it's Friday."

After the apologies, he was measured and fitted in a flash. Someone fetched him a cup of coffee while the alterations were made on a suit off the rack.

Bernie left in a blue pinstripe jobby with a white shirt and a subdued blue tie, the kind the tailors knew Little preferred, with assurances the balance would be ready tomorrow. They gave him change from one of the twenties. Bernie paused to examine the overcoats. Winter was coming, after all.

Maybe later, he thought.

Bernie snapped the brim of his new fedora and stepped out into the city, heading deeper into the Third Ward. Night had come on strong. The crowds on the street had thinned. Bernie knew many of the men were at *shul* and their women were home "making *Shabbos*."

Not his own father, though. Pop's usual Friday night routine consisted of staying out late, getting tanked, and losing his paycheck to Little Meyer's bookies.

His mother would be home, "making *Shabbos*" as best she could. There would still be a meal on the table, but no candles or finery like in most of the other apartments. At least he could show off his sharp clothes and eat with her. His mother would fawn over the suit. Not much else would get through to her, now or ever again, it seemed.

He entered the tenement where they lived and started up the stairs. With his newfound status, he would have to steer clear of his father for a few days, which would be no problem tonight. Mom would be in, singing to herself.

Bernie strolled through the front door of their one-bedroom apartment. It opened into the kitchen. Dirty dishes filled the sink and grime stained the floor. A surprise! His father sat in state, ruling from the cheap table with a glass of schnapps instead of a scepter. His mother, Pesha, hung off his father; she was a small, thin bird-like woman, the shiner over her left eye turning from saffron to purple. She rocked back and forth. Her lips moved soundlessly.

"What in the hell is this?" his father yelled.

Isadore Rosenbaum rose to his towering five feet six inches. His arms protruded from rounded shoulders and a sunken chest. His fleshy belly jiggled with rage.

"What in the goddamned hell is this?" Isadore's spittle flew. "You look like a gangster-whoremonger! You one o'them gangster-whoremongers now?"

"Dad—"

"This is all your goddamned fault!" Isadore shouted at Pesha, bringing his right hand to his left ear.

Bernie knew the gesture well. His father meant to strike his mother across her face with a terrible backhand blow.

No more, Bernie thought. He was with Little Meyer now. He knew Little would not put up with this for a minute. Bernie had two inches on his father. More importantly, he had lots of days with Big Meyer out at the farm. Big had shown him punches, straights, crosses, and roundhouses. He had shown Bernie how to block and weave, fall, throw, and roll. He had taught him the knife. And Bernie had a rage all his own.

He shoved his father. The old man proved quicker than expected and tagged Bernie with a solid punch to the nose. Bernie hit Isadore with two crackling jabs, stunning the old man, and followed up with a right cross to the jaw that sapped the strength from his father's legs. In slow motion, he sagged to the floor, a confused look on his face.

"Oh, oh, oh!" Pesha shouted. She tried to negotiate her way through the cramped space to Isadore, but she tripped over a chair and fell on top of him.

"Get the hell off me, you rummy bitch!"

"You two slay me, you know that?" Bernie had reached the end of his rope. He was with Little Meyer now. There was no reason he had to put up with the drinking, yelling, and fisticuffs of his home life anymore.

He walked out.

Bernie cleaned up in the restroom of a coffee shop outside the Third Ward, dabbing a wet napkin on the blood staining his tie and wiping more blood from under his nose. The waitress sat him at a small table, and he settled his mind over a cup of black coffee. When she came around with a refill, he ordered a plate of meatloaf and potatoes. He finished and threw down a twenty-five-cent tip without a care, smiling at his magnanimity.

He wandered back to the hideout. Reb Shenkler had long since closed up and gone home. Bernie fiddled with the locked rear door, then quit. He would have to wait for the gang outside.

The temperature dropped. Bernie could see his breath as he waited, leaning against the cold bricks. The row homes on the block glowed with warm yellow light. Sabbath candles burned in some of the windows. He pulled his new suit jacket snug and folded his arms across his chest.

Thoughts of his parents crowded into his mind. They had lived in a row house of their own when Bernie was little, but one day, they had abruptly moved to the apartment. His father added gambling to his drinking and beating to his yelling. His mother receded from life, slowly and certainly.

He wrestled with the idea of walking over to the First Ward in case the former adversaries, the gangs led by Richie the Boot and Little Meyer, had signed a deal and were celebrating. On the one hand, he had not been invited. On the other, icicles were growing on his nuts.

The hell with it, he thought. Little Meyer's men don't dither, so he headed on over.

The Italian neighborhood bustled with activity. Big Meyer had mentioned Spatola's and a garage. There were several garages in the vicinity of Spatola's restaurant. No one paid Bernie any attention. The treaty must have gone through, he convinced himself. No member of Little Meyer's gang would be able to saunter so freely in Richie's territory unless it had.

At Spatola's, Friday night packed 'em in like sardines. Bernie cupped his hands around his eyes, leaned on the front window and searched for his friends. He didn't see anyone he knew, but he couldn't see all the way anyway. He randomly picked the throughfare heading east out of the nearby intersection and peeked inside the first repair shop he came to. Empty. And so it went, shop after shop, until he checked a run-down two-bay filling station set back from a pushcart-wide street five blocks away.

He peered through a cracked pane into a shadowy office area. Light spilled out of the open doorway from the garage. An arm sheathed in a white shirt poking out the end of a suit jacket lay on the floor. The pale hand rested palm-up, thumb and fingers slightly curled. Dread squeezed Bernie's chest, choking off his breath.

He tried the front. No dice. Lifting either bay door would surely attract attention. He walked down the alley between the garage and the neighboring factory. A single lamp on a pole threw a weak yellow spot on Abe's and Big Meyer's cars.

A cold gust rattled the weatherbeaten back door in its frame. Bernie saw rot where the deadbolt met the jamb. He kicked it once, twice, and it swung on the third try. He stepped inside, closing it behind him.

There they were, all seven of them. They had fallen in a neat row and rested in a large common pool of blood. Big lay face-up, his visage an unrecognizable red mass, the back of his cranium peeled open like discarded fruit with bone, fascia, and skin attached to the rind. Forty-five caliber shell casings carpeted the floor by the bay doors. Abe and the rest had been tommy-gunned by a line of shooters. Misses had blown circular chips out of the blood-splattered gray cinder blocks to the rear. Dead men marked the hits.

Little's own .45 had skidded out of the blood puddle, a black pistol with ivory grip panels. They had flipped him over and shot him twice in the forehead.

Blood rushed in Bernie's ears. His heart pounded in his chest. Anger trumped what little teenage judgment he had. These were his friends. Fathers. Older brothers, maybe. Whatever. He loved them.

Bernie would have to do the right thing. He realized he could not possibly get all the Italians, but he would at least get some. Perhaps he would fall in an act of glorious revenge, one of the gang to the end.

Then despair set in. What could he really do, being only a kid? He started to cry. Bernie thought of Big. Big wouldn't be sitting on his keister, bawling like a little girl. He wiped his eyes dry. Big would close this deal, that's what he would do.

The anger came rushing back.

Big liked to say a person could never have enough money. Bernie forced himself to walk into the blood and touch the dead. He went through Little Meyer's pockets and found cash. He searched a few of the other guys, taking their bills. The viscus fluid congealed in the cold and covered his hands. He almost threw up the meatloaf.

Bernie picked up Little's fancy .45. Sliding the magazine out of the handle, he could see Little had managed to fire three times. Good ole' Little. Those Meyers. He would do what they would have done.

Big also liked to say you could never have enough ammunition. Bernie collected Little's extra magazines. Armed with a pistol and a hell of a lot of cash, he hurried toward the exit. He wasn't afraid Richie the Boot's boys would return. He was afraid of the cops showing up, paid or tipped off.

A thought stopped him. Maybe Big would want him to use one of his pistols. Big had never let Bernie shoot his good automatic, the one Big wore on his right hip, so he left that one alone. Big always had him shoot the old one he carried in the small of his back, however. After much grunting and pulling, he got the old pistol and more magazines. The process made him want to cry again.

He steeled his resolve. He would have kissed Big on his forehead, had any of it remained. Instead, Bernie knelt by his side. Embarrassment spurred him to glance around, but he lifted one of Big's hands to his lips and kissed the knuckles of the only man who had ever given a damn about him. He put it down neatly and backed out of the garage.

Some of Richie the Boot's gang must be at Spatola's, he thought; it was popular with them and a good place to start.

Bernie loped to the restaurant. The crowd had thinned somewhat. He studied the customers through the plate glass, hunting for some of Richie's guys. A bar extended along one side and heaping family-style platters of food were hitting white linen throughout the narrow eatery.

Earlier, the trade was three-deep at the bar and filled every seat. Now, despite active drinkers and many diners, there was room enough. Hate kept Bernie focused. He concentrated on the clientele, table by table. As the last member of Little's gang, he knew what he had to do.

He thought he caught a glimpse of one of Richie's guys in the back. The thrill of the hunt fueled the fury in his heart. Bernie didn't think, he acted.

A floor captain stopped him at the door and told him they were committed for the rest of the night. Bernie maintained eye contact with the man but couldn't come up with a next move. Then he remembered something Big used to do. Big taught him when the guy at the door gets a hefty tip, he lets the bartender and waiters know they've got a real butter-and-eggs man on the hook. He gave the floor captain one of the bills from his pocket without looking at the denomination.

"Just the bar," Bernie said.

"Yes, sir!"

Once inside, he took in the rest of the restaurant. Murals of the old country—Venetian gondolas, hills with funny pine trees, the Coliseum—were painted on the walls. Half-high russet wood paneling and brass accents were set off by burgundy curtains and a black-and-white checkered floor. Bernie thought he saw two more members of Richie's gang, heads together at the bar, but he wasn't positive.

"Get anything for you, sir?" a bartender inquired over the heads of other patrons.

Sure enough, the guy Bernie had seen from the window was one of Richie's. He was big and fat, laughing robustly, food in his open mouth. One corner of a napkin was jammed into the collar of his shirt. He playfully hit the man next to him on the arm with a fist grasping a fork full of veal. A new round of laughter burst forth. Bernie recognized the other two as Richie's guys as well. One of the four had his back to Bernie.

"Hey, we were here first!" a patron cried, objecting to the attention the bartender was paying to Bernie.

"Make room there, you," the bartender ordered. "Okay, what would you like?"

"Beer," Bernie said. Then, to avoid a confrontation, he added, "And drinks for my friends," gesturing at the man who had yelled at the bartender. He had seen Big do that once.

"Mighty good of you, my boy," the man said, disarmed completely. "Ain't you a little young to be in here?"

Bernie slapped a bill on the bar and took his beer. He sipped at it to cover his checking around. He could not see any more men he recognized as members of Richie's gang, just the four eating and the possible two at the bar.

His nervous yearning for murder dissipated and he could breathe again. He knew what he had to do. Big always told him he had to keep his mind on the job at hand.

"Anyway, thanks for the drink, buddy. I'm Angelo."

Bernie's mood shifted again. He wanted to bolt from the Spatola's and run home, except he could not go home. Before, he could have at least gone to the hideout. Now he couldn't even go there. Little and the gang had been his friends; he had been one of them. Now he had no one.

He became dangerously angry again.

"Buddy, I said I'm Angelo. Who're you? I like to know who I'm drinking with."

Big Meyer had told Bernie to always have a plan. His plan was to shoot the four diners and then make like a tree and leaf. He'd escape past the guys at the door on speed alone. Even mad, Bernie realized he could not look for more members of Richie's gang after he'd shot the first members. He would have to run hard to stay alive and maybe try for more the next night.

"I said—"

"See you later, alligator." Bernie weaved his way through the tables until he faced the fat man. A second man sat to Bernie's left. The other two were on his right.

"Wha' choo want?" the fat man asked.

Big had always taught him not to grandstand, repeating the lesson so often that sometimes he heard it in his sleep: "Make the deal and hit the road, lad." Well, school was out, and Big would have to forgive him this one time.

"I'm with Meyer's gang."

"Hey, get a load of this kid!" the fat man yelled, laughing. "What gang? There ain't no Meyers no more. We took care o' dat. Get the hell outta here—"

Bernie pulled both pistols out of his waistband and trained them on the fat man, who froze in shock, mouth open mid-chew, his food-laden fork stopping halfway to his face.

Bernie fired. The resulting roar drowned out the noise of the restaurant. The fat man fell over backward. Using the .45 in his left hand, Bernie shot the man on his left in the face.

He tried to get both pistols pointed at the man on his immediate right, but that man started to get up and reach for his own weapon. Instead, Bernie hammered his pate with the barrel of the Colt in his right hand, knocking the man into his seat. Then he spun his left arm across his own body and shot the fourth man, the one on the far right, in the chest.

That brought his hands into alignment, and he fired at the man on the far right again with both pistols. The double impact jerked the man in his chair. Bernie stepped back and discharged another double volley at the man shaking off the effects of his pistol-whipping. Two rounds hit the man in the side of the head, spraying brains and blood.

Silence filled Spatola's and cordite hung in the air. Bernie's ears rang. He remembered he needed to run, but people traumatized to torpidity blocked the way to the door. He raised his Colts and parted the crowd like the prophet for an angry deity. However, the two gangsters he had seen at the bar were on course to intercept him.

They clearly had not been taught by Big: they moved together as they drew their weapons, upper arms touching, making an attractive target. Big would have told them to spread out. Bernie let loose with his Colts and the two men fell away. He cleared the door and joined the people on the sidewalk, then, scurrying to the corner, he slowed to a purposeful walk.

Bernie tossed the guns into a trash-strewn alley, immune to the prevailing rush of the curious, looking down the whole time. The ringing in his ears subsided, and the taste of gunpowder faded. He followed an almost innate desire to head for the Ironbound neighborhood, where the Portuguese mob held their own against Richie the Boot. The cold invaded his arms and legs. He had lost his new hat somewhere along the way.

Eventually, he crossed under some railroad tracks running on a viaduct constructed of massive grayish-black granite stones. He thought of trains. Did he need to run farther than out of the First Ward? Maybe. Maybe if he stuck around, Richie's gang or their paid coppers would find him before sunup. He followed the line north to Pennsylvania Station.

"Where to?" the thin old clerk at the ticket counter asked.

That was a damn good question, Bernie thought. He wanted to ask someone, but then he remembered that he was alone. A passenger waiting in the wooden pews read a paper. War news dominated the front page: German threats, French initiatives.

"Mister, we ain't got all night," the clerk said.

The Canucks were in the war. He would go to Canada and join up to kill sour-krauts. Big fought in the Great War. Hell, Hitler and Mussolini were buddies. Maybe he would get another crack at some dagos. That was the ticket, all right. He would enlist in the Canadian army and go to war.

"Canada."

"Can you narrow it down a little, professor? It's a big country, Canada is."

The wind rocked the wooden car as it sped down the rails, flying north along the Hudson River. Bernie rested his head on the window. Chilled, he turned up his collar.

What had he done? What the hell had he done? He had killed maybe six guys, definitely four. What the hell had he done?

Regret for his actions increased until the loss of Big Meyer and the other men crashed into his consciousness and knocked the remorse away. Them Eye-talians had played, so they had to pay, he told himself. Those fools left one of the gang alive. They thought they had gotten all of them, but they hadn't. No matter what, Bernie would be one of Little's guys forever. Tonight, he had proven it.

Sleep pulled at him; his limbs grew heavy. His situation didn't look good, even though he had almost eight hundred dollars in his pocket. As far as he knew, agents of the FBI, the G-men, would get him at the border. He should do something about his name. A new moniker was necessary to beat this rap. He pondered the problem as the train rolled through the night.

It came to him in a flash of the insight available to him, his not having graduated from high school or travelled farther out of Newark's First Ward than the Passaic River for a summer swim.

"Barry Rosen," he said, testing it.

That was the cat's meow, all right. No one would ever know he was the First Ward Shooter, or even that he was Jewish, probably.

1

The line of dead men in the Newark Garage, an image from six hard years ago, jolted Barry Rosen awake. He was riding shotgun in the cab of a deuce-and-a-half, as the large olive drab army trucks were commonly called. Leoshan, an American Negro soldier, drove fast. The bright sun, surrounding verdant forest and the cold cobalt of the Bavarian sky caused the dream about the gang to fade. Giddiness came upon Barry; he felt glad to have made it this far, to the autumn of 1945.

Lots of guys hadn't.

Barry had chosen to wear his dress greens on his first ride to the camp, without a coat. He should have known better. Leo had the canvas top down. It was okay for him, he wore a field jacket and a green wool hat with its small brim in front. Still, Barry enjoyed being alive to feel the cold. He remembered another cold ride, on a train, late at night, his run from Newark six years prior.

He had ridden, walked, and sailed a lot of miles since then.

His thoughts returned to the moment. The logistics of his move from Munich to Furstflarn, a borough nestled in the foothills of the Alps and nearest the camp, had been a real pain in the neck, but at least he was settled now. Two members of his gang from Austria were here also. They had gotten a place of their own and were, he hoped, looking for a suitable warehouse, as opposed to sampling whores, which Barry knew to be their preferred pastime.

There was the nightclub, too.

The layout of modern Furstflarn had been influenced by Munich. The central squares carried the same names, *Marienplatz*, or Mary's Square. A similar memorial column rose in the middle as well. Barry didn't know or care who had engineered the civic plagiarism or what the column commemorated. Probably some German-sponsored European slaughter pre-dating the one he had recently managed to survive.

The *rathaus, burgermeister*'s bureau and a large domed church bordered the square. Four- and five-floor apartment buildings roofed with red terracotta tiles made up the surrounding neighborhood, with residential and commercial districts radiating outward. The rail station, with its one line to Munich, was to the west of *Marienplatz*.

After he had moved his personal gear and his small gang to the area, Barry had gone to Munich to meet Leo, Staff Sergeant Washington's man, on his return from a Switzerland run. They'd found each other at the depot yesterday and had spent the night on the town, such as it was in October, 1945, then had left before dawn. He didn't want any of Washington's men to know exactly where he lived. Washington was his partner in a black-market racket and they got along, but one never knew when the play would turn to shit. Barry directed Leo to the entrance of the nightclub and had him note its location, after which they drove to the camp.

The gates were open.

"I guess this is it, Mr. Barry," Leo said, stopping in front of a two-story clapboard building with white paint peeling off in sheets.

"I guess so too," Barry reflected, not altogether impressed.

In the years since his flight from Newark, he had grown into his ears and reached his adult height of five feet eight inches. He thought he cut a lean, fit figure in his new greens, a uniform that an accommodating hausfrau in Austria had tailored perfectly. Barry wore his mouse-brown hair pursuant to army regulations and a white pinstripe scar ran down his jawline from left ear to chin, which he thought helped age his youthful countenance. Despite six years of war, he was not yet twenty-four.

Barry climbed down from the cab and walked around to the driver's side.

"Thanks for running me out here. You've got the package for Staff Sergeant Washington?" Barry rubbed his hands together to warm them up.

"Sure do," Leo grinned slyly.

Barry grinned back.

"You did good on the Switzerland run. Otto told me he was very impressed." Barry pulled a small roll of US currency out of his pocket, not script, the fake cash the Occupation authorities issued. On principle, he didn't want to be caught holding any when the big shots decided it wasn't worth anything anymore. Practically, he never gave script to his friends, either. He held the real money out to Leo. "A bonus. For you."

"Why thank you for sure, Mr. Barry."

"Lots more jobs needing to be done right coming down the road. I'll be keeping you in mind."

"Sure, sure. You need me to wait on you? For the ride back?"

"I'll be okay. Tell the others I'll meet up with them tonight on the street outside the club. Tell the Staff Sergeant I'll be in touch."

Leoshan revved the engine and left in a cloud of dirt and fumes. Beyond the wire of the Gaufering Displaced Persons Camp, formerly the Gaufering Slave Labor Camp, peaceful fields rolled in front of the picture-perfect town in the distance. The backdrop of undulating forest stretched out under a cloudless sky and the angular snow-covered peaks of the Alps dominated the southern horizon. Barry knew the clear air made them appear closer than they were. Nothing is ever as it seems, he thought.

He slipped inside. Displaced persons wearing dull dresses and mismatched suits pressed against a counter of rough, warped wood and vigorously complained about small issues to a staff of other displaced persons, in comparable garb, manning the barricade. Based on bureaucratic instincts finely tuned by years of army service, Barry concluded little was accomplished here. Guessing camp authority had something to do with the staircase on the right, he climbed.

A room came into view at the top of the stairs, and he walked through the open door as if he owned the place. A layer of dense dust started where the unevenly plastered walls met the scuffed and gouged wood floor and faded upward. A smaller square office had been built into a far corner, seemingly as an afterthought. Bright light streamed in through bare windows.

"But Rivka, you could come with me. To America," a short, pudgy American army corporal was saying. "It's a better life there, not like here in Europe." He held up a diamond ring as he spoke to a petite woman in her early twenties.

"I do not know, Howie. I...can't..." she stammered, looking at the ground, her accented English failing her. Retreating, she bumped the front of her desk.

The woman glanced up and locked eyes with Barry. Her thick black hair fell in ringlets that she had gathered at the nape of her neck. She wore a threadbare cardigan over a washed-out summer print dress of blues and yellows and her bare legs ended at a pair of worn but sensible brown shoes.

Her pale skin fit tight across the bones of her face, creating an almost macabre effect, except for lively dark eyes. Her eyes grabbed him and held on as she met his gaze. He could have studied her all day, but he forced his attention to the rest of the room.

To Barry's left, three men huddled together at a table in front of one large open volume. The diminutive man in the middle, gray-haired, skull-capped and improbably old considering recent history, examined him with rheumy eyes peering out over a matted beard. Barry nodded at the old man, who made like a statue as his two younger compatriots flanking him fidgeted over the book.

"But Rivka, you have to know this is my last day. I have to leave for Munich after my replacement gets here. You could give a boy an answer," the corporal pleaded.

"She already has, Corporal," Barry interrupted. "Besides, you might want to try nylons; they will get you further than a ring she can't eat or burn."

This boy was completely inept. If an American couldn't get a local to marry him in post-war Europe, he just plain wasn't trying. Double true for displaced girl-type persons.

"And just who in the heck are you?" the corporal asked, in a high-pitched whiney voice, before noticing the stripes.

"Technical Sergeant Barry Rosen, United States Army," he replied calmly but with hard authority. His arms bore the weight of large chevrons, three gold stripes pointing up, a small field of black, and two rounded stripes down, commonly referred to as rockers.

"I'm sorry, Sergeant. Um, I'm Howie Epstein, I—"

"Howie?" Barry's question stopped the corporal dead, his forehead wrinkling as he concentrated.

The corporal wore his own pair of stripes on each arm and one row of give-away ribbons over his left breast pocket, making him a chair-borne commando, soft and scared.

"Oh, I mean Corporal Epstein. I'm the chief administrative officer here—"

"Clerk."

"I'm sorry?"

"You're a clerk. A clerk who don't know enough to give nylons, then diamonds. Your girl's legs are cold. Ain't you leaving today?"

"I...yes, Technical Sergeant."

"Why don't you show me the camp before you go?"

Howie stared dumbly, eyes unfocused, lower lip sagging. Barry didn't care for these Remington Raiders, boys who had sat out the fighting in warm offices.

"Now would be good," Barry said.

"Oh!" the corporal squawked. He crossed to a third table, one covered with papers and ledgers.

"Do I got to guess who these guys are?"

Howie gestured at the old man. "This is Rav Hirsch, *Rosh Yeshiva* of *Yeshiva Beis Rashi*. He was—"

"What's his game?" Barry squinted at the old man bundled up in the ratty black overcoat.

"He's a great rabbi. He learns. My father—"

"Good morning, Grandfather." Barry tapped the book with a smile. "Keep reading."

"Here are students of his who survived the camps," Howie continued, referring to the men in their mid-twenties on either side of the great rabbi. "Rav Hirsch has just given them *smicha*."

"Huh?"

"*Smicha*? The rav has ordained them as rabbis themselves, but they are still learning. This is Pinchas Shammi, Sergeant," Howie indicated the junior rabbi on the left, a tall, skeletal, hawk-faced man wearing a fedora, a brown jacket torn at the shoulder, and a dingy white shirt. "And here is Shimshon Gutkin." Gutkin's pleasant features were already softening and rounding due to the healthy diet brought about by the end of the war. He had a spotty beard growing in haphazardly and wore a skull cap and a once-white shirt made seedy with repeated washings.

"What are they supposed to be doing around here?"

"Why, I let them learn with the rav."

"Okay. Who's your honey?"

"My honey? Oh. This is Rivka Shapiro, Ambassador Resnick's secretary."

The girl evaluated Barry without expression. Her neck was all muscle, sinew and veins. This time, he didn't turn away. Finally, she dropped her eyes while guiding a stray ringlet behind her ear with thin fingers. Overall, she had no more substance than a sparrow, except for her breasts, their shape apparent through her otherwise baggy clothing. He found the contrast captivating, but there was work to be done.

"All right Corporal, what is it you do all day?" Barry moved to the cluttered surface he figured was Howie's desk.

"I track supplies for the camp, arrange for and record maintenance, handle administration for the displaced persons, DPs we call 'em, and other personnel and organize the care packages," Howie said, with an air of great importance. "I order—"

"I got it. Where are the records?"

"I use these journals." Howie rooted through the loose papers and pulled out a large cloth-bound accounting ledger. "This one for supplies, this one for aid, and displaced persons in this one."

"Where do you secure the files for the army personnel assigned here?"

"What army personnel? It's only me, and my file is at the depot in Munich. I need to swing by there today."

Good, Barry thought. Only one dogface, just as he had heard.

"You know, Sergeant, no one informed us you would be here," Howie remarked.

"Well here I is. Corporal."

"So! Today is the day!" A trim man in his mid-thirties, American, stepped into the office area. "Isn't that right, Howie?" Dapper in a navy pinstripe suit, bright white shirt, and shined leather shoes, his face neatly shaved and hair combed, the man smiled and waited for a reply.

Rivka and the three religious men stood. "Good morning, Mr. Ambassador," they chimed simultaneously.

"Oh, really, sit down all of you," Dapper Dan said, with what struck Barry as false modesty. "Do we have something to celebrate?"

"Mr. Ambassador, may I introduce Technical Sergeant Rosen, my replacement? Sergeant Rosen, Ambassador Jeremy Resnick."

"Replacement? What replacement? My God, Sergeant, did you win the war single handedly?"

"Sir?"

"Your uniform. Some people say I'm an expert in military heraldry. A Bronze Star with an oak leaf cluster, a Purple Heart, also with clusters, and two more rows of the rest of the lesser decorations, correct?"

"Yes, sir." What a goofball, Barry thought. "Heraldry my ass," he wanted to say. This nancy-boy should have earned some himself if they impressed him so much.

"A Combat Infantryman's Badge and American Jump Wings on the right and, oh my, what are those? British Airborne Wings?"

"Canadian."

"Canadian? I see. And your unit, the 101st Airborne. But what's on your right shoulder? An arrowhead with 'USA' and 'Canada' written on it?"

"Yes sir. The First Special Service Force."

"I've never heard of it. I see. Welcome. I would love to meet with you, however, I'm staying but a moment. Meeting in town, you know. Came by to give my congratulations and dearest regards to Howie and Rivka here."

"Mr. Ambassador, Corporal Epstein made a tactical error and failed to achieve the objective. He'll show me the place and then scat."

"Howie, what does he mean?"

"I'll be leaving by myself, Mr. Ambassador," a crushed Howie reported.

"I see." The ambassador's eyes narrowed. "Um, Sergeant? The stripes on your arm? You seem young for that many."

"It was a stepping-down present."

"Stepping-down present?"

"I was a lieutenant. I was commissioned in combat. Temporarily, it turned out. Both me and the army thought it best I come back down to enlisted, considering the war is over and all."

"Interesting, interesting. Well, Howie, stop by on your way out." He entered the corner office and closed the door behind him.

Barry happened to catch Rivka looking at him; they made eye contact, and then she suddenly became absorbed in the papers on her desk. Howie stumbled and mumbled, not sure what to do next.

"Corporal, how about a USO tour of the place?" Barry asked, referencing the type of tour a visiting celebrity would get.

"The USO don't come here, Sergeant."

"Oh? My mistake," Barry said dryly. "Let's go."

Howie drove up and down the camp's rutted dirt roads in a battered jeep that leaned to the left, introducing Barry to the leaders of the camp council and the various groups that had formed inside the fence line. There were religious Zionists on one side, non-religious Zionists on the other, non-religious non-Zionists and religious non-Zionists here and there, and even a small band of European assimilationists.

There were four barracks of Eastern Europeans, mostly Poles but others too, Russians even, filled with people who didn't want to return to countries controlled by the Soviets. Their presence was unexpected, he had not heard of them when he selected Gaufering.

Howie's shoulders were slumped, and he fought back tears. He touched Barry's arm at the door leading into the administration building.

"Technical Sergeant?" Howie asked. "Do you think I could hang around for a day or so? I think maybe I startled Rivka this morning. Maybe after a good night's sleep, she'll change her mind."

Barry needed this Remington Raider out of the camp. He didn't give a rat's backside if someone's girl changed her mind. He had picked this specific camp because he would be the sole US soldier in it, and he wanted it that way right now.

"Corporal, what's going to happen tonight is you will track her down and find her with the boy who's taking her 'round the bases. If you choose to sneak up on 'em, you'll hear 'em making fun of what you tried to do today."

"You think she has a boyfriend?" Howie asked.

"You taking her 'round the bases?"

"You wouldn't ask if you knew her."

"Well, somebody is."

"Do you think so?" Howie's confidence in Rivka's virtue dissipated instantly.

Barry kept his face sympathetic but felt like rolling his eyes. "See here, I've been playing baseball all over Austria and Germany since the end of the war. They ain't even sure their men are dead yet. Why is this broad any different? Broads is all the same. You should have given her some nylons and played some ball yourself."

This perspective slackened the corporal's suety face, until some resolve-producing conclusion firmed it up.

"Wait here, Technical Sergeant. I'll just need a minute to get my stuff." Howie charged into the building. He emerged ten minutes later carrying a cardboard suitcase and an olive drab duffle bag, attempting a sarcastic sneer. It came out more sad sack than tough guy. "She wanted to talk to me, but I didn't want to hear it."

"Good for you, Corporal. Get in the jeep." As they drove to town, Barry changed topics. "Buzz is this camp is lousy with the black market."

"Um...um, well...."

"Is there a black-market problem?" Barry asked, faking surprise.

"I wouldn't call it a problem, exactly." Howie worried his hands in front of his stomach against the blustery airstream flowing around the windshield.

"Come on, Corporal. You wouldn't want CID to get the idea you was one of them conspirators, would you?" Inserting the army's Criminal Investigation Division into the conversation was a refined touch, the mark of a true professional.

Howie had panic in his eyes. "Are you going to tell?"

"Tell what? You ain't answered me yet."

"But—"

"If I find out you was involved in shenanigans after you're gone, I'll have to report it straight away. I won't be able to help you."

"But—"

"Goddammit Corporal!"

"Mrs. Levenson controls most of it. She got lots of the goods sewn up. Nobody can get nothing to sell unless they go through her. There is a Russian in supply who stands up to her. He sells out the back door of the supply warehouse."

"That so?"

"Oh, yeah. He sells the relief agency stuff, no questions asked. Problem with him is, he wants cash up front. Mrs. Levenson gives credit, but she wants to know where and how the stuff is going to be sold and such, which a lot of us don't like."

"She trying to control the market out in town?"

"A little. She mostly works the camp. Some of her trade goes out to the Germans, but not much. Truth is, there ain't so much stuff available to sell." Howie paused. "For those of us in the camp, it's the only way to make a dime."

"There's that 'us' again. What's up with you?"

"Up? Nothing, sergeant, but yeah, us. You know…Jews."

"So you don't do nothing about it because you feel bad for Jews?"

"No, Sergeant."

"No, Sergeant?"

"Yes, Sergeant."

Barry figured the corporal thought he had swum into hot water. Best thing for a junior enlisted man to do in those circumstance would be to retreat to a "yes sir, no sir" position.

"Um, Sergeant? You gonna do anything? 'Cause if you are—"

"So they don't like Levenson, either?"

"Not really."

"What does Levenson look like?"

"Huh? Oh, she's big and she's got great big—" here Howie put both of his hands over his chest in the universal male pantomime for breasts.

"You sure do like your sisters with big ones," Barry mused.

Howie's juvenile cheeks flashed red.

"Anyway, what does Resnick say?"

"Nothing. He talks big, but he hasn't said anything to CID."

"Ever see him talking to Levenson?"

"Um, yeah. I've seen them talking."

"What about the Russian?"

"What about him, Sergeant?"

"What about him?" Barry mimicked. "What do you think? Does Resnick talk to him?"

"No, I don't think so. I've never seen them talking. I work mostly in the office, but I've never seen Mr. Resnick there, at supply I mean. I go for him."

Barry glanced away from watching the road. Howie hunched over to use as much of the windshield as possible to block the slipstream.

"Getting cold?" Barry asked.

"Yes, Sergeant."

"Not used to it, are you?"

"No, Sergeant."

Barry all but threw Howie and his bags out of the jeep, barely stopping at the Munich depot. As he drove to Furstflarn, with the wind battering his head and shoulders and once again regretting his lack of a decent jacket, he reviewed the intelligence he had gathered.

This Resnick probably got his piece of the illegal action from the Levenson broad in return for pretending he didn't see it. After Barry got Levenson on the team or took care of her, it seemed like it would be good business to regularly hit Resnick with some payola. He floored the accelerator and pushed the jeep hard.

He parked by his building at sunset and changed into a gray suit and his gray fedora. The club was in the neighborhood, so he set out for it on foot. It took him three false turns before he found the front door, freshly painted in forest green. Barry wondered how Ulrich had managed that as he knocked. A small hatch, two-thirds of the way up, slid open. A lone eye peered out and asked a question in German.

"I got dollars," Barry said in English.

He heard a bolt being thrown and the door swung in. The eye belonged to an old party in shirt sleeves sitting on a stool. Barry tipped him some script and walked through to the bar where he ordered a whiskey and waited.

Dim electric lighting and flickering candles threw shadows on the bare brick of the half-finished interior. Six inches of tobacco smoke abutted the ceiling. A small stage of raw wood had been built along one wall, several feet from a door guarded by a formally dressed thug. Patrons ate and mostly drank while a Victrola spun a record—some Glenn Miller swing, God bless him.

"It is good to see you again this soon," an elegant man said in German-accented Oxbridge English arriving at the same time as a pair of whiskeys. "Somewhat ahead of schedule, yes?"

Ulrich Genscher was ten years older than Barry and taller by almost six inches. His blond hair had been greased down and his shiny brown eyes, normally sharp and attentive, revealed that he had been recently dipping into his own stock. His narrow, colorless lips grinned out from under a well-shaped patrician nose and his lean fit body indicated recent active military service. Tonight, he wore a dark blue suit, striped shirt, and a baby-blue silk necktie.

"Yeah. Where did you get that suit?" Barry's had come from a grateful Austrian widow.

"Its former owner has no further use for it, I'm afraid," Ulrich sighed. "Not the clothes or his wife. So how do you like our fair town of Furstflarn?"

"Not bad. Less damage than Munich. I rented a flat nearby."

"And how do you like the club?"

"Swank. You've done a lot in a short time." Barry turned from the coarse bar to face the main floor. "What's behind the door over there?"

"Gaming," Ulrich smiled slyly.

"You smoothie!"

"Thank you, thank you. None of this would have been possible without you. By the by, how does the camp look?"

"It will work, I think. There ain't any other army personnel and the only other American is the nancy-boy running the place. I'm told he's a former ambassador. I have to see how much trouble the ambassador will be. What are they eating?"

"The American roast beef you sent and German potatoes. Shall we take a table?"

"Right here is fine. I'm famished."

"He is not quite an ambassador," Ulrich said, before instructing the bartender to bring over a plate of the night's offering.

"No?"

"No. He spent the war on some staff at the US embassy in London. The DPs delude themselves about his celebrity."

"You kidding me?"

"Perhaps you do not know? Ah. Word is he wanted the position Isaac Stone was appointed to in Nuremberg. He thought because he was Jewish, he had the job. They offered him this, and his consideration was based on his knowledge of Jew."

"Jew?"

"Sorry, how you say, the language of them?"

"Yiddish?"

"Yes, Yiddish." Ulrich jabbed his cigarette into a cut-down brass artillery shell serving as an ashtray. The bartender placed a steaming plate of food, a cloth napkin and some flatware on the bar. "*Ach*, thank you. Another whiskey for him and one for me, please."

"How do you know all this?" Barry picked up his knife and fork.

"See there?"

The so-called ambassador, the dapper boss of the camp Barry had met earlier, held court across the floor. The aftermath of a meal, including two used plates and an empty bottle of wine, lay in front of him and an adoring young blonde woman hung off his left arm.

"She works for you," Ulrich said.

"Us," Barry replied, emphasizing their partnership.

Ulrich nodded his thanks.

"I'm feeling better about him by the minute. Keep me posted on our ambassador, will you?"

"Of course. After you eat, I would like to introduce you to someone in the gaming room."

Barry finished his rare roast beef, and they took fresh drinks into the gaming room. Three card tables were moderately populated with suckers, their women trying out their post-war finery, drab and sad as it was.

"New dresses to sell would be a big score," Barry whispered. "It's all cards."

"I have commissioned a roulette wheel from a carpenter, and I am teaching the dice game to an accommodating young woman. We will have these things shortly, yes? This way." Ulrich walked toward the leftmost chumps.

"How's our friend the forger?"

"He wanted to live in Munich, not here. He's settled nicely in the rubble."

"Let's get him started on Canadian passports and International Red Cross papers for all of us."

"As you wish."

Barry noticed a man watching him intently from the far wall. He was tall and blond, clearly cold capable muscle. They stopped to watch four people draw cards for blackjack. An older man with a low prehistoric brow, his large head sitting directly on broad sloping shoulders, played farthest away, a slim brunette hovering over him, giggling each time a card hit the green felt.

A young man, an imbecile, participated one spot over. He wore his brown hair, the consistency of straw, parted on the right. The skin of his face was pulled tight over his bone structure, in contrast with the rest of him. His eyes and mouth were slits. His torso had the same general dimensions as a quarter keg of beer and pudgy fingers manipulated his face-down card. He came up to the shoulder of the young buxom woman on his left.

The imbecile asked to be hit. The dealer threw him a deuce, taking him to twelve on the face-up cards. The imbecile held after the next card, showing sixteen. The dealer flipped his hole card and held at twenty. The man with the big head had fifteen. The imbecile reversed a five with quiet satisfaction: twenty-one. After gleefully pulling in his winnings of script and cigarettes, the winner faced Ulrich. They jabbered in German until Ulrich gestured with his burned-down cigarette.

"This is the American I spoke of, Barry Rosen," Ulrich said in English. "Barry, Kurt Speidel."

"Ah, yes. Ulrich and his kind failed to consider the American Jew. Is that not so, Herr Rosen?" Kurt responded with a thick accent and stuck out a fat ugly hand.

"What was that, now?" Barry shook hands, silently admonishing himself for judging a book by its cover.

"The Nazis. They failed to consider the difference between the European Jew and the American kind."

Barry decided to kill Kurt right here. He wasn't going to rehash the "Jewish Question" with any German, much less this freak. The muscle would have to go first, for sure.

"Do not jump to think me bad," Kurt took off his jacket and rolled up a sleeve. A number had been branded on his forearm in black banality of efficient horror. "They put me in Dachau just because I ugly. But I smart, like you. Now I with the former sub-commandant's daughter."

The buxom woman looked incredibly sad. Kurt spat something in German. Her eyes snapped into focus, and she activated a megawatt-bright smile.

"Hello," she articulated slowly.

"That is her English, neither do the others speak it. How about the dealer?"

"No English there," Ulrich verified.

"And your boy on the wall?" Barry asked.

"Please not to worry about him." Kurt opened a gold cigarette tin. "Ulrich says you want to do business in town, Herr Rosen?"

"Call me Barry. Now that the war is over, a man's gotta do something, somewhere." He politely refused Kurt's offer of a cigarette and produced his own textured silver cigar case.

"May I?" Kurt reached out and rotated Barry's wrist for a better view of the cigar case.

The case was made up of three tubes. The eagle with swastika emblem, wings spread across all the tubes, graced the front. A dent and a short, ugly gash rendered the middle tube unusable. "Quite a special item. Something you…" Kurt trailed off, confused, and questioned Ulrich in German.

Barry bristled at the touch of Kurt's sweaty hand, but kept his mouth shut.

"Purchased?" Ulrich hesitated.

"Purchased, yes," Kurt confirmed.

"Gosh, no. The fellow this belonged to won't be needing it no more."

"I see." Kurt let go of Barry's wrist. "Reich Security, I hope?"

"Not that man, no."

"Are you interested in taking over the town?" Kurt produced a delicate silver lighter with vertical detailing, igniting his and Ulrich's cigarettes.

Barry and Ulrich had been contemplating exactly that. Now that he had seen the territory, however, Furstflarn and the camp that is, doubt crept into this analysis. He had not realized how large everything was. The place was going to be a stinking money factory and take up his time accordingly.

Barry also hadn't expected to find a smooth operator like Kurt so evidently well entrenched this quickly after the war. To survive the camps, he thought Kurt must be tough and tenacious. He would probably have to kill Kurt to get rid of him. Both men watched him closely, waiting for an answer.

He extracted a brown cigar from his case.

"What's on the table?" he asked.

Kurt examined the green felt tabletop, then exchanged some rapid-fire German with Ulrich.

"Herr Barry," Kurt said, grinning, seeming to have figured out the slang, "you must be a reader of the mind. At first, Ulrich and I were thinking of getting rid of you. But after meeting you, I think I need to have you killed to be rid of you. Why do we not do this? I will take the town and you the camp take. Ulrich will this club have. Any time I go to the camp, I split the money with you. When you come to the town, we also split the money. What do you think of that?"

"I've got a better idea," Barry gushed, inspiration striking like George Patton. "I'm going to bring in black market goods and sell them to the DPs. They're going to come to town and hopefully go up to Munich, too, to sell the stuff." Here came the innovation. "You let the DPs sell their stuff without a hassle, even protect them from the police, and I'll share a cut of the profits, after expenses, of course."

"How could I protect them from the police?"

"Don't give me no guff, now." Barry risked a questioning glimpse of Ulrich, who lifted his shoulders slightly in return.

"Okay, okay," Kurt said, putting his hands up in mock surrender. "How much?"

"Three percent."

"Oh, my. First, my expenses, your expenses, whatever. We must the gross talk. I would need at least twenty percent gross for what you say."

Three percent had been a wild guess, but now Barry's gut told him that Kurt was lying, that he was actually thrilled to be counted in at all.

"Since we are talking gross, seven."

"Attention! For seven, I might as well go back to Dachau and ask the Nazis to take care of me. Sixteen."

"Eight."

"Thirteen?"

"Eight."

"Eleven? Police are expensive."

"That's why you're getting eight."

The conversation paused. The atmosphere was neither tense nor calm. Barry manipulated his cigar but made no move to start it. He could see Kurt losing his fight not to smile.

"Done and done for eight," Kurt said.

The men shook hands.

They discussed some minor details before Barry slid his cigar into the carrier and proffered his excuses for an early evening.

"You know, you are quite well formed for a Jew," Kurt commented with a leer. "We should get along sometime. Without Ulrich, yes?"

"Do you mean 'together?'" Ulrich asked.

"Of course. Together," Kurt took Barry's hand in both of his own and squeezed gently.

"Together?" he asked, uncomfortably. "Yeah, together. I'm sure." Barry pulled away and left the two of them in the gaming room.

He walked slowly down the deserted streets of Furstflarn, doping out his way to his flat. Soon two large men were following him. He turned onto a side street and slowed even more, shivering, and jammed his hands into his pockets.

They closed in.

"I don't have all night. It's cold," Barry grumbled, just above a whisper, in his immature Yiddish. His voice bounced off the stone buildings, amplified in the frigid nighttime air.

The two men quickened their pace until they caught up with him. They were Hitlerian stereotypes of Jews personified. The sight of their sizable irregular noses, thinning brown hair, umber eyes and thick lips made Barry glad, as these were the features of the Safek brothers, and they worked for him.

The shorter of the two, Elya, dwarfed Barry. Elya's brother, Menachem, stood a hand's breadth taller still. They both wore ill-fitting suits and overcoats Barry had bought for them, remembering Little Meyer's lessons. Elya had lively focused eyes that always followed the action, indicative of natural intelligence, while Manny, as Menachem had been dubbed, was as dumb as a post.

"Sorry, Boss. Where are you going?" Elya asked.

"My flat."

"It's back there." Elya pointed over his shoulder.

"So?" Barry, still speaking Yiddish, using the universal "*nu*," which could communicate many things; in this instance, it moved the conversation along, covering up his annoyance with himself for screwing up in front of his employees. "What did you see in the club?"

"We were in there for a time." Elya's suave old-country Yiddish flowed smoothly. "Ulrich was doing some good business. Nothing irregular."

"We think the meat was horse," Manny added.

"*Swell*," Barry said in English, scrunching up his face. "What's the story on Kurt what's-his-name?"

"He leads the local gangsters. He sells girls and possibly boys and has gambling elsewhere. They say he can get black market goods, but we haven't seen much for sale. He has good relations with the police." Elya shrugged. "That's it."

"Any army in town?"

"A jeep with MPs drives through once, sometimes twice a day."

"Storehouses?" Barry scanned furtively up and down the street and stomped his feet and rubbed his hands.

Elya handed over a folded piece of paper. "This man has three. Two are empty. His name and address, and the addresses of the storehouses, are on the paper."

"Good work. You need anything? Money?"

"Yes, I need—" Manny started to say, before his "little" brother cut him off with a punch to the arm.

"No, we have everything," Elya said.

"But...?"

Manny scuffed the toe of his right shoe on the stones like a child caught at some mischief.

"All the expense money," Elya confessed, "went to the fräuleins. He wants to ask you for some of the money in his Swiss account. I told him that money was for tomorrow."

"What are you doing tomorrow?" Barry asked.

"Not 'tomorrow.' *Tomorrow*, as in when we get to America. We will need money in America, no?"

"Yes. You'll need money in America." Barry dug in his pockets and came up with some script and two packs of cigarettes. "We work tomorrow night. Find some gasoline, a small can will do, and a broom. Come to my flat at eleven. Good job, you two." He gave everything to Elya.

"Boss, come with us," Manny said in his earnest thick voice. "We know where some girls are."

Barry wanted to say yes, but the image of a petite, thin young woman, her pale skin set off by her black, black eyes and raven ringlets appeared in his mind's eye. "It's late. You go. I'll see you tomorrow."

He wondered why Rivka should come to mind and pushed her away to concentrate on finding his place. The ornate façades of the neighborhood struck him as universally ominous in the depth of the night.

He'd passed his building by a few steps before realizing the door looked familiar. Inside, linoleum, a wide staircase with an ornate wrought iron balustrade and a high ceiling dominated the foyer. He started up the stairway. On the first floor, the door to the landlady's flat opened. The landlady, a hausfrau without a man but with real estate to manage and children to take care of, shoved her daughter out. The door closed gently but firmly behind her.

The girl wore a discolored bathrobe, which she gathered at her throat with her right hand. She held her left arm protectively across her narrow waist. He noticed her eyes jumping from side to side and her rapid breathing.

Barry had seen her before. He and the landlady had negotiated over tea. The girl, not older than eighteen, had served. She was very pretty. This turn of events was probably his fault. He must have gotten caught peeking down her dress as she bent over with the tea tray or, more likely, he had leered at her throughout the visit.

Her expression changed. Fear made some room for inquisitiveness.

He wished her a *Guten abend* and tried to walk by.

"*Bitte*," she replied, eyeing him and then the stairs.

Her fine blond hair fell in gentle waves to her shoulders. She wore some red lipstick and rouge, just enough to make Barry think of a child dressing up. Her soft brown eyes were both requesting and nervous. The robe covered her up pretty good, but he knew her to be slender, graceful, not too much in the breast department but a solid looker overall. This hausfrau was a real hustler, specializing in apartments and daughters.

A genuine businesswoman.

Barry figured from the girl's demeanor that her mother had told her to land the client or else. He understood her predicament, so he smiled and indicated she should use the staircase, even though he had no intention of making it with her. She smiled back, relieved and fearful at the same time.

They walked upstairs to his place on the second floor, where he unlocked the door and stepped back, blocking her from moving forward. When he was sure he could not hear anything from inside, he turned on the light switch by the door and scrutinized the room. He sniffed. Normal. Only then did he let the girl go in.

The apartment had high ceilings, excellent plaster and crown molding throughout. It had weathered the fighting well. Even all the windows were intact. He recognized it as the type of luxurious home he could not have ever aspired to before the war.

"Hungry?" he asked in English.

She flashed him a brief smile, uncertainty all over her face.

"Hell yeah, she's hungry. The whole stupid country is hungry," Barry muttered.

He had stacked field gear in the second bedroom. Among the equipment were combat rations, cardboard boxes of tinned dishes and accompaniments designed and perfected to keep a soldier fighting. Barry no fresh food. Drinking, however, was another matter. He had a bar's inventory of various alcoholic beverages.

After draping his coat and suit jacket over an arm of the couch and laying his hat on top, he motioned toward the bedroom. Her face fell and she shuffled off in her slippers. He laughed privately because while she was attractive enough and literally the girl next door, she was a child.

He grabbed several tins from the rations and rummaged through the gear for a canteen cup. He opened a bottle of white wine and filled the cup halfway. He arranged everything on a serving tray and carried it to her.

She had gotten undressed and slid under the covers, the panicky expression returning. Barry, not completely scandalized, handed her the tray. A powerful urge to ravage the girl hit him hard. The image of Rivka may have trumped the idea of whores, but here was a real live sweetheart of a girl. Naked. A wonderful opportunity, except he could plainly see how scared she was.

She held the covers against her chest until she could get them situated under her arms. She accepted the wine with a questioning mien. He winked, produced one of the miniature can openers issued with the rations and cut around the tops of the tins.

Her countenance switched from quizzical to alarmed.

Barry followed her eyes down to his right hip where she had spotted the Colt he wore in a leather holster.

"Don't worry about that." With practiced economy, he positioned crackers, a fudge disk and a sandwich cookie on two plates and sprinkled sugar from a small paper packet on the crackers.

She licked her lips and swallowed nervously.

"Go ahead, eat," he said, handing her one of the crackers, trying not to spill the sugar.

She reached across her chest and put the wine down on the night table, then went for a cracker. The sheet fell away, revealing one baseball-sized breast, peach and pink. She blushed and managed to re-situate the sheet. After nibbling at the cracker and waiting a moment, an embarrassed smile lit up her face and she gobbled up the rest. Then the girl eyed Barry's untouched food.

"Go ahead."

She cleaned his plate and drank down the wine.

"Okay. Enough. Good night." He walked to the bedroom door.

She was clearly confused.

Barry didn't speak German and wasn't confident that "go to sleep" was the same in the languages he knew. Instead, he brought both of his hands together, palm to palm. He oriented them horizontally and placed his head over them. She finally got it and laid her head on the pillow. He turned off the light and closed the door. The last thing he saw was the smile on her face.

He stripped down to his skivvies in the second bedroom and, using the blanket, flung gear from the bed to the floor, causing a clanking racket. After he put the .45 on the nightstand, he lay down, pulled up the covers and fell asleep before he could change his mind.

2

Early the next morning, Barry waltzed into the camp office, threw two packages of nylons in front of Rivka and began wading through paperwork. He saw right away that he would need to lay off most of the tasks Howie had done onto the staff to free up his diary for his own agenda.

He caught her flipping one of the packages over, her brows furrowed in thought. It made him happy.

As Rivka typed at her desk, the rabbis studied the same book from the day before. Barry decided it was time. He walked to the middle of the room with two fresh ledgers.

"From now on, you guys are going to work," he addressed the rabbis in English, dropping a green bound notebook in front of each of them. "Not you, *Zaydeh*," Barry said to the old man, using the Yiddish word for grandfather.

"*You speak?*" Shimshon Gutkin, the shorter, rounder rabbi asked in Yiddish.

"Yes."

"*So by Howie, we learned every day already. We are yeshiva students and this is the rav.*"

"I understand," Barry replied in English, not trusting his childhood Yiddish. "But you have to work. No free rides."

A flurry of Yiddish burst forth from Rivka, concerning regulations and Howie, but otherwise it came too fast for Barry to comprehend entirely. Shimshon frowned.

"*He must be an animal,*" Pinchas over-articulated his words, looking at the older rabbi but clearly intending them for Barry. "*He does not understand you are the rav and we are the only two of your students to survive. Everyone else is dead, our families, your family, all the other teachers and students. He is an ignoramus.*"

The insults made Barry hot enough to switch to Yiddish. "*I understand. You work a little, you learn a little. Work first, until lunch. After lunch, learn.*"

Barry waited for the next salvo from the aggrieved parties.

The old man spoke at last: "*Torah and an occupation is the best way.*"

"*No!*" Pinchas slammed a hand down on the wooden table. "*You are the rav! Who does he think he is, Joseph by Pharaoh's court?*"

"I think I'm Technical Sergeant Rosen," Barry said in quiet English, "and if you guys want to eat here, you work here. Pinchas, you get the morning supply count. Document everything that has come into camp since the previous morning, and I mean everything. Shimshon, you get me the count of camp residents. Every morning. Each day you get an accurate count of inmates in the camp from the leaders of the different groups. At least once a week, you, yourself, count the people in each barracks. I don't care who is eating on whose ration card. Just worry about who is really here. If they are, I want to know, and if they ain't, I want to know that, too."

Rivka translated his instructions to the two men.

"Howie let them learn all day," she said neutrally.

"Howie's gone. *You eat,*" Barry confirmed for the clergymen, "*you work.*"

Pinchas mumbled something under his breath.

"What?"

"*Like Hitler, may his name be erased. You and the Germans, what's the difference?*"

He yanked Pinchas up out of his chair and half over the table by his scruffy lapels. "Here's the difference, dummy," Barry castigated the refugee while Rivka interpreted. "If I were German, you'd be dead." He let go of Pinchas's jacket and grabbed him by the hair with one hand, tugging until his face stopped inches from the rows of martial ribbons on Barry's tunic. "I fought. I won. Now I make the rules. If you had fought for yourself and lived, maybe you could make the rules. But you didn't." He released the young rabbi and then threw a ledger out the door. It landed on the soft wood with a loud slap. "*Work now.*"

Pinchas, glaring, walked to the ledger and picked it up. Shimshon scuttled out the door, his ledger held protectively across his chest. Barry's muscles quivered with adrenaline. Rav Hirsch busied himself in his book. Rivka worked on. Barry calmed down and resumed ruffling through the paperwork he had inherited from Howie and refused to worry about his popularity in the office.

A half hour or so went by when Rivka waylaid him with a jam sandwich made on thick slices of white bread, a mug of tea and the slightest of smiles. Barry spent the rest of the day figuring out what other work there was and how much of it he could put off on the staff. By early evening, tired of the camp, he drove to town.

Later, Barry, in a single-breasted brown suit, and Ulrich, wearing one of broad pinstripes, met at the club with a weary *geschäftsinhaber* who oozed wealth. Although the German business owner wore finely tailored clothes and still had an ample waistline, skin sagged where he formerly had a double chin, and his collar was too big for his neck. The bags under his sad eyes, however, were full. Over drinks, Ulrich and the *geschäftsinhaber* negotiated in German until Ulrich quit.

"He says 'no.'" Ulrich took a drag off his cigarette, which he had secured in an enamel holder. "He thinks because you are here, there is US government interest in the warehouse. He would rather wait for the official contract. He thinks we want to cut him under."

"Undercut him? How so?" Barry asked, wondering where that stupid cigarette holder came from. Who did he think he was, Roosevelt?

"We rent it and then, through you, rent it to the army for twice as much."

"Smart guy, is he? You were right. I shouldn't have come. Dammit." Barry could not hide his disgust. "How many warehouses does he have again?"

"He has three in good repair. Two are ready to rent."

"Swell. Tell him thanks and get rid of him."

Ulrich and the *geschäftsinhaber* concluded their conversation. The businessman rose to leave.

"I sorry," he said in English.

"Not as sorry as you're going to be." Barry waved the man away.

He surveyed the club. It was early. Patrons were sparse. The working girls lazed in their chairs like lionesses in a zoo. One or two regarded him with the same frank appraisal he directed at them.

"War is hell." Barry shot the last of his whiskey.

"Huh? What is it that you say?"

"Is Kurt on board? And the police?"

"Yes, yes. Everything is arranged."

"Okay. What's on the menu tonight?"

"Sausage and kraut. I have also located several extra barrels of beer, so one glass is free if customers pay for a meal."

"Great. I'll take a plate and a beer."

"And dessert?" Ulrich grinned in the general direction of the girls lounging at the tables.

"Not tonight. Got work to do."

Barry ate and then lingered over coffee, the beans for which he had directed Staff Sergeant Washington to steal from US military supplies. The club slowly filled, and a steady stream of players made for the gaming room. Suckers like his father. After the beer with supper, he didn't order any more alcohol; instead, he smoked half a cigar. Long after sunset and with a nod at Ulrich, he settled up on his way out.

Barry buttoned his tan trench coat and pulled his fedora low over his brow. He had gotten a break; an overcast sky dimmed the moonlight. He rendezvoused with the Safek brothers at the designated corner, now quiet, right on time. They looked like proper commandos, dressed in US army clothes stolen for them: work pants, olive drab medium-weight field jackets and black wool watch caps. Elya carried a broom and Manny hauled two five-gallon Jerry cans, one in each hand.

"It's on," Barry said in Yiddish, by way of greeting, "let's go."

Elya took the lead as the three men walked out of the city center through the cold deserted streets.

"Can I help with the gas?" Barry asked Manny.

"No, I do it."

"Here it is." Elya stopped in front of a small warehouse.

The brothers had done the necessary reconnaissance. Barry had told them they would set up on the smallest one. Coincidentally, it was the one the old bastard had already rented.

He had the Safeks stay where they were, then walked the perimeter of the building, a one-story structure with a loading dock. Two large bay doors, facing the street, were locked and no cars or trucks were parked nearby. A second door allowed access from the alley.

The businesses in the neighboring buildings were quiet. Barry could not tell if they were abandoned because of the war, their employees dead in some Russian or French field, or if they were merely closed up for the night.

He completed the circuit and beckoned for the Safeks to follow him; they walked up to the side entrance. Barry pointed at Manny and then the door.

"Yes, boss," Manny whispered, putting down the Jerry cans and slamming his right shoulder into the heavy wood.

There was a loud, solid *thunk*, but the door didn't budge. He gathered himself for another try. Barry sighed and tapped the large man on the arm. Manny faced him with an expression of eager expectation.

Barry struggled over Yiddish vocabulary. He gave up and asked Elya, in English, "What is the word for pry bar?"

Elya nodded. Facing his brother, he said, "Pry...bar?" in accented English.

Manny's eyes bounced from Barry to Elya in confusion, then Elya slapped Manny's thigh. Manny unzipped his jacket and slid a crowbar out from inside his trousers, where it had hung over his belt by the claw.

Barry took it and shoved the straight end between the door and the jamb. He eased the crowbar to the right and bent the jamb enough to clear the deadbolt. He slowly pushed the door with the toe of his shoe, ushered the others in and followed, gently closing the door behind them.

He could barely discern the wooden crates that had been stacked in a logical manner to make a grid of walkways over the concrete floor. After waiting to be sure no watchman was on duty, Barry had Manny sweep up all the dust he could find and pile it in the middle of the space, and then he instructed Elya on how to pour out the gasoline. After some work arranging dust and pouring gas, they were ready to leave.

"Why the sweeping?" Elya asked in Yiddish.

"Without dust, only fire," Barry replied.

"And with it?"

"You will see. Pour out the last of the petrol to the door."

"No more."

"What you mean 'no more'?"

"There isn't any more petrol." Elya winced like he expected to get hit.

"Shit. Okay, outside."

The two men left Barry alone. He wondered how he kept getting into these situations. He should have watched Elya closer. Damn amateurs were going to get him killed, he thought.

Barry grabbed the broom and produced his lighter, then hesitated. Playing with fire always gave him the willies. He wrestled again with the reality he was going to significantly hurt the owner's ability to earn a living.

Perhaps they didn't have to torch the place, he thought. No one would blame him for quitting. They could store the stuff another way.

Barry's resolve stiffened like it always did before a jump or when rushing into a firefight. It was simple, this was his territory now and, in his territory, people played ball or bad things happened.

It was the way it had to be.

"Stupid shenanigans." Barry ignited the bristles.

Flames consumed the business end of the broom and, when ready, he threw it at the closest gas puddle and sprinted for the door. From behind him, he heard a loud whomp and felt a hot blast. He knew the burning gas had done some kind of chemical thing to the dust, resulting in an incendiary explosion of some kind. The army had trained him well. By the time he caught up with the Safeks, a conflagration consumed the contents of the warehouse.

"Go on, get lost," Barry said in English, then he switched to Yiddish. "See you tomorrow at the club."

The two smiling brothers wished him a good night. After they left, Barry faded into the shadows and waited. The fire brigade, surely a pale imitation of the pre-war service, responded to a fully engulfed warehouse. Police and spectators came to stand by them and watch the roof fall in, liberating orange arms that reached up into the cold cloudy night, blasting heat and sparks over the town.

Eventually, Ulrich and the *geschäftsinhaber* arrived. The property owner wore a coat over flannel pajamas and worried a hat in his hands, crushing the brim. The dancing blaze illuminated his lined tired face. Ulrich rested a sympathetic hand on the *geschäftsinhaber's* shoulder. Barry sidled up to them.

Ulrich bobbed his head. It caught the attention of the owner.

"I sorry," Barry said, mimicking the businessman.

The *geschäftsinhaber* nodded his thanks and returned to his immolated property. A minute later the owner's eyes focused and he glared sharply at Barry, then at Ulrich and then Barry again.

"Ulrich, tell him we would like to rent the other storehouse, not the one on the main street but the out-of-the way one. I'm sure you won't have to say you expect a fair price, just make sure we get one."

Ulrich spoke in German. Understanding flowed over the businessman's features, followed by anger. Then the sharp expression on the old face that had seen the big war, the Nazis and this last war come and go, faded. Resignation took its place.

He nodded.

Barry had what he wanted. He lifted his chin toward Ulrich in farewell, confident they would strike a deal since the owner now knew the lay of the land.

At his building, a tired Barry slowly mounted the stairs to his floor. His flat came into view, a sliver of light shining from under the door, deepening the shadows in the hallway. Suddenly, he was crackling with nervous energy. He thought it could not possibly be the police, or worse, the army's Criminal Investigation Division, so who the hell was it?

Drawing his pistol, he laid his ear on the worn wood but didn't detect any sounds. Then, stepping to the side, he gently tried the doorknob with his left hand as he thumbed back the hammer of the .45 in his right. The knob rotated freely. He opened the door but remained in the hall.

Light footfalls raced to the door. Barry reached from the hallway and grabbed. He caught a handful of cotton cloth and pulled. The business end of his heat ended up under the chin of the blonde girl from downstairs, the landlady's daughter.

"For crying out loud," Barry said, forcing her into the flat.

He made sure they were alone before he let her go. The apartment had been cleaned and organized since the morning. Barry kicked the door closed behind them. She stood in the middle of the living room, quiet and subdued in her sad chaste nightgown. He lowered the hammer of his pistol and returned it to its holster.

"*Bistu gut?*" he asked, trying Yiddish, seeing if she were all right.

She thought for a moment and then said, "*Geht es dir gut?*"

Barry could not sus out her meaning. "Yeah," he said in English, "sure." Then he decided to go with their common word. "*Gut?*"

"*Gut.*" She smiled.

"Did you do all this?"

That was all she needed to switch from subdued to animated. She took him by the hand and gave him the grand tour. The kitchen counters were clear. In the second bedroom, Barry's gear had been stacked along one wall. The blankets and sleeping bags, pack and duffle bags, booze bottles and boxes took up much less space now. His uniforms and suits had been pressed before they were arranged carefully in an armoire. The covers had been folded back in the main bedroom. The viola case rested on top of a dresser. He didn't care for the landlady keeping a key, but he sure liked the results.

Back in the kitchen, he searched through the cupboards. The girl skipped around him, showing him where she had put the combat rations. After some initial confusion caused by the two of them competing for cooking rights, Barry surrendered unconditionally, and she commenced warming beef stew in a pot.

They ate in silence off porcelain plates and cutlery that had not been in the apartment the night before. Once they had finished and cleared the table, things became awkward. Barry realized that the girl was making herself available to him. She was everything a hard-fighting soldier could ask for. Such opportunities had come frequently since the end of the war and his habit had been to accept every one of them. Tonight, as he escorted her into the master bedroom, his intent was to celebrate some more. They paused at the bed, and he put his hands on her shoulders and faced her. He prepared to make his move, then thought again of how young she was, how threadbare her nightgown, and of Rivka's dark eyes.

Barry leaned in and kissed the girl's forehead before retreating to the second bedroom for the night. He lay there for some time, alternately berating and congratulating himself for not taking advantage. In the end, lust won out. He yawned, planned to get up in a minute, but fell asleep instead.

3

"What about you, Ernst? What will you do when we get home?"

In a pretty little corner of southern Poland, a group of German prisoners of war were killing time and trying not to be noticed by their Russian captors.

Ernst Hoffmann looked up from where he had been examining the frost covering the dirt. He formed a row with his fellow prisoners, their backs to the bitter wind. Clouds raced across a blue sky, far above problems of human life and death.

In addition to their group, there were others in the compound, the ragtag remnants of a once great war machine, inconveniently persisting in dilapidated tents whose wooden sides under canvas roofs indicated a dispiriting sense of permanence. Cruel barbed wire fencing and crueler Russian guards kept them in. A fallow field and a distant colorless tree line marked the final boundary between them and a world no longer at war.

"I trained as a lawyer, Gerhart," Ernst replied, tramping his freezing feet. "I want to go back to the law. Maybe become a professor."

"Rich lawyer, that's the ticket. And you, Rudiger?"

They were all in a bad way, but Rudiger had it the worst. While Ernst, a tall blue-eyed blond from northern Germany with an aquiline nose set in an oval face, was thin, starvation had vitiated Rudiger. Cavernous lines framed his eyes and mouth, his own blue eyes were clouded and perpetually unfocused and his filthy pale hair had started falling out.

Before their capture, Ernst had been able to get pieces of an Army uniform. Rudiger, already sick, had been too slow. He had been detained wearing his black leather SS overcoat, and the Russians had taken note. They refrained from finishing Rudiger off for the sport of continuing to beat him regularly.

"Rudiger, what are you going to do when we get back?" Gerhart asked again.

"I'm not going to make it back," Rudiger muttered.

They could barely hear him over the wind.

"You will! For sure you will!"

Gerhart's shouting and anger were common these days.

Rudiger slowly swiveled his head in the negative.

Gerhart shoved Rudiger, who would have fallen if Ernst had not propped him up.

"Now men, it's nothing." Ernst took his friend by the arm and steered him away from the others. "Let's walk. It will be good to get the blood flowing."

Ernst had never been a true leader. Childhood failure on the playing fields had left its mark on his psyche. Shyness and a crooked right incisor had made him self-conscious. Their current situation, however, had brought out an element of decisiveness in him.

"I will not ever make it back to the Fatherland," Rudiger repeated, his halting gait impeding their promenade.

He was far from the gay blade of earlier times and Ernst understood why. The Russians barely fed them, and the constant craving ate at their wills. Hunger, penetrating cold, and the frequent beatings had reduced them to walking shells.

"Don't be dramatic," Ernst said in as playful a tone as he could muster. "I told you, we are going to escape."

He, too, was not the same man who had been captured as a *Schutzstaffel* captain. Ernst had never been a stand-out in life, but an older friend of the family had suggested he join up; the experience would season him and the connections would be good for his career. The friend had even made some introductions, and the friend had been right, Ernst had grown in confidence once he donned the sharp black uniform. Service in this new branch, protecting the Reich, had been ennobling.

After the war came, he had been able to justify his actions in the name of saving the Fatherland, at least until he went east. In the east, he had become an administrator for the *Einsatzgruppen:* "deployment groups" of mobile execution squads formed to "handle" the Jewish question, the Gypsy question, the questions about those who were abominations in front of the Lord, and finally, the question of prisoners of war. Now he was here, an answer to someone else's question.

"You know, Rudiger, I have been in uniform for a long time," Ernst confessed. "I even wore my uniform to church."

Now, in the hell of this camp, he realized how wrong they had all been. The people who had made up the answers to the questions of his government, the questions he had helped answer, had felt the hunger, the cold and the fear he felt now. If he and Rudiger didn't escape soon, the two of them would succumb as millions before them had succumbed.

"It becomes you, Ernst."

He laughed at Rudiger's small joke. "Rudy, don't give up. We'll make it. We have almost enough food to escape."

Rudiger smiled sadly.

They had come to the east and starved people. They had torn families and communities apart. They had hunted down the "undesirables" and killed them outright. They had caused so much pain. And now the Russians were doing it to them. How wrong they all were. He started to sink in a sea of shame and sadness. To stop the emotional drowning, he focused on his plans instead.

"I want to go home and teach about what we did, Rudy. I want to work hard to prevent anyone from doing it again. We are all God's children."

"Home." Rudiger's face screwed itself up in misery. Eyes tightly shut, his mouth opened in a silent cry. He sagged against Ernst, who marshaled all his strength to hold his friend up.

"No, Rudy, stay strong," he whispered sharply. "We are going to escape. We need to be strong for the journey. I have food. We will steal clothes. We are going to walk across Poland and go home."

His friend started slipping to the ground. Ernst thought the others might help him get Rudy into their tent and turned to call them over.

The Germans were running, scattering everywhere, as a group of smiling Russian soldiers, clad in their baggy green sack-like uniforms, bore down on them.

In another moment, the Russians were on them. He tried to hold on to Rudy, but they were pulled apart. Ernst suffered some sharp blows. The Russians laughed. They swarmed all over Rudy, taunting him over his black leather overcoat. Someone spun Ernst and punched him once, twice, a third time in the face. He struggled to stay on his feet, but his thighs failed him. The dirt of the camp yard rushed up at him and—

4

In another Polish camp run by different Russians, Zalman Finkle, the shoeshine boy, scurried into the well-built barracks that housed the Soviet officers. In each hand he carried a pair of black jackboots buffed to a high gloss.

"Comrade, here they are!" he called out in his poor Russian.

"Give them over." The officer's orderly held out his hands for the boots. "You did well. Tomorrow, I need some alterations done. Very fine work. Can you handle it?"

"Sure I can handle it. Should I meet you here?"

Zalman liked the officers' quarters because a coal fire burned there all the time. He had been moved to the Monowitz displaced persons camp with the other survivors of the Birkinau concentration camp, both in Poland. They shared the installation with a small Soviet garrison. Although safe from imminent murder, they faced a scarcity of coal and wood for heating. The roughly constructed, rotting former inmate barracks could not withstand even the autumn temperatures and were always cold.

"We can even work here," the orderly, a great big Russian peasant, said. "Show up at half-past nine. I have something for you." He produced a cloth bundle as big as his massive hand and peeled back the corners, revealing four of the fried cakes Zalman liked. They were doughy and greasy and wonderful.

"Thanks, Comrade." He re-folded the cloth over the cakes and snatched them away.

"Don't worry, no one will take your cakes. Why don't you eat them now?"

Zalman thought the orderly must have given over more than he wanted to. Maybe he thought they would share the cakes and he would get two back. Four was a lot for shined boots.

"Sorry, Comrade, I need to sweep out the political officer's day room."

Fear crossed the orderly's face. Mere mention of the political officer scared these Russians like by a *dybbuk*. Zalman had to admit he enjoyed the large soldier's discomfort, even though such thoughts did not show good character. He raced out the door, shouting "See you!" and dashed down the dirt road separating the dilapidated wooden barracks.

The dull sky looked pregnant with snow. Zalman, appearing closer in size and maturity to ten than his actual age of fourteen, wore *Heer* trousers he had altered himself, a gray wool shirt and a green alpine sweater. He slowed to a walk on his way to the infirmary.

At liberation, he had been emaciated. Years of deprivation had left him too thin and small, but he had recovered and now there was new life in him. His straight brown hair had grown in. Energy sparkled in his hazel eyes. Freckles covered his wide nose.

Yankel Shapiro was also healing, but at a much slower rate. Zalman entered the building for inmates who were improving. During the war, the Germans had them sleep on large wooden shelves. Yankel, still skin over bone despite regular meals, rested on the straw mattress of an individual bed assembled out of the former shelving. His thick black hair and dark eyes accentuated his pale complexion, paler still since he held a letter.

"Yitzie Strasen made it back to Roszowice," Yankel said, gesturing with the letter.

Zalman sat on the bed. He produced the cakes and offered one. "A blessing. What does he write?"

"Are they kosher?"

"They're food. What does Yitzie write?"

"The Name didn't bring us through evil to see us eat lard."

"Lard? Do you think Mrs. Linowitz fries with lard?" It wasn't exactly a lie, Zalman thought. Merely a question.

They were not exactly friends, with Yankel being six years older, much more religious and very opinionated, but they were both from the same town. The Shapiros, with their house off the square and a stables even, had not associated with his more modest family.

"Oh, Mrs. Linowitz. Well then." Yankel took the cake, said the blessing over baked goods and took a bite. "Yitzie says two things. One is not to come home. The other is—" and here he could not contain his smile, "Rivka is alive."

"Rivka!" Zalman shouted, spewing crumbs all over the bed. "That makes four from Roszowice: me, you, him and Rivka! Where is she?"

"Rivka had sent a letter to town. Someone posted it on the old *shul* wall. It said she was alive and in a DP camp near Munich."

"Good luck! She's with the Americans. Why did Yitzie say not to come to Roszowice?"

"He writes that Jews who return are being run off or beaten. Some have been killed."

Zalman chewed thoughtfully on the last cake, savoring the greasy mess in his mouth. "Let's go to the Americans. We can tell Yitzie to meet us. I think it's warm where Rivka is. I think she has what to eat."

Yankel thought for a minute before declining. "I want to go to Roszowice. My family's factory is there, our home, everything. If I don't go back, the Nazi has won."

The war has turned Yankel into a common law idiot, Zalman thought. The Nazis *had* won. He knew this because of what they did to his family.

His father had been a pious tailor of some reputation in town, and he had started teaching Zalman the trade in the afternoons. He had always been of good cheer in the tidy little shop and Zalman had adored their conversations as they sewed, sitting shoulder to shoulder.

The Nazis came before his *bar mitzvah*. His father, a slender scholarly man, refused to defer to a big loud German in uniform. He watched as the German knocked his father to the gutter right outside their shop and smashed his head open with a rifle butt, making nine-year-old Zalman the man of the house on the spot.

How old did that make him now? One or two years past *bar mitzvah*, something like that?

With his mother (oh Mama! His always-present despair surged and threatened to swamp him before slowly receding) and younger sisters, he had survived the march to the ghetto and their internment in it. They had even managed to stay together during the round-up and transport.

But on the ramp after the train ride to the camp, he had let himself be pulled away from them. He had believed the Germans, with his mother's encouragement. The Germans had told him he would see his mother and sisters again after their de-lousing and showers.

A veteran inmate soon set him right. "They're up the chimney," the man had said, gesturing skyward with his thumb.

Yankel the fool.

Of course the Nazis had won.

Zalman wet the tip of a finger and used it to capture crumbs from the blanket. He licked them off his finger and chewed them between his front teeth. He thought Yankel was crazy. He should write to Rivka and tell her they were coming to Munich. That was good sense. Not this grandmother story about factories, like someone would give it back to Yankel because he showed up and asked.

Nu? Zalman thought. If Yankel wanted to go to Roszowice, so be it. Zalman would go with him. Where else did he have to go, and who else did he have to go there with?

5

Gitta Peled had spent the last three of her eight years mostly in the farmer's root cellar, coming out briefly at night for a quick run around the yard. The isolated farm consisted of a few hectares in the countryside, a long, long walk from Roszowice. The farmer had let Gitta's uncle and cousin fix it up for the four of them. They had made wooden steps and a rough floor, but the walls were still dirt. Her uncle and cousin had gone out to find food one night and had never come back. Mama said they were with The Name, in The World to Come, with everyone else.

Gitta, small for her age, with stringy brown hair and expressive eyes the color of milk chocolate, a heart-shaped mouth and a sharp chin, had lived underground long enough for her unhealthy yellowish-white visage to match her Mama's, whom she favored. She went barefoot, as she had outgrown her shoes. Her dress had long since deteriorated to a rag with sleeves.

She and Mama slept on a pallet in a pile of old blankets. Three wooden boxes held all their belongings, chief of which for Gitta was her blonde doll, Dolly. Dolly originally had a fancy party dress. Over the years in the cellar, the dress had become soiled. Most of the sparkles were gone.

Gitta's mother coughed wetly in fits so strong they bounced her torso off the pallet, then she fell back with spittle foaming in the corners of her dry cracked lips. Her eyes were closed. Gitta crawled over and patted her shoulder.

"You'll feel better, Mama," Gitta said by rote, because Mama didn't get better, but she didn't get worse.

Her mother, eyes closed, struggled to smile.

The door banged open bringing light, cold fresh air and a stomping farmer with a cloth-covered metal tin in one hand and a bucket in the other. Gitta was scared of the big, barrel-chested man and his gruff voice, but she was glad to see him. More precisely, it was the food and water that made her glad, the first since midday yesterday.

"You must go," he stated, by way of greeting.

Mama coughed weakly and silently pled for mercy with moist eyes.

"The war ended five months ago," he whispered fiercely. "You have to go! The Missus is getting suspicious."

"I'm not well," Mama said quietly. "Just a few more days."

"You keep saying, 'a few more days,'" mocked the farmer.

She flipped aside the blankets and faced away from Gitta.

Gitta knew what that meant. She scooted over to the far corner with Dolly. When the farmer got on top of Mama and bumped up and down, grunting, Gitta was supposed to kneel in the corner and remember the Sabbaths they used to have with her grandmother. She tried to tell Dolly about the Sabbath once, but the farmer shouted. Now she thought of it in her head like she was telling it, but she didn't actually tell it.

Spending the Sabbath at her grandmother's house had been beautiful. On Friday nights in the winter, a large fire in the oven warmed all the rooms. Grandma and Mama and her sisters would light candles. After prayers at the synagogue, her Papa and the boys would come home and say the blessings over wine and two (not just one, but two!) braided loaves of bread. There would be meat and potatoes and cake. They would sing and Gitta would fall asleep on the couch before the Grace after Meals.

Gitta heard the farmer's belt buckle. He muttered something. The grunting started.

That's what Mama told over about the Sabbath, anyway. All Gitta remembered was how warm Grandma's house had been and Grandma smiling and the bright candles. She could not remember her Papa and her brothers. They were gone a long time now. In her head, she repeated the Sabbath story to Dolly and tried to ignore the food in the tin.

"It is only a day's walk to Roszowice," the farmer said, after.

"Maybe you could take us in the wagon?" Mama asked.

"Enough taking, just go already." He stomped up the stairs and slammed the door shut.

Gitta heard some rustling. Her mother called her. The tin was open on the dirt next to the pallet and Mama gestured at it. She scuttled over. A lump of bread, some meat in gravy and cut up chunks of potato were inside. Mama nodded and Gitta reached in.

"Take the bread first, Gitta."

She knew what Mama wanted. She held up the bread and said the appropriate blessing in Hebrew: "*Boruch atah Hashem, elohainou melech ha'olam, hahmotzi lechem min ha'ortez.*"

"Very good, cuteness, now eat."

Gitta wolfed the food down with her fingers, eating it all up, then she brushed several stray locks out of her eyes and smiled.

"Oh Gitta, you put gravy on your face and in your hair." Mama leaned back on the pallet and cried.

She always cried.

"You'll feel better, Mama," Gitta said by rote.

6

Roszowice, Poland, lay one hundred and fifty kilometers to the east of Yankel and Zalman's displaced persons camp and one hundred and twenty kilometers to the west of Ernst and Rudiger's prisoner of war camp. At the center of town, a brick three-story county seat with a copper roof and a tower, a Roman church with a cathedral-like steeple, and a domed Greek Orthodox church all faced one another across the manicured park. Buildings with shops and cafés on their ground floors and professional offices above bordered the park and buildings.

A cobblestone square one block southeast anchored the most fashionable neighborhood in Roszowice, where the residences had white stucco walls, red tiled roofs and tended gardens. A small gathering watched as jeering young men beat their victim down to the gray masonry.

Sixteen-year-old Jan Pulturzycki came upon the scene and witnessed the victim curl into a ball to weather the savage kicks. The assailants tired of their sport and meandered off. The beaten man relaxed his protective curl. It took a few seconds, but Jan recognized the bloody face.

In his excitement, Jan jogged home to a less fashionable neighborhood. His wooden house had flat dark tiles on the roof and a farther walk to church. He burst through the front door and stopped to catch his breath in the foyer. Light flowed from his mother's warm bright kitchen to his right.

The stairway on the left rose to a second story of bedrooms, and the hall to the common rooms opened in the shadows.

"Pop! They are beating Yitzie!" he yelled, gulping air.

Jan had survived the war in the village of his birth as the German and Russian armies came and went. He attended school, walked out to the fields for work and, to help out, foraged for food as best he could. At close to six feet tall already, dressed in an old cotton shirt and thick wool trousers, he had a lean wiry build and an oval face with a sharp nose. He jerked his head to send a shock of straight blond hair to the side, out of his clear blue eyes.

"Yitzie who?" his father, Hipolit, asked from the top of the stairs, suspenders hanging down from his waist.

"Yitzie Strasen!"

"Well, isn't that just too bad. He should have stayed away." Hipolit dried his hands on a towel. At over six feet and stout, with the same blond hair and blue eyes as his son, he towered over his family.

"Next thing you know, they will all come back," Uncle Boleslaus said, from behind Hipolit. Uncle Boleslaus was not quite as tall and not quite as wide as his older brother.

"No, not all," Hipolit said.

They both laughed.

"Pop, what if Mr. Shapiro comes back and—"

"No!" Hipolit charged down the staircase and poked Jan in the chest with a rigid finger. "The Jews abandoned their property!" He took charge of his temper and calmed down. "See here, they left and won't be coming back. Now, clean up for dinner."

"Yitzie came back," Jan stated, head bowed, examining the toes of his boots.

"Clean up for dinner," his father barked, ending the exchange.

Jan climbed the stairs, yielding to his sneering uncle as they passed, not meeting his eyes. This house, with its paneled dining and living rooms below and a stables on the alley behind, was so much nicer than their old one. Three substantial area rugs covered the floors downstairs, and each bedroom upstairs had white plaster walls.

Jan's father's former boss, Mr. Shapiro, had lived here. Before the war,

Jan had been a visitor inside it once. The tide of advancing Germans had risen through and past Roszowice, washing the Shapiros and the other Jews away. Shortly after, the Germans had given the property to Hipolit.

At the dining room table, as they were eating a chicken and dumplings supper, Jan felt quarrelsome.

"If the Shapiros come, they should get their house back," he said.

Silence took the place of conversation and the clinking of cutlery on china.

"I decide what this family does, not you," Hipolit said quietly.

"But what if—"

"They won't be coming back. They got what they deserved, and they won't be coming back."

"But, Pop, Yitzie—"

"Damn it to hell! The Jew filth won't be coming back!" Hipolit yelled, red with rage. He balled up a massive fist and banged it on the table so hard half-filled glasses jumped, then he exhaled forcibly and seemed to deflate. "I earned this house, working for those bastards. I decide what we will do with it. Now get out of my sight."

"Hipolit," Jan's mother gently interjected.

"He is to get out of my sight!"

"Don't shout at Mama!" Jan stormed out of the dining room and made his way up the Shapiros' stairs to his bedroom.

7

In a city to the west, on the far side of the Polish-German frontier, the brick on the middle of the sidewalk brought Volkmar Baur to a dead stop in cold moonlight bright enough for shadows. Where the buildings used to be, swells of debris appeared to roll as if they were the sea. The street had been swept.

The battered brick needed to be with the rubble, not on the sidewalk. He reached out for it, but his right hand held the crowbar. The soft moonlight glow gave the crowbar a silver glow, except where a dark viscous liquid covered the hooked end.

The brick, thought Baur, belonged with the rubble. He could not figure out a way to pick it up. He still had his left arm and hand, but the right way to pick things up from the walk was with one's right hand, and his hand held the crowbar.

A flying pig could see why he could not put the crowbar down.

Baur, tall, broad-shouldered and shaved, surveyed the city center. What the Tommies and the American mutts had done here proved their barbarity. Two corners of the baroque Cathedral of Our Lady jutted up from the waves of wreckage, and the Town Hall Tower had somehow survived. Otherwise, no one brick stood on another.

He had not meant to kill anybody tonight.

Baur forced himself to pass the brick and walk south along the Elbe. He knew he could find his apartment if he followed the river downstream.

He had gone to the Royal Technical University here for a year before the invasion of Poland. He had, of course, enlisted immediately. He had expected it of himself after seven years in the Hitler Youth.

Baur walked on.

He had walked on and on in the Hitler Youth, where long hikes and paramilitary rituals were the rule of the day. He had seen combat in Panzers and eventually in the Twelfth SS Hitler Youth Division. He had driven, used, and repaired the metal monsters in battle with the Russians and Brits and Ami mutts, surviving to return to the city they had pummeled and burned and raped. Marta had survived, too. After it was all over, he had moved in with her and her mother. All he wanted to do was go back to school and marry Marta.

She knew that, and she took up with the Communist hooligan anyway. The *Führer* had been right to resist the Communist hooligans and Jews. The skeletons of destroyed buildings and the rolling heaps of rubble pressed in hard against Baur. His beautiful, ruined city.

Marta, too, they had ruined. Yes, it had been him who had delayed their nuptials; he planned to graduate first. Sure, they had been hungry. And he had been quiet. Well, in reality he had alternated periods of brooding with bursts of loud fury. The war had made him unsettled. He would smooth out once classes began. You don't fight all over the world for years and afterward expect to get along as if nothing had happened.

But Marta had taken up with a Communist hooligan occupier. They fought over it. She said things she shouldn't have. He beat her. Oh, how he had beaten her. He beat her until she cried out tearfully again and again that she would stop seeing the Communist hooligan.

Baur had believed her.

Now out of the city center, he walked through a neighborhood of upright walls. Baur knew daylight would reveal tragic gaps where the roofs had been. The first night of the three days of the Allied horror that had occurred nine months ago, commenced with their delivery of tons of high explosive munitions.

He had believed Marta until she started coming in late again. Food had also come into their home. She ridiculed him with the food. He had searched for work. He had his tool pouch and carried it from garage to garage, looking for a situation. No positions were to be had. No one had any money. She derided him with her food and painted lips. He knew she was seeing *him* again, so he had followed her.

After the high explosive bombs had blown the roofs off, the English and the Americans had dropped incendiary devices. The exposed wooden frames of the roofless buildings had ignited easily. He had fought in the west as Dresden burned. His parents and his sister had died in the inferno. Marta had survived to fornicate with a Communist hooligan.

They had been right to trust in the *Führer*.

Baur had taken his crowbar with him to force his way into their flop and not for any other reason. He wanted to talk to her. She had to know the Russian was an animal. Probably a Jew animal Bolshevik. Baur had thrown open the door and found them picnicking on a bed. A coal fire glowed in the brazier, the heat causing the Communist hooligan to unbutton his tunic.

Under Baur's anger, he wondered where the Communist had gotten the coal. Theft, undoubtedly.

His beautiful Marta laughed at some joke, but the mirth froze on her face.

Then mirth morphed into terror.

Baur had come to talk. It made him mad that Marta felt fear when she saw him. How could she be terrified of him after all they had shared? The Communist must have put unhealthy ideas in her head.

The Communist had not yet moved his hand toward the flap of the pistol holster hanging from his leather belt. Somehow, Baur was in the apartment. The hooked end of the crowbar smashed into the side of the Communist's head, knocking him off the bed. The crowbar followed the Communist down to the floor, hitting him hard all the way until the man stopped moving.

"Please don't hurt me," Marta had sobbed.

Baur felt ashamed. How could she have thought he would hurt her? Then the anger came back with even greater force. Wrath filled his consciousness.

"You do not judge me!" he had roared. "You do not judge me! If you had not whored with the Communist Jew Bolshevik, this would not have happened! This is your fault! You cannot judge me!"

Marta screamed and scrambled wildly to get away from him. The bed linens were in disarray.

He had wanted to talk, that's all. She had no reason to be afraid.

She managed to get clear of the sheets and fall to the floor and crab her way to the door. Hate roiled in Baur's chest. Why wouldn't she talk to him? Why was she afraid?

"Wait, little one," he had said, in a tone of soothing gentleness.

Marta had stopped moving. She had reached the doorway, but no farther.

"Honey?"

Baur's lungs heaved. He knelt by her. The back of her head had been reduced to pulp. He did not remember the Communist assaulting his Marta.

He wanted to turn her over, but he held the crowbar in both hands. He could not put it down, so he stood and lifted her shoulder with the tip of his boot. Marta did not respond. Baur removed his foot and she fell, a limp doll. The silence seemed physical. He could not fathom how her beauty had transformed itself into a gooey mess of red and bone.

All that had happened earlier. Now, the moon was setting. The half shadows grew longer. By the time he reached his building, he was chilled through and through. The power was off so he fumbled his way up the stairs and wondered what he might say to his future mother-in-law. Maybe he would ask her if Marta had come home yet. Some simple questions to occupy her mind. He hoped Marta was warm enough, wherever she was.

At their door, Baur tried to arrange the thoughts swirling in his confused mind. He hoped Marta had gotten home before him. But that could not be right. As he opened the door, concern for Marta's well-being and his growing befuddlement evaporated. He smelled burned tobacco. Not Russian, but a more refined blend.

"Herr Baur, do come in," a deep velvety voice said.

A match flared and ignited a candle's wick. Frau Ostwald, Marta's mother, stirred and feebly raised her hands against the light. She had been dozing in an overstuffed armchair in their sitting room. A thin-faced man with receding brown hair and pockmarked cheeks relaxed on the couch.

"Cigarette?" the stranger offered. "They are interesting. 'Lucky Strikes.' From America, I believe."

The stranger, in his early forties, had sharp brown eyes and his calm demeanor did little to hide his natural authority. He wore a viridian green sweater underneath a black leather overcoat. Baur guessed him to have been a major or lieutenant colonel.

"I'm Schmidt. Here, take one." The newcomer held out two of the American cigarettes.

Baur walked over to Schmidt and reached out for it with his right hand, but he could not take it. He still held the crowbar.

Schmidt squinted as he examined the crowbar. He put both cigarettes in his mouth and lit them. He studied Baur through the smoke.

Baur thought Schmidt understood what had happened by the calm way his eyes took it all in. Schmidt grasped a dry place in the middle of the tool and gently tugged.

"Why don't we put it down?" he asked in soothing tones.

A reasonable question. Baur tried to let go, but his fingers would not relax.

"Herr Baur, I will take it." Schmidt's voice sounded pinched from his efforts to speak and not crush the cigarettes in his lips. He pulled on the crowbar with a little more insistence.

It slid out of Baur's hand.

"Oh good." Schmidt placed it on the floor.

Frau Ostwald whimpered. Schmidt handed one of the cigarettes to Baur. The mild smoke felt wonderful in his lungs.

"Sit, Herr Baur." Schmidt settled onto the couch, crossed his legs and pointed toward the other end, inviting Baur to sit. "Your skill as a mechanical artificer is well known among those who love Germany, so please excuse me for being inappropriate. I mean no disrespect, but I have come by to inquire regarding your prospects. I am sure you are currently engaged. Even so, might you be interested in a position? Something in motorcars?"

"A job, Herr Schmidt?" Baur asked. Schmidt struck Baur as someone

one spoke to with respect, but even so, he thought the man joked. "I have been everywhere. No one is hiring. I will do anything."

"Good. I have heard you are talented with tools."

"Yes, Herr Schmidt."

"And motorcars? Can you fix engines? Suspensions, too?"

"Sir, I have been playing with Panzers these last few years. Motorcars will be fun."

"Of course." Schmidt motioned at the crowbar. "Considering all things, would you be interested in coming with me tonight? You can stay with me. The position will require relocation anyway. I'm sure this is not a problem?"

Baur nodded.

"Good. Maybe we should go now."

Baur used a second candle to beat the shadows back in his and Marta's bedroom, where he packed in a trance. At first, Baur wondered where Marta had gone, but then he remembered what had happened earlier, although the details were fading.

Baur felt lucky Herr Schmidt had picked him. He shoved undergarments into a cloth sack. Marta would not be coming back, after all. He could tell he would be happy, obeying such a leader.

Marta, why? Why did you leave? He dawdled in the little pool of luminescence by their bed and came to a stop, holding socks. His deflated sack lay in front of him.

"Let's go now." Schmidt materialized, taking the socks and tossing them into the sack. He pulled the drawstring tight, then guided Baur out of the room with a hand on Baur's arm. "Do you have tools?"

"Oh, um...yes." He had forgotten the dirty army utility bag made of rough canvas. "They are next to the bed. There is also, the, um...."

"Where is Marta?" Frau Ostwald called from the sitting room.

"Of course." Schmidt passed the sack to Baur and retrieved the tool bag. "We go."

Once again in the sitting room, Schmidt picked up the crowbar.

"Shall we?" He held the tool bag out but kept the crowbar.

Baur accepted his tools. Schmidt opened the door and Baur left the apartment.

"Where is Marta?" Frau Ostwald, kneading her hands, began crying outright.

Schmidt followed Baur out and pulled the door closed behind him.

8

A hard rain had rolled through the Gaufering Displaced Persons Camp. It was gone by sunset, leaving mud and a bitter, cold wet wind behind. Barry blended in with the evening shadows, watching his whole plan go right down the toilet.

Leoshan had driven his deuce-and-a-half to camp with the cargo bed full of goods for the black market. Along with the Safek brothers, Leoshan was supposed to be selling the stuff to the waiting crowd. Instead, Leo glanced in Barry's general direction from the cab of the army truck, concerned, and the Safek brothers, positioned at the rear of the truck, tried to calm the angry DPs and still their shouting in Yiddish. They had no currency or script but wanted the stuff anyway.

"This SNAFU is going nowhere," Barry said, out loud, to no one.

He wore a regulation shirt and tie under a tanker's jacket. His American Jump Wings and Combat Infantryman's Badge were on his left breast, and the Canadian Jump Wings were on the right. The large technical sergeant chevrons and his unit patches were on each arm. His green trousers were bloused into shined but mud-stained boots, and he had balanced his overseas cap, with airborne device, at a cocky angle. A Colt hung from a canvas web belt in an army holster, complete with suicide flap.

Barry threw down the chewed stump of his cigar and tramped over to the truck. He had expected this first load of aid packages and staples such as flour and sugar, diverted by Staff Sergeant Washington, to be snapped up by all the natural entrepreneurs of the DP camp. The idea had been to sell the goods to the DPs. The DPs would then, ideally, black market the goods in town.

He reached the truck as a woman as petit as Rivka, but with a full head of gray hair, slammed Manny with a formidable handbag, large enough to have provided cover and concealment to an infantry platoon on Anzio beach.

"You people, what are you doing!" Barry shouted, in his best army non-commissioned-officer voice. "You there, get over here!"

The crowd started to loosen up. These were people who knew the risk posed by an armed angry man in uniform.

"And you in the truck! Show me your papers!"

That did it. DPs scattered. Barry waved the Safeks into the back of the big Deuce. They scrambled up the gate and Barry threw it shut. He marched toward the cab, head high, shouting once again for papers before jumping inside.

"Hit it," he ordered.

Leo popped the clutch and tires churned, throwing mud all over dawdling onlookers. He drove so fast the truck fishtailed left and right through the turns, all the way out the camp exit. Barry told him to head for their warehouse and then, like the experienced soldier he was, fell asleep.

He woke when the truck stopped, and he sprang out of his seat, immediately alert, and opened one of the large wooden doors of the warehouse. It had originally been built for carriages and horses, but the stalls had been removed and concrete poured over the dirt floor. Thankfully, the big truck fit, despite his personal crap he had left here because it would clutter up the apartment.

Leo had brought over all of Barry's belongings from Austria. It struck him again and left him astonished at how much shit he had accumulated since May, but there was plenty of room for supplies, inventory, tools and equipment, and even a car, now parked under a canvas cover.

Leo pulled inside and killed the engine. Barry closed the door and the Safeks climbed down from the bed. Leo joined them.

"You ain't sore, is you Mr. Barry?" he asked.

"Oh, hell no. Just a SNAFU. 'Course, the woman who hit Manny was in a pet," Barry grinned. "It coulda been murder with her bag, big as it was. You okay?"

Both Safeks smiled at him hesitantly. Neither one was especially competent in English. He must have lost them; his half-assed Yiddish would have to do.

"The grandmother hit you good," Barry said to Manny.

"Good? Like with bricks she hits." He rubbed his arm for emphasis.

"Sorry we couldn't make any deals, Boss. Are you mad?" Elya asked.

"No, we just need to think of something else. Let's go to the club." Barry switched to English and addressed Leo, "Can you stay another day or two while we work this out?"

"Well, I guess so. I won't get no grief from Staff Sergeant Washington if I'm staying with you."

"Yeah, stick around. We'll try again. In the meantime, leave the truck here. You and I will change into civvies and we'll go to the club." Barry swapped languages for the Safeks. "Let's meet at the club in an hour."

An hour later, they were all sitting at a table in front of plates of pork chops and potatoes, explaining to Ulrich how their great plan had failed. A quartet of musicians was setting up on the stage. Working women prowled the floor.

"I know what you mean," Ulrich said. "My day, too, was a, how you say, bust? The bank does not want to grant me a loan. Can you believe? I have the only active cabaret in town, and they will not lend me money." He spat the words out in disgust.

"What do you need to borrow money for?" Barry picked at one of the pork chop bones.

"I want to buy a building for this club, with flats upstairs, you know? They won't do it."

"We have enough in Switzerland if you want to do it. You want to?"

"I want it to look a-okay-dokey to the authorities. I have to live here, not like you. One day you will leave for America, but I have to stay. Well, maybe Munich."

"I won't be going back to America any time soon, Ulrich," Barry shared.

"Why not?"

"It may be some folks got their eyes out for me at home."

"You never said. Might it be the G-men? Or is it some old associates?"

"Could be. Hard to tell."

"Mr. Barry, them girls is giving me the eye," Leo said.

"Yeah, they got an angle. They're professional gals."

"Oh. I see."

"You game?"

"Well, you know..." Leo trailed off uncertainly.

"Here." Barry put three packs of cigarettes on the table.

"Hey, there!" Leo said.

"Hell, boy, spend the night. I'll meet you here tomorrow for supper."

"Thank you, Mr. Barry." Leo scooped the cigarettes up and headed over to the women.

"May we—" Elya started to ask, in Yiddish.

"We'll meet here tomorrow for supper." Barry waved off the Safeks and shifted to English to speak to Ulrich. "How much for all this chow?"

"You know, as one of the owners, you are entitled to eat for free. Even the services of the girls, too, if it's not too often."

"Let's keep everything square." Barry threw more than enough script down. "I'll take my end out of the profits. You could buy me a drink, though, since you're giving stuff away."

He and Ulrich walked over to the bar. They ordered whiskeys. Ulrich fitted a cigarette to his holder and Barry prepared a cigar.

"Too bad about the bank," Barry said.

"Yes, one day they will crawl out from under their minds and money to me throw," Ulrich said, striking a match.

"Whatever." Barry worked the cigar in his mouth. He leaned over to draw on Ulrich's match. "Let's play cards. Maybe our luck will change."

That night, Barry gambled and drank too much. He lost a little, then a lot. He left the club in a generally bad mood. He went over the failure of his scheme again and again. At his apartment building, he managed to stumble by the landlady's flat without waking either the landlady or her daughter.

The next day, he was late to the administration office and Shammi and Gutkin were out on their rounds, Rav Hirsch had settled down in front of his ancient tome with a cup of tea, and Rivka, wearing her nylons, typed away. At least he had beat Resnick to work. Barry's desk was clear, he had transferred enough of the routine work to the others so that he had time to steal or supervise, whatever came up.

He wore what had become his standard office attire, a long-sleeved shirt, tie, boots, and tanker's jacket, and he had taken to carrying a scuffed-up black leather satchel, which he now threw down on his desk. Barry unzipped his jacket and hung it up. His shirt sported the same insignia as the jacket, a CIB and American Jump Wings on the left and his Canadian Jump Wings on the right. He pulled a book out of his satchel.

After the first jam sandwich, Rivka stopped bringing him food. If he wanted tea or coffee, he had to get up and get it himself. This morning, the landlady's daughter had come up and fried him some Spam, so he was satisfied, although he could always use some coffee. He had been meaning to bring in some supplies to augment whatever Rivka had been organizing, but he had not gotten to it yet. He had no idea how the people in the office were eating and didn't really care, but he didn't want to rock their boat, either.

Various pursuits occupied the staff. A typewriter clacked away in the background. Barry read until he came to a rough passage, then he shut his book and slammed it down on the desk.

"Godammedsonofabitch!" he yelled and hopped up to pace the office. "Sorry," he continued, embarrassed, "but this guy, Murdstone, the bastard, just threw this boy away. His mom died and he just threw him away. Son of a bitch!"

Rivka translated her way through the English and clarity washed over her face, followed by radiant joy.

"You read *Copperfield*? The Dickens you are having?" she tentatively walked over to Barry.

"Yeah, sure. I picked this up at a rest center." He handed her the pulpy paperback produced for the war effort.

"I love Dickens." Rivka ran her hands over the cover.

"You've read Dickens?"

She blushed. "I read with my tutor. I wanted to learn literature at university. But you? You read much?"

"Not really, but I like it." Barry reached for his wallet. "Lieutenant Mac gave me a list once. Junk I should read." He unfolded a worn piece of paper and smoothed it flat on his desktop.

"Look at this, *Beowulf*, Chaucer, Shakespeare." Rivka leaned in to examine the stained, ragged sheet with names and titles written in faded ink. "So! Austen and Brontë. Who is Crane?"

"An American. *The Red Badge of Courage*?"

She wrinkled her nose. "You recite to this Mac after you finish?" she asked with new life in her eyes.

"Oh, no. Lieutenant Mac is dead." Barry thought for a minute. "All the Canadians are. Dead or shot up. 'Course, Beane's 'chute didn't open. He got it before everyone."

"I don't understand."

"I started out in the Canadian Army. I crossed the border in '39 and joined up. My first regiment went to England. Then a bunch of us went from England to Fort Benning in America for airborne training. After, we were sent to the First Special Service Force where we were assigned with Americans. I switched armies there 'cause I'm an American."

"No! An American? Really?"

"Sure, can't you tell?"

Rivka laughed at him. "Everyone can tell." Her smile made her beautiful.

"Anyway, all my Canadian friends were shot up or killed, and come to think of it, all the Americans we started with got it, too. By the end of the war, I didn't know anybody in my platoon."

"May you know no more sorrows," a suddenly subdued Rivka consoled quietly.

"Hell, even my mom was dead by then. The Red Cross told me in 1943."

She reached out and rested her hand on Barry's arm. Rav Hirsch coughed audibly, and she pulled her hand back.

"We Jews have books, too," Rav Hirsch observed in Yiddish.

Instead of his usual tired expression, Rav Hirsch scrutinized Barry intently.

"What books are those, Grandfather?" he asked, humoring the old man.

"The Torah."

"So, what's in it?" Barry knew the Torah was the first five books of the Bible; he joshed the old man a minute was all.

"One of our great sages once said it was about not doing to others what you would not want done to you. The rest is commentary, and now we study the commentary."

"Right now?" The old rabbi was pretty funny. Barry wanted to share the joke with Rivka, but she hung off Rav Hirsch's every word.

"Take, for instance, the Ten Statements. The whole Torah can be found in the Ten Statements."

The two young people moved toward Rav Hirsch.

"Ten what?"

"The Ten Commandments," Rivka said.

Rav Hirsch sighed and shook his head slightly. "The Ten Statements contain all the Torah. The Name, blessed be He, instructs us to have faith in his being, not to worship idols, not to use His name in vain oaths, to observe the Sabbath and make it holy, to honor our parents, not to murder, not to know another man's wife, not to steal, not to be a false witness and not to covet. The complete Torah can be found in these statements."

Rav Hirsch scowled severely in Barry's direction.

"Let us consider the good deed of not stealing for a moment," Rav Hirsch said.

Pinchas, the tall, thin rabbi, staggered into the room with a face showing evidence of having recently stopped more than one punch. His left eye had swollen shut and his right eye peered out at the world though a mere slit. Blood trickled out of his nose, and his lips were split, black and blue sausage casings. Dust covered his clothes, and he had lost his hat.

"What the hell happened to you?" Barry asked, in English.

"I still have it," he murmured, gesturing weakly with his left hand, which held the supply ledger. "He wanted it, but I kept it!"

Rivka hurried out of the room. Barry helped Pinchas sit in a nearby chair. She reappeared with a moistened rag and started cleaning his face.

Barry adopted a casual air and tried out his Yiddish again. "Who did this?"

Pinchas answered in a sentence, but all Barry could understand was the word "Russian."

"What did he say?" Barry asked, switching back to English.

"The Russian, the boss of the supply room," Rivka interpreted. "He did it. He's a White Russian and he doesn't want to go back."

Barry knew exactly what to do, having already heard of this "Russian from supply." He pulled a holstered pistol wrapped in an olive drab web belt from his satchel.

Barry unfastened the black leather holster flap and drew a Colt .45. Dropping the magazine out of the handle, he made sure the chamber was empty. He released the slide, which slammed forward with a loud metal on metal crash and pressed the trigger. The hammer fell with an audible click, then he replaced the loaded magazine and slid the weapon into the holster.

"Let's go," Barry said to Pinchas as he secured the web belt round his waist.

"What are you going to do?" Rav Hirsch asked in Yiddish.

"I'm not going to do anything. He is," Barry said in English, pointing at Pinchas.

Rivka translated for them.

"What do you want Pinchas to do?" Rav Hirsch asked.

"Pinchas is going to fight the Russian," Barry said, in Yiddish.

"Fight the Russian? Can't you see? He already did!"

Pinchas's one visible eye zeroed in on Barry.

He didn't want to imagine the hate that would have been on Pinchas's face, had it been able to form an expression. Pinchas must think him crazy.

"Pinchas has to do it again," Barry replied in English. "Let's go boy. Up! On your feet!"

"You do not make him go there," Rivka pleaded. "Please not do that."

Pinchas gently pulled the damp rag out of her hand and wiped his swollen eyes with it. He slowly rose.

"We go," he agreed, placing the ledger in front of Rav Hirsch.

"Sergeant Rosen," Rivka called out, just before they walked out of the room.

He expected some girl-like whimpering as he faced her.

"Everyone I know is dead, too," she said quietly.

Rivka stood in the middle of the room. Light streamed in through the windows behind her. Her hair seemed so black it drank the radiance; her skin fairly shimmered.

He nodded, dry-mouthed, before they left.

Outside, clouds left only patches of blue sky, and a crisp breeze spoke of the coming winter. Barry set a quick pace on their way to the supply building, with Pinchas struggling to keep up. Barry arrived at the loading dock and jumped onto the landing.

The large warehouse door was split down the middle and hinged on both sides. He threw the latch and pulled open the right side. Cold air surged in. Slavic shouting erupted immediately from a group of men in shirt sleeves.

"Which one of you did this?" Barry waved to his left.

The nearest men started laughing.

Barry turned, expecting to see Pinchas, but no one was there. Twisting farther around and looking down, he found Pinchas struggling. Both hands and a foot were on the truck-high concrete platform, but the rest of him hung below eye level. He dangled there, grunting with effort.

Barry sighed and grabbed a shoulder, helping Pinchas roll up onto the landing. Pinchas gracelessly scrambled to his feet and caught his breath.

The little group of workmen parted, and a mountain of a man ambled through the gap. The foreman's squinty little eyes were set back under a protrusion of bone over robust round cheeks. Wads of muscle made a forty-five-degree angle from his ears to his shoulders. He was large in girth, width and height, and wore a work shirt with sleeves rolled up over thick forearms, suspenders and dusty trousers of a rough material. He sneered with merriment and malice and spoke to the group in a language Barry didn't understand. The large man rubbed bloody knuckles with a dirty rag.

"So this must be the Russian from supply," Barry commented. "I guess you're not going to beat him up after all."

A confused Pinchas asked Barry to speak Yiddish.

"Never mind."

Barry pointed forcefully with both index fingers into the warehouse. The workers fell back, perhaps in testament to Barry's command presence. Barry and Pinchas followed. The Russian produced a steady stream of verbiage. He and Barry maintained eye contact.

Barry quickly developed a strong dislike for the foreman. Obviously, with a man like this, there could be no business. The foreman would need to be the boss all the way. He sighed again.

"Supply boss want to know what you here for," someone in the group yelled.

"He can't go around beating up my staff." Barry didn't take his eyes off the Russian.

"He say little Jew bastard with gun not ever his chief."

Barry growled at the worker doing the translating, who instantly threw up his hands, palms forward.

"He say, not me. I not say,"

Barry signaled they should move even deeper into the warehouse. "Shall we dance?" he asked.

There was no reason for Barry to believe the Russian knew American slang or even English, but he must have grasped the context because he grinned and nodded at Barry's pistol.

Barry unhooked the belt and rolled the holster up in it. As he did so, the foreman beamed broadly and started walking backward. Pinchas came abreast of Barry, who slammed his bundle into Pinchas's chest. The tall rabbi grabbed it with both hands.

They all drifted farther into the warehouse until they reached a spacious area amongst the industrial shelving. The Russian man spread his arms in wide welcome, smiling, nodding, sure of his impending victory.

Barry shed his tanker jacket and placed it on a box with his overseas cap. The foreman circled. Barry followed, calmly unbuttoning his cuffs and rolling up his own sleeves. As usual in situations like this, an edgy kind of fear hit him.

Workers jockeyed for position, presumably to watch their boss pummel the little American. Barry risked one more glance at Pinchas, who stood off by himself, clutching the gun belt, nobody bothering him.

With a yell, the foreman rushed Barry like a bull on the charge, probably hoping to end it right there with a brutal roundhouse. If Barry had stopped learning how to fight on the tough streets of Newark, New Jersey, it would have. Those skills would not have been enough to overcome disadvantages in height and weight.

But the war intervened. His timing honed by training and combat, Barry waited until they were close. The foreman launched his punch before planting his feet. Barry grabbed the foreman's shirt-front, dropped his left foot back and rotated at the waist, flipping the foreman over his hip. At the same time, he tried to up-end the foreman to smash his cranium on the concrete floor.

Barry threw his opponent cleanly, but the up-ending didn't work. Barry held on a second too long and, defeated by mass, lost his balance and fell. He went over and rolled up into a fighting stance, securely crouched with his hands in front of him.

The foreman had hit the concrete and slipped into some shelving. He wobbled up onto his feet. Anger and better judgment seemed to vie for the limited available space in his brain. Anger won out and he charged again, yelling the same way. This time they were farther apart. He extended his arms, intending to grab Barry, who managed to get both of his own hands between the foreman's arms.

He grabbed the foreman's shirt again, planted his left boot in the giant's fleshy middle and tumbled backward. At the top of the foreman's arc, Barry let go and thrust upward with his leg, tossing the man away, then rolled sideways and whirled to his feet.

The foreman landed solidly on his back, losing all his air in one great exhalation. Barry hoped it had knocked the fight out of him, but the large man righted himself, got up on one knee and rose.

Barry closed the distance and hit the man with a straight right to the nose and a left to his Adam's apple. The foreman kept rising. He chopped the foreman in the side of his throat and slapped his ear. As targets passed upward, Barry nailed them with hard punches to the clavicles, solar plexus and floating ribs. The foreman reached his full height, and Barry never saw it coming.

The bear of a man swiped at him in pain and petulance with a massive paw and sent Barry sprawling. The blow blurred his vision and slowed him down considerably. He gained his feet, and the big man came on again.

The foreman circled, moving fists like a nineteenth-century English boxer. Barry had marked him; the Russian bled from his nose and mouth and held his head at an angle to the left.

Barry threw strikes the foreman easily parried as he punched as well, slow would-be thumps meeting air where Barry had been, until Barry moved in too close.

The Russian enveloped him in a bear hug. Barry tried to move his hands up between their torsos, but he didn't have the room. Jolts of pain shot out from his middle. He jammed his fingers into loose flesh and grabbed the foreman's floating ribs as best he could. The foreman roared as Barry pulled up on the ribs, trying to break them off the spine. Barry head-butted his captor once, twice and a third time. The foreman's hold weakened just enough.

Barry kneed the man in the testicles. The foreman let him slip. Standing on his own, Barry gave him the same again, landing a blow with the point of his knee after a satisfying wind-up. The big man felt it. He started blubbering. Barry stepped to his left and kicked the foreman in the side of his leg, driving him to the concrete, then chopped him in the back of the neck, and the foreman ended up on all fours, head down.

Barry scuttled behind the foreman, aiming to punt those gonads over the goal post, but he didn't have to. The large man collapsed and rolled onto his back. He held his hands up in surrender and said something in a series of hard consonants, sounding an awful lot like the Russian version of "uncle."

Barry caught his breath. He walked over to Pinchas and, with a wink, pulled his pistol out of the holster. He grabbed the translator by his shirt and dragged him over to where the foreman lay, breathing heavily. Barry leaned over the big man, pinched his mouth open and jammed the Colt in it.

After Barry made sure Pinchas was out of earshot, he spoke to the translator.

"You tell him if he sells any more stuff out the back door of this place without paying me, I'll come in here and finish the job," Barry snarled through clenched teeth.

"What you say?" the worker translating asked in a confused panic.

"No more sell! Only through me!"

The translator understood and translated. The foreman nodded vigorously.

Barry indicated Pinchas. "You beat him up, or anybody else that works for me, I'll come back and finish the job."

Translation complete, Barry let go of the man and drew the pistol out of his mouth. As an afterthought, Barry put the barrel of the semi-automatic against the foreman's forehead, making the foreman cross-eyed.

Barry thumbed the hammer back. "You beat up any more Jews and I'll come back and finish the job."

"Okay!" the Russian yelled, not needing the benefits of translation by then.

Barry gently lowered the hammer down on the empty chamber.

Standing by Pinchas, Barry holstered the pistol, tucked in his shirt and adjusted his gig line. He clipped his web belt around his waist. A respectful silence lay over the men of the loading dock, even Pinchas. Barry pretended to ignore them as he put on his jacket and overseas cap.

"What are you looking at?" he finally asked Pinchas.

"Yehuda ha Maccabi."

The hero of Hanukkah.

"You're a goofball," Barry said in English, smiling. "Let's go."

He and Pinchas walked to the office. Barry was starting to form some idea of respect for the tall rabbi. After all, in spite of a terrific beating, he had seemed willing to fight back.

"Well, well," Barry whispered. "What do we have here?"

An intimidating middle-aged woman waited at the entrance to the administration building, still some way ahead of them. She had gray and brown hair styled in a firm helmet the breeze could not sway, and she wore a bulky frayed overcoat in a drab green and umber color scheme, increasing her girth greatly. She watched their approach calmly.

"So, this is the new American officer?" She spoke in Yiddish when they reached her. "What happened to you?" she asked Pinchas.

"A Russian," he replied, smiling.

"So by the Americans, a beating is something to laugh about?"

"So? Maybe you should ask what happed to the Russian?" The tall rabbi touched Barry's arm. "I'm going to go upstairs. Thank you." Pinchas scuttled away before Barry could answer.

"Good morning, Mrs. Levenson," Barry said.

"How did you know my name?" she asked warily.

Barry shrugged.

"So, let's see," she gestured at Barry's hand. "From what Pinchas said and your raw knuckles, I think maybe you happened to the Russian?"

He nodded.

"So it must also be true that you are going into the black market business?"

"Black market is illegal," Barry deadpanned in his hesitant Yiddish.

"Illegal?"

"Yes."

"So?" Mrs. Levenson laughed. "Beating Russian supply foremen is illegal too."

He swallowed his rebuttal.

"Anyway, it's fine. He needed to learn some manners. You know, the black market is the single business we can do. It is like the old days. No jobs for us. Moneylending maybe," she said, followed immediately by a short burst of humorless laughter.

"And you are willing to help your fellow DPs?"

"Someone must."

They measured one another for a long moment. He'd have thought a man in uniform would intimidate her, considering her experiences during the war. She gazed at him without fear, but with a great amount of sadness in her eyes.

"You are going to try to control the black market, I see. I tell you, it will not be as easy as you think, new American officer."

Barry took a breath in preparation to speak.

"Don't you say anything," Mrs. Levenson interjected. "I understand you. You will see." She started to walk away. "You will see," she said again, over her shoulder.

"That's right, sister. We'll both see," he grumbled.

9

An unexpected frigid gust sucked the air out of Rivka's lungs as she left the administration building at the end of the Gaufering DP Camp workday. She had seen the clouds thicken but had taken no notice and now, without a jacket, she embraced herself and scuttled, hunched over and knock-kneed, down muddy lanes toward the barracks.

The coarse low structure had been her home since her imposed relocation to Germany and remained so now. Light fled out of the barracks between gaps in walls fashioned from irregular slats and Rivka shivered as she thought of January, February and March. True, some of the men had come by and divided what had been one large bay into rooms, but it would never be more than a temporary building the Nazis had constructed for people they thought of as temporary as well.

Inside, she hurried to the middle section. There, Mrs. Kugel had organized a kitchen of sorts. Hot plates, an icebox and some gouged cabinetry holding liberated German utensils for the use of the single girls and women. Mrs. Kugel did her best with what she had, and they were thankful for it.

"Hello, Mrs. Kugel," Rivka greeted the small sharp-featured woman whose silver and black hair had grown in sufficiently to be pulled into a bun. "How are you?"

"Almost ready, dear." Mrs. Kugel handed Rivka a bowl. A fried potato pancake smelling wonderfully of onions and chicken fat covered the bottom. "Stand by me, dear. Potato soup with leeks." She beamed as she stirred a pot simmering on a hot plate. She ladled the soup over the pancake and placed a spoon in the bowl. "While it's still hot, dear." She spun Rivka from her shoulders and nudged her toward Hannah.

"Wait, I need another spoon, not this one!" Rivka said.

A swastika decorated the top of the handle.

"Oh my," Mrs. Kugel switched it for simple flatware.

Rivka walked quickly to the small, partitioned area where she lived with two other girls, carefully holding the bowl by her fingertips. Rich odors emanated from the wholesome food.

"When I smell that, I know the war is over." Hannah Blimah was awake and watching from her bed.

All of them were thin, but Hannah Blimah had not put on any weight since liberation, remaining emaciated. It concerned and worried everyone that she was no more than skin over bone. Eyes sparkling with intelligence and mischief were the only remnants of the vibrant teenager the Germans had captured. She lay under a frayed wool blanket and a clean white sheet.

Their living space also had not recovered from the war. Attempts at decoration were limited to a dingy painting of yellow flowers and dull curtains liberated from the former camp commandant's house. The warped planks of the softwood floor were gouged and stained. A rag posing as a tablecloth covered a small round stand.

"Mrs. Kugel's revenge on the Nazis." Rivka forced good cheer to camouflage her concern for her friend's health. "Food so good *they* would die for it."

Hannah Blimah tried to prop herself up. After several attempts, Rivka put the bowl down on the table and helped. Hannah seemed less substantial, even just compared to yesterday.

"It hurts Mrs. Kugel's feelings when you don't eat everything she makes." Rivka moved a simple wobbly chair close to the head of the bed. "She thinks you don't like her cooking." Taking the spoon and bowl in her hand, she began to feed her friend.

"Mmm, delicious," Hannah said, after a sip of the soup. "Tell me, what's going on at the administration building?"

"Here, try the potato pancake." Rivka cut off a small piece and presented it, slathered with the hearty soup.

Hannah took it and swallowed. Rivka watched the bulge of food visibly travel down her neck.

"Tell me," Hannah insisted, "do you miss Howie?"

"I don't know if I miss him." She scooped up another serving. "He was nice, a nice boy, but...."

"What more do you need? Like by a Rothchild, you're so wealthy you can wave goodbye to a nice American boy?"

"He was nice, and American, but he wasn't, I don't know, he wasn't at all like, you know. Take Sergeant Rosen, for instance—"

"Don't tell me! You're sweet on Sergeant Rosen!"

"No, I am not!" Rivka felt herself blushing, so she ducked her head to cover it up and tried to give Hannah more soup at the same time.

"Yes, you are—I hear he is a rogue."

"He is not a rogue," Rivka said indignantly. She put the spoon down in the bowl. "He happens to be a very nice boy."

"A nice boy doesn't end up wearing the uniform of a war hero."

"How do you know what he wears?"

"Other people talk to me too, you know. They say he is handsome."

"I don't know." Rivka swirled the soup around the bowl, her face burning furiously now.

"I see how much you don't know."

"You don't understand. He started learning Torah with Rav Hirsch."

"Oh, a scholar he is. *Mishnah* or *Gemara*?"

"The Ten Statements, if you must know."

"The Ten Statements? For children, the Ten Statements."

"He did not learn them when he was a child...he had to work. He comes from a poor family," Rivka lied.

Barry never discussed his background, but she could tell he had not gotten much of a Jewish education growing up. She imagined he had had to help support the family. Why else would Jewish parents neglect the education of their children?

"Anyway," Hannah said, "I hear he needs to study the Ten Statements. Especially the one about stealing."

"And what do you mean by that?"

"Well, I hear things."

"You hear things? I'm working in the camp office. What have you heard that I haven't?"

"That the American officer Rosen is in the black market."

"You don't know." Rivka shook her head defensively.

"People talk."

"The Language of Evil they say, and this is what you hear." Rivka frowned.

"I don't think so. Why did he come here? I think it's right. He wants to be in the black market."

"He's a top American officer in the army." Rivka spooned up more soup. "They don't choose where they go. Besides, he makes money. He doesn't need any black market."

"If you think so."

"I think so."

"I also heard he gave what-for to the Russian in the supply warehouse."

"What—that just happened, how did—oh, never mind. Eat!" Rivka trained the spoon on Hannah's mouth.

She ate several grams before waving off the rest.

"But the last of the potato pancake," Rivka said.

"I can't, not another bite. When we were freed, I thought I'd eat until I blew up. But now I can't eat much at all."

Rivka absentmindedly dragged the spoon through the leavings. She debated bringing it up again, but her curiosity got the better of her.

"So what have you heard about Sergeant Rosen and the black market?"

"Well," Hannah warmed to her subject with a grin, "I might have heard something about a Sergeant Rosen and the black market, but I'm sure it couldn't have been your Sergeant Rosen. He would never!"

"You are so bad. Tell me."

"Well, I heard he tried to sell goods to us for resale last night. A Black in an army truck came with two Jews in the back. They wanted cash! Who has cash? Anyway, when they wouldn't give credit, the people became a little agitated."

"What happened?"

"Mrs. Deinstein hit one with her bag." Hannah laughed.

"Really?"

"Really. The two Jews were pretty low types, and they would not give her a single thing on credit. Then your Sergeant walks up, screaming for papers, so everyone made like they ran away. They all saw him jump in the truck with them and drive off. Does he think we're idiots? They are all working together. They could be hoodlums! 'Give me your papers,'" Hannah mimicked, forcing her voice low and adopting an exaggerated authoritarian manner.

"Come quick, dear," Mrs. Kugel interrupted, "they are looking for you. Something happened with one of the men from Operation Judgment."

Rivka put the bowl down on the little table and followed Mrs. Kugel out.

10

Barry finished his last notation in a ledger, alone in the Gaufering DP Camp office. It took more effort than he had planned to set the situation up the way he wanted. Luckily, Howie had laid a good foundation—sloppy records and delinquent communications. The complicated part came from maintaining the proper level of efficiency, or rather inefficiency, regarding the camp's affairs. They needed to be messed up enough to hide things but not so messed up someone would want to visit or call for an inspection of the place.

He shut the ledger with a bang, sending echoes through the empty office. Rivka was gone, the rabbis had left before sundown and Resnick had missed the whole day. Barry signed Resnick's name on several letters, sealed the envelopes and put them in the outbox. He slid on his tanker jacket and headed out the door into the cold night.

Instead of getting into the Jeep, he decided to take a stroll and see what went on in the evenings. To be sure, he grazed his fingertips along the top of the leather holster at his side. Only the occasional DP walked by. Barry assumed most of the residents (Campers? Inmates? He didn't know what to call them) were inside eating. Everything was quiet, until he heard something off to his right.

A car with a long snout and small cockpit idled in front of one of the barracks, parked sideways. He paused and watched from the shadows. Satisfied but wary, he entered the housing unit.

A group of men clustered by a bunk. One man, dressed in a tweed jacket, fine wool trousers and a shirt and tie, did not belong. In his mid-thirties and oozing health and energy, he was taller than the rest, with blond hair and a slender build. Barry had not seen him before, in camp or out in town.

Barry moved closer. In the bunk, another man sweated, grimacing in pain. He had brown hair, olive skin and bad teeth. He pressed a rag to his middle, but it wasn't helping with the damp red stain at all.

The men detected the camp's authority figure, and the small group dissipated. The injured man was beyond caring, but his tall partner assessed Barry from top to bottom. His expression displayed neither concern nor fright, nor any emotion at all.

Barry knew he presented the same poker face. They were both waiting and ready for the next card. He thought he should say something to get the ball rolling. After all, gut-shot guys did not show up to his camp every day.

At that moment, Rivka slipped by him. She appraised the man on the bed and sucked air audibly.

The tall man smiled at her and it knocked years off his appearance. They had a rapid exchange in a language familiar to Barry but that he could not identify at first. Then it came to him, they were speaking Hebrew, but not with any accent he had heard before.

"Sergeant Rosen, this is Paul Featherstone," Rivka said. "Paul, this is Sergeant Rosen, the new camp director."

"Administrator," Barry corrected, making no move to stick out his hand.

"I expect this might seem somewhat awkward to you, Sergeant," Paul said in the King's English.

Barry had spent enough time in Great Britain to recognize Paul's poshness, and in the army to recognize Paul's expectation of being obeyed.

The doctor from the married barracks shoved his way in. A green canvas US Army medic's bag hung on a wide strap from his shoulder. He issued some orders in decisive Yiddish, and everyone slowly moved away. Paul ended up next to Barry, with Rivka close by.

"So what's the skinny?" Barry asked.

"That's why I like Yanks, Rivka. Highly efficient. Are you an MOT, Sergeant?"

"What the hell is an MOT?"

"A Member of the Tribe?"

Barry laughed. He had never heard the phrase before. "Yes," he said. "I'm Jewish."

Paul and Rivka had another quick exchange in their funny-sounding Hebrew.

"Rivka tells me you were moderately active during the war," Paul said.

"I did my part."

"But you served in a combat unit?" Paul guided them toward the door.

The three of them walked outside. The brisk night air discouraged bystanders, and they were now far enough away from anyone else to ensure some measure of privacy.

"Listen, this ain't about me. Now I can tell you're someone used to being in charge, maybe an ex-Rupert even, but this is my camp. Who's your wounded and what are you doing here?"

The Englishman glared through squinted eyes. Eventually, he nodded.

"Dudu, my friend in there, and I were soldiers with the Jewish Brigade of the British Army. Do you know it, the brigade?"

"Yeah, what of it?"

"It was raised from Palestinian Jews, fought in Italy and garrisoned in the low countries. You know its operational record?"

"Whatever. What's going on?"

Paul and Rivka had another quick discussion in Hebrew.

"Have you heard of Operation Judgment?" Paul asked.

"Look," Barry said, annoyed, "Last time. What's the skinny?"

"I guess you haven't at that. It applies directly to Dudu. Operation Judgment is the effort to mete out some justice, as it were, to some of those most responsible for the recent unpleasantness our Jewish relations on the continent have suffered. Do you follow me?"

"You're going around greasing them SS guys, right?"

"Ah," Paul started. "Well…simply put but veracious, in the end."

"So what happened, a kraut get the better of you?"

"You're a quick study. Yes. The fat old bastard got the better of us. Dudu took a few in the belly. Now the race, as they say, is on. Can I leave Dudu here while I attempt to return the favor on our adversary?"

"Where is he?" Barry glanced from side to side as if the former SS man was in the camp.

"We think he's in town. We caught up with him in Munich, but he was heading this way. That's where the unfortunate business with Dudu happened. The monster's mum lives here. Can you believe it had a mother? I have an address, and I hope to catch him at her house tonight. I'm concerned if I wait too long, I might miss the opportunity."

"You and who else?"

"Just me, I'm afraid. Not much of a staff in this Operation Judgment. We're doing it on the cheap."

Barry considered the situation. As a provisional lieutenant, near the end, he and his scout section had stumbled over a subcamp. He remembered what he felt that day—incredulous, revolted disbelief and pity turning to anger upon learning that the stacks of emaciated dead were Jews.

Even so, he didn't come to Gaufering to right wrongs or get involved in revenge. Big Meyer had always told him killing was something to avoid unless absolutely necessary. He said it was bad for business. He'd also cautioned Barry—murder had a habit of coming back on a fella.

"No coincidence it's a sin," Big used to say.

Now, this English twit and his boy had already gotten the wrong end of the deal, and the twit wanted to go out and get more of the same. And what were these SS types anyway? Just a bunch of dirty coppers nobody was ever going to bring to "justice." Barry was here to make money and nothing else. Well, maybe have a little enjoyment as well. Rivka gazed at him expectantly, her expression saying everything. This broad was all business, he thought.

"So we taking this smooth ride or what?" Barry asked, indicating the two-tone coupe.

He was shocked. He had intended for something completely different to come out of his mouth.

"Well, I say, Sergeant. Yes. Yes, indeed and it would be my pleasure to have you along," Paul said. "We haven't a moment to lose."

English restraint prevented a greater demonstration, but Barry recognized Paul's gratification at the answer he had evidently not expected either.

The three of them walked to the red and cream sports car. Paul opened the driver's side door. Rivka blitzed by him, pushing the driver's seat forward and wiggling into the back.

"Now wait one minute, sister," Barry reprimanded from the passenger side. "There is no way in—"

"If I may, Sergeant, I should fill you in on Rivka's operational history before you put the old foot in the mouth," the Englishman suggested.

"Humph. What is this thing anyway?"

"An Audi 920 Cabriolet convertible. Took the keys right out of the hands of a former camp adjutant we caught up with just after the surrender. Nice, isn't it?" Paul pressed the accelerator, and the engine rumbled its desire to run.

"Dead hands?"

Paul laughed a slight, proper little laugh.

"None of this is good news." Barry unlatched the passenger door.

They sped out the main gate toward town. Barry glared over his shoulder at Rivka. She met his stare evenly.

"So what makes sister's operational history, as you call it, so special?" Barry jerked his thumb rearward.

Again, Paul and Rivka conversed in Hebrew. After a brief pause, Paul switched to English.

"She was a communications runner for the resistance in Poland. At great risk to herself, she ran dispatches from ghetto to ghetto and from the towns and cities to the fighters in the forest. She was among the most reliable and steady of the runners."

Barry twisted to half face Rivka. "This true?"

"I assure you it is," Paul replied for her. "Getting Rivka to confirm it would be like prying special operations executive information out of you, I'm afraid. Anyway, they caught her because she tried to gather up some children for an escape attempt out of the Lodz Ghetto. They were all captured in one of the final roundups. She ended up in the forced labor system. Small hands, you see."

"I see."

They were all quiet until Barry spoke again. "What did the jerk we're going for do?"

"First, he was SS Supervisor of Soviet guards, those that turned coat and worked in the camps, and later, execution supervisor at Budzyn. He directly supervised the mechanics of killing at that camp. He was promoted to deputy operations officer there then acting operations officer until the Soviets arrived. By the end of the war, he was doing the actual selections. Witnesses say he fled just before the death march out. He finished up at Mathausen on staff. We were put on to him in Bremen and found him in Munich, but we made a mistake. We gave him a chance. He's a right wily bastard. If you get to him first, do not hesitate." Paul tapped the rim of the steering wheel with the ball of his hand.

"What's he look like?"

The Englishman laughed. "Mussolini, actually. Bull head on powerful shoulders and a big fat middle. As tall as me. Bald. I may have winged him, but I'm not sure."

"All right. Let's do this thing, then. But I'm not going in uniform. Let's swing by my place so I can change."

"We don't have time, I'm afraid. Need to get straight to it."

"We ain't got the firepower either. I need civvies and at least a second heater. Only take me a minute."

At his apartment, Barry changed into a suit, skipped the tie and secured another pistol. He considered the viola case but ruled it out. This copper will be long gone, he thought. With his hat jammed down and his unbuttoned overcoat flapping behind him, he scurried out to the car.

They roared away, and Paul and Rivka started speaking in Hebrew again. Barry's ear was getting used to it, and he made out the address the Englishman gave her and the directions she provided. Leaving the city center, they entered a neighborhood of neat cottages north of town. After more turns, Rivka indicated they had reached the right street.

"Shall we park it here and walk in?" Paul slowed to a stop by the side of the road.

"Maybe we should try a quick reconnaissance," Barry recommended. "Just drive by, real calm like, to see if anything's going on."

Paul mulled it over. He checked with Rivka via the rear-view mirror. She didn't respond and he offered up a silent shrug before putting the Audi in gear and easing down the street.

"It comes," Rivka said in English.

"How do you know?" Barry asked.

"This town I know already."

Barry saw one car parked on the street, on his side, four houses down. Suddenly they were next to it. Light glowed out of the gaping front doorway of the nearest house, highlighting the silhouette of a tall, wide man; his head sitting directly on broad shoulders, a figure matching Paul's description of their target. The man held a suitcase in each hand.

"There he is!" Barry said, tugging his door latch.

He put one foot onto the running board, planning to step into the street as the car moved on. He figured this would allow him to clear the coupe and engage the man. He hopped off.

Unfortunately, Paul slammed on the brakes. The Audi halted with a lurch. Barry, moving to account for his momentum, had not expected this and crashed into the inside of his open door. He fell backward, the hard landing knocking the wind out of him, but even as he struggled for breath, he scrambled to his feet.

Their target ran for the house but tripped on the low step leading into the cottage.

Barry dashed toward him, pulling his Colt from its holster. The fat man rolled onto his back and began yanking at something in his right coat pocket. Barry arrived at the doorway just as the fat man produced a Walther P38 pistol. Barry aimed a kick at the Walther, with fear giving it plenty of oomph. He nailed the fat man's hand, and the pistol spun off into the night. Barry dropped straight down, landing knee-first on the man's torso. He heard people running up behind him.

"Is it him?" Barry punched their target twice in the face with his left hand.

"Old boy, I—" Paul started.

"Is it him!?"

Paul leaned in and scrutinized the fat man. "Yes, it's him."

"Sure?"

"Positive."

Barry eyed Rivka with an unspoken question on his face. She answered with a terse affirmative nod. He stood up and pointed his big automatic at the downed man's chest.

"*Nien*," someone said.

A gray-haired old woman with the approximate dimensions of a meatball from Spatola's hovered in the doorway. Barry eyeballed her hands for a weapon. They were empty. He forced himself to focus past her, on the inside of the cottage. He did not see any other movement.

Barry pulled the trigger twice. The man's body jerked. Then Barry shot the SS man once in the face. Blood flowed out of the neat hole between and above the target's eyes, and a crimson puddle grew behind his bean on the stoop, forming an unholy halo; the precious fluid streaming out of an unseen exit wound.

"Let's go." Barry started backing down the walk.

Paul and Rivka froze, mute witnesses to the man bleeding out.

Barry holstered up as he walked away, backward. He toppled over one of the suitcases and fell down again.

"Crap! Hey, do we want these? And what about the car over there? It could be his."

The questions got the Englishman moving. He took Rivka's arm and maneuvered her down the walk.

"Leave the car," Paul said calmly. "Take the bags and we're off."

Barry picked up both bags and wrestled them into the back seat of the coupe, next to Rivka. In his last sight of the cottage, the old woman, with her rounded back, stood in profile over the body.

A solemn mood settled on the Audi 920. With the exception of Newark, he had taken life exclusively in combat. True, he had threatened more than one German and Italian prisoner, but he'd never killed one. Bopped 'em on the head occasionally, but that was no crime. And, if the good officers of the Winchester City Police in Britain ever laid hands on him, they'd likely want him to confess to having tried to take off a few of the local wiseguys when he was stationed there, the ones in the life that did not appreciate Yankee competition.

He unconsciously scratched the scar along his jaw.

Those had been misses, those English toughs. Tonight, he had killed in cold blood. This time he had had no official reason. It made him melancholy.

The dead guy had sent only God knows how many up the chimney in the camps, Barry thought. And all those Jews he had run through the machinery of the Final Solution, doesn't their target get the blame for that? And Dudu.

"Anyway," Paul uttered, "he was with the SS."

"That's just what I was thinking," Barry said.

Rivka chimed in with, "How did you know what I was think?"

Barry wanted to face her, but a feeling akin to embarrassment prevented him from looking backward.

"I see we are of the same mind." The Englishman had eased his tone. "Sergeant Rosen, you are quite the technician."

"Technician?" Barry asked, confused. What'd he fix?

"In these matters, it would seem so. Well done back there."

"Indeed, my lordship," Barry replied, imitating a smart English accent. "I daresay, falling on my arse was quite the technical achievement."

Rivka giggled. Barry snorted. Soon all three of them were laughing.

"Too bad poor Dudu won't be alive to hear the news," Paul said after they had calmed down.

Yup, too bad.

Back at the camp, Barry unlocked the chain securing the gate. He had a passing interest in how loose the gates were secured. An adult needed to be able to slip through. They drove to the barracks to see Dudu.

Paul went in but came right back out. "He's unconscious but breathing. I'm going to sit with him. Don't worry, we'll be out by morning."

Barry nodded.

"Perhaps it would be best if I did not hold you up any longer, Sergeant Rosen. I notice you make the natives restless."

"I guess so. Good luck to you."

They didn't shake hands.

Barry didn't want to leave Rivka with the Englishman, but he could not think of a politic way to take her with him. He admitted defeat and slowly walked away as they conversed in Hebrew, making him jealous. Well, he could always go home and clean his Colt, he thought.

Just then, footsteps padded toward him from behind and he felt a tap on his shoulder.

"Would you like a tea?" Rivka asked.

They left the overhead bulb off in the administration office, and Barry moved his chair over to Rivka's desk. She poured hot water into his cup. The shadows caused by her weak desk lamp made her face skull-like. She grimaced sadly.

"Not...not," she struggled for an English word, "pleasant...tonight?"

At first, he wanted to laugh it off. He could say, yeah sister, he killed SS guys all the time. Play the tough guy.

"No. Not pleasant," he said instead.

She shifted into the gleam, illuminating her face. She was beautiful.

"But it needed to be done," she half queried, half stated.

Those bastards were evil, Barry thought, but the SS coppers would never get their due. It was the way of the world.

"I think so," he finally agreed, sipping his tea.

Rivka nodded thoughtfully.

"So what's your story?" he asked quietly.

"What?"

"Your story. Runner for the resistance? Dangerous work."

"Ah." She studied the inside of her cup. "Someone had to do something."

"Just like that?"

She put her cup down and faced the opaque window. She rubbed her thighs.

"Like that," she said.

"Hey," Barry replied. "You can tell me. We're buddies."

"Buddies?"

"Yeah...like comrades. We hit that fat guy together. We're in the same gang. Could you see Howie out there, doing that?"

"No, not Howie." Rivka shrugged, mostly to herself. "Oh-kay." She sipped her tea. "In our village, my father owned first a store. Then he bought a factory. It made...clothes and, uh, textile? We were religious. He was a leader with the men.

"They came in 1939. When I was almost fourteen. They burned our *shul* right away. The Nazis came for my father very fast. They took him and my two older brothers. They were gone for two weeks. When they came back, they were very scared. They did not say what happen to them. After, we had to wear the *Mogen Dovid* on our coats.

"At first, the Nazis left us be. Eventually, they brought a woman, two soldiers brought a woman to our home. A Polish woman. She took it. We could not take anything. Only a suitcase and some things. We moved to a flat in a not-nice place in town."

"Wait, she took it? What did she take?"

"Our home. The whole home. Everything. Then they took the factory. They took the store before. With the factory gone, my father and brothers were not safe. The factory was for the war. It made cloaks and coats, so my father and brothers were safe. But they took it and gave it to a German. A little after, they came and took my father and brothers. So only my mother and younger sister and me.

"It was like the first time. We had no news of them. I started running for the resistance. Me and some of the other children. Most people did not do anything. All this the Germans did and nobody did anything. A few in the resistance did something. I ran all over. I sneak out and look for them. Someone told me the men had been marched out of town. The men were taken away. There was shooting. I have not seen my father and brothers since."

Rivka spoke in a monotone. She gazed at the desktop while she remembered.

"I started running for them," she continued. "I guess because I was small, the Germans didn't notice me. In return, the resistance gave us food. This was how we stayed alive. One day they came and made the ghetto."

"Made the ghetto?"

"Yes. They put a wall up around some streets. All Jews had to move there. Our flat was in there, so we did not move. I stay with my mother and sister. I would go out with the resistance sometimes."

"How?"

"I would go through, um, how you say? Water? Like from the street, you know, pipe?"

"Sewer? Through the sewers?"

"Yes, that. Sometimes I bribed guard, sometimes a sewer. Anyway, one day they came. They made all people go to the football stadium. I was out with the resistance. I get back in the night. The ghetto was empty. I try to find my mother and my sister. The Germans took them from the stadium to a building.

"I try to bribe a guard to find them and bring them out. The guard, the guard, he said, he said he would…he said he would help. He did not. He took me behind, behind a building where no one could see—"

Rivka turned her head away. It didn't matter. Barry knew what came next.

"Hey there," he reached out to touch her hand and comfort her.

She flinched. He pulled back. Rivka sniffed loudly. She smiled. Her eyes filled with tears, but she didn't cry; instead, she straightened her spine and squared her shoulders and gave Barry a lopsided grin.

"Buddies," she said.

He nodded. "Yeah. Buddies."

"After the guard, I could do nothing. They took them and I have not seen them since."

"Did you get nabbed?"

"You mean arrested? Not then. I went out to the resistance. I thought I would fight, but when I try, I could not shoot. I could hold the gun at them, but I could not do the trigger. So I did the messages. I went to town and made reports back. This I do for a long time. I go in and out of ghettos, in and out of towns, until they start to…uh, close ghettos. Everyone was taken to the camps. So some fight. I help with reports and to take out children.

"In Lodz, I was taking out children. There was a Polish woman there helping. She was saint. She arranged for safety for them. I go to get the last of children and get caught. Me and all children. Because I am so small, they think me one of the children. I not get shot or inter—how do you say?"

"Interrogated?"

"*Tak*, that. That not happen. I was sent to a work camp in Poland. The Russians come, the Germans marched us here." Rivka hugged herself. "Here it is."

"Here it is," Barry agreed.

This girl had moxie for sure. God alone knows what she left out of the story.

"What about you?" she asked.

"What about me what?"

"You fight?"

"Oh yeah," Barry said. "I fought. Not at first, though. I joined up with the Canadians. That's where I met Lieutenant Mac and the guys. I trained in Canada, then went to England and trained some more. Over in England, Mac got word they were starting a new unit. It was going to be joint Canadian and American. Mac heard it was going to be real fast. The First Special Service Force, it was called. We made our way back to Canada to volunteer. We got all sorts of training and had been at it so long, I guess I lost sight of what was going on. It surprised me when our war started. We went after the Japs first and then went to Italy. Mac and them got killed or shot up.

"The army couldn't keep up the training of replacements, you know, the quality. We was becoming ordinary, so we got disbanded. It was sad, but I didn't know nobody by then anyway. I went over to the 101st. I was a provisional lieutenant. They didn't know what to do with me, so they put me on staff until the West Point lieutenants needed the slots.

"I got a platoon; they made it a scout element, and we stayed out in front looking around and doing every little job no one else wanted. It was a squad by the end. Even less, really. The war ended before my little squad ran out of people entirely. My commissioning paperwork had never been done or some such, so they played like I had to go back down to slick-sleeve."

"Slick-sleeve?" Rivka asked.

Barry slid his left hand down his right upper arm, from shoulder to elbow, in a dismissive gesture, brushing away imaginary dust. "A bare arm, a private soldier. I wasn't having any of that, so I asked for master sergeant, but the adjutant came up no farther than buck sergeant, so—"

The adjutant was a major who, for whatever reason, couldn't play baseball out in town. Barry paid for a girl to be very friendly with the major, *very friendly*, and the major gave him technical sergeant in return for what had looked like an innocent introduction.

He decided to skip this part of the story.

"Yes?" the beautiful Rivka asked.

"Sorry. Yeah, so we split the baby, and he gave me tech sergeant. Austria was our last place. From Austria, I came here."

She didn't say anything. He tried to sip some tea, but the cup was empty. They enjoyed a companionable silence in the half-light until she spoke up.

"We buddies, yes?"

"Well, sure."

"May I say, I mean...."

"Go ahead."

"You know, about the black-market goods."

Great, just great, Barry thought. This broad don't miss a trick.

"You could give credit," she suggested. "For the goods you want to sell. The people can go to town with them. They can sell them and then pay you. They will do it. There is no other way to make money."

"I don't know what you're talking about," he said defensively.

"I am sure." Rivka smiled wryly. "If you give them credit, they will sell and then pay you."

It made sense, he thought. Not much of a risk. After all, he knew where all of them lived.

"And also..." she trailed off to silence again.

"Go ahead—you're in this deep."

"And also, Mrs. Levenson could organize it for you."

Barry's first instinct was to yell because he had taken an immediate intense dislike to Levenson. Her superior airs, based on her half-assed peddling, rubbed him the wrong way. He wanted to ruin her.

"Mrs. Levenson knows everyone," she explained. "She already has a plan. She just needs goods."

Well, it would be one less thing for him to do, he thought. Other than to beat the Levenson broad at her own game, why should he start from scratch? Big Meyer would have said it was good business, Rivka's way.

"How'd you get so smart?" Barry asked.

"I study."

"You study. Sheesh."

11

Sunset came with a cruel cold wind, causing the soiled canvas of the tent holding Ernst and the other German prisoners of war to snap and crack like gunfire. A prodigious gritty gust blew through the POW camp, driving itself mercilessly through the mismatched slats of the wood walls, chilling him to his core. As he tried to wipe the grime out of his eyes, he figured they would have to get out there and tighten the roof again at first light. The Russians wasted no coal on their German POWs. The cold caused them to cluster, and he and Rudy shivered together on the dirt floor.

Rudy, eyes open and staring sightlessly upward, raggedly inhaled. He stopped, as if consciously holding his breath, then exhaled weakly. He had not regained consciousness after the most recent beating. His breathing progressively slowed through the night. Ernst had played nurse, but the false dawn brought truth.

Ernst laughed quietly.

Rudy had eaten less and less until he had ceased altogether. Ernst had carried on collecting both their rations and now his pockets were full of stale bread and whatever he had been able to fish out of the soup.

Some joke. Ernst was ready to escape and had enough food to at least get a good start on the way to Germany. For the two of them.

He laughed again, a bark of humorless emotion.

Soft irregular gasps escaped Rudy's mouth. His yellow skin had more in common with parchment than a face, and his cheeks were hollowed out like bunkers.

After one particularly serrated exhalation, Ernst waited for the inhalation, while studying Rudy's chest and oddly colored mien. The pause dragged. Tension built in Ernst's shoulders, compelling him to check. His friend's grimy hands were stiff and cold, his inner wrist still. There was no pulse.

Rudy would not be going anywhere.

Ernst did not know whether to laugh or cry. Laugh, because all of his planning and hoarding was for naught. Rudy had already escaped. Cry, because of the injustice of it, of being treated this way in this camp.

Wouldn't someone come to help them?

Ernst dutifully dusted off the black leather coat that had caused Rudy so much trouble. After patting his friend's arm, his chin puckered as he bowed his head, gasped and fought off his tears. A soul-rending sadness tried to pull him down into a dark, dark place. Then he did start to cry, soundlessly, lest he should wake the others.

The time had come to go. He'd already seen hell and whatever lay ahead couldn't be worse than this. Ernst gazed down at Rudy and gently brushed the man's eyes closed.

"Goodbye, my friend," he whispered.

He decided to step out for a quick reconnaissance of the camp. The vicious northern wind blew small snowflakes sideways. A dusting of white accented the gray yard, tents and buildings, leaving eerie streaks on two steel behemoths by the front gate.

"Tanks!" Ernst hissed.

Long cannon barrels protruded out of their turrets at gentle inclines. The general-purpose machine guns, located by the main hatches on top, pointed straight up, and ammunition belts hung down from their breaches.

Light crept into the eastern sky. He moved closer, thinking he might be hallucinating. The tanks became firmer and more defined. He heard the low rumbling of their idling engines and discovered, beyond the tanks, the camp gates were wide open.

Ernst scanned the area for Russian soldiers and found none. They must be in the headquarters building, he thought. There, or in the warm armored beasts.

A field lay beyond the camp, bisected by the road leading through the gates and into the tree line two hundred meters distant. If he ran for it and was caught, they would surely shoot him. If he stayed, he would end up like Rudy. Maybe tomorrow, maybe next week, but eventually he would meet the same fate.

And there were the tanks to consider. They had never come to camp before. Whatever reason brought them here now, it did not bode well for the Germans. Why were the machine guns loaded?

Ernst's heart pounded in his chest. A personal voice argued that the tents, with their wooden walls and his German comrades, were the best place to be. After all, the war was over.

The tanks must be passing through, the voice said. Perchance the crews wanted to spend the night. The Russians would serve breakfast. True, it would be two hundred grams of hard bread and the usual dishwater soup, but it would be breakfast nonetheless.

He needed to wait it out. The circumstances would surely get better. The Russians were hardly barbarians, the voice said. Running would take effort, and he was so tired.

"No!" Ernst rebuked himself. He clenched his teeth and rolled his fists tight.

That was how they had gotten the Jews. How many times had he done staff work for the *Aktions,* the operations liquidating villages and ghettos? How many times had small units of German *Einsatzgruppen* rounded up countless more Jews than the *Einsatzgruppen* had Germans, ten times, one hundred times, and herded them to field or forest, where the *Einsatzgruppen* shot them down without any difficulty at all?

Their secret weapon had been engineering this kind of thinking, this *waiting* and *hoping* on the part of their victims. They created ambiguity, which led to exploitable fear. They added hunger to turn the Jews into pathetic shells, much like Ernst was now, to cause a persistent anxiety that gnawed at the victim's judgment until there was no judgement left. The pathetic shells, flotsam in a sea of panic, had seized on an overconfidence in the sanctity of civilized men. Ernst and his colleagues moved fast, so the shells didn't have the opportunity to realize men were not civilized.

He overcame this secret weapon through understanding. He would not make the same mistake of trusting his foe to change and do the right thing or even just stop. Forcing one foot and then the other to move forward, Ernst's mission made him brave enough to run, to fight, to survive.

His mission was to stand as witness to what had happened, what was happening and what must not be permitted to continue into the second half of the century. He was a witness, a participant and a victim, all in one. The Father, Son and Holy Ghost had not only left him alive but had given him directives as well. He had to endure to testify, to accept guilt and to teach. The Heavenly Court had promoted him to apostle in a ministry of justice and civilization, and called him to preach against, and if necessary, personally prevent, future mass murder.

Freedom beckoned.

The tanks were malevolence personified. Terror grabbed Ernst's heart and he fought it to walk, one footfall at a time, toward the metal brutes. Tears coursed down his cheeks. No Russians appeared.

He navigated between the creatures and after clearing the gates, loped out across the field. It took an eternity to cover the open ground. He crashed into the tree line and fell onto the dirt.

After a rest, Ernst moved deeper into the forest, keeping his back to the breaking dawn. He walked until he thought it would be safe to pause for a small taste of his meager rations. He ate a bite of his hoarded bread and bent to scoop some snow into his mouth. As it melted to water, moistening his tongue, the thudding of machine gun fire broke out a ways behind him.

Ernst froze in place, eyes wide. Definitely two guns, the competing rhythms of the firing were discernable to the experienced listener. It went on and on. The gunners were not conserving ammunition. It was an unending stream of deafening high-caliber automatic weapons fire that hurt the ears.

The firing stopped abruptly, as if cut by the Hand of God.

The sounds of the forest did not return for some time.

12

Zalman was a witness; the news that Rivka, Yankel's sister, was alive had made a new man out of him. On the day the news came, Yankel struggled out of his infirmary bed in the displaced persons camp run by the Russians and took a few unassisted steps. Now he walked twice a day around the camp perimeter as religiously as he prayed three times a day.

Zalman burst into the infirmary. "Look, an overcoat!" he shouted, waving the heavy wool garment.

Yankel smiled. "How did you get it?"

"The Name provided. It will fit you, I think."

"Oh, for me?" Yankel slid his arms into the sleeves. It hung from his shoulders as if he were a scarecrow. "Now we can go."

"Go?" Zalman asked, flabbergasted. "You must want to live to one hundred and twenty! Look, you need a hat, gloves, and boots at least. What's the hurry? You think the rav is going to hold a lecture you might miss?"

"Don't be wicked. Now that Rivka is alive, I have to get home. I must provide for her. Even if she does not come, like you say she would be crazy to do, I could get money for our property. She will need it to marry."

What a grandmother story. She didn't need money to marry. Zalman saw people marrying every day with no more than lint between them. Such a marriage might happen days after the bride and groom were reunited if they had been from the same village before the war. He did not share this with Yankel, who was a little stubborn. Well, maybe more than a little.

"So, we'll go home. Let me see what else I can organize for you."

Zalman had been working on his project to clothe Yankel for some time, trolling the camp for odd jobs and errands, accepting script or property for barter or sale as he procured equipment. What he needed now, he needed in a hurry. He would have to steal items the garrison guarded closely and sold dearly, if at all: their gloves, hats, and boots.

He found a Russian barracks in need of cleaning with a soldier in charge who was willing to pay. While he swept, he peered around for unattended and unsecured clothing, with no luck at all. Winter loomed and Zalman wanted to be someplace warm before it burst upon them. The idea of trudging to Roszowice through cold and snow plagued him.

He decided to see his friend the orderly. Perhaps there were some boots to shine. He knocked on the door and entered. The big, broad-faced orderly stood at attention, getting yelled at by the political officer. The political officer, a shorter, rounder, meaner Russian, saw Zalman, whose lack of fluency in Russian did not stop him from understanding most of what came next.

"You should emulate this worker. He survives by his honest labor. Come in here, you! This worker could have all this done in a day, I'm sure. You two get started. There will be no more delays." The political officer jammed his round service cap on his head by the leather brim, rammed open the door and stamped out.

"Thank heavens, Zalman. Look at this!" The orderly spoke in their personal Russian/Yiddish mix, waving at five pairs of muddy boots and gloves, and five wet hats. The green hats had fur-lined flaps that could be lowered to cover the ears and the back of the neck. "All this must be inspection-ready by tomorrow! Some of these gloves need darning and the coats have to be brushed. And I'm missing another coat. I simply do not have time for all of this. Can you help me?"

"Can I help you, Comrade?" Zalman hoped the manufactured nature of his enthusiasm did not show. "After all you've done for me? I'll take the work to the barracks, and my friends and I will be done by morning!" His performance bordered on over-the-top, so he relaxed. "But I'm forced to mention, there is the question of cost...."

"Anything, if you can finish these on time! I need to find the missing coat!"

"Comrade, I'm your man," Zalman said, scooping up all the boots, gloves and hats he could carry.

He backed his way out the door, making repeated assurances everything would be fine and asking if he had ever let down the orderly before? As soon as he was certain he was not being followed, he turned sharply and headed to the infirmary, where Yankel paced the room, annoying everyone.

Zalman threw the cold weather gear down at Yankel's feet.

"Blessed be The Name! He has been generous with us!" Yankel exclaimed. He started trying boots on for size.

Ignoramus, Zalman thought. He could not imagine how Yankel made it this far without learning how to hide his feelings. He had mastered the skill in the camps quickly. One's life literally depended on keeping a straight face in front of the Nazis. Expressionless, he laughed inside at how Yankel the Torah scholar, a man so religious he would not eat non-kosher when starving, enjoyed the results of theft.

"Pick what you want so I can get the rest back," Zalman said.

"Never mind. I will dress and we will leave," he said, tossing aside a boot and reaching for another.

"We're leaving now? It's a good thing you didn't wait to the last moment to tell me. I must go to my barracks. I'll be back soon."

A distracted Yankel waved as he examined each boot as if he were a fancy customer in his family's store. Zalman sighed in exasperation.

Outside, he walked slowly to his quarters, concentrating on the details of their trip. Someone grabbed his arm. Zalman, frightened to his core, responded instinctively and instantly; he jerked the caught arm hard, breaking free of the grip, then dashed for the nearest building, intending to dive under it and roll out the other side. The maneuver had saved his life more than once in the last few years.

"Where are you going?" his friend the orderly yelled.

Zalman slowed to a trot. The war was over. Russians were running the camp. There was no need to escape. Fear seeped out of his chest, and he breathed deeply as he relaxed.

"Comrade, I'm sorry, I didn't know you," Zalman said.

"You know me!"

"I mean I didn't know who grabbed me."

"Oh, I see." The orderly looked away. "I must ask you...you know the missing coat...I must ask to see your quarters." He wiped his hands and licked his lips. "I'm sorry."

"Not to worry, Comrade, all is kosher."

They started walking toward the barracks where the single Jewish men lived. The low wooden buildings in this section formed neat rows and had doors on each end. Zalman's mind raced, but at least the orderly wouldn't find the coat. Yankel had it. Zalman led the way into a building.

"This isn't where you live," the orderly noted.

"No, but I'm cold. Let's walk through."

Zalman examined the watching residents for a potential ally. He did not see any friends, but he did notice the anger the appearance of the uninvited soldier caused. He thought maybe he could use that to his advantage.

Zalman made eye contact with one of the men and raised a hand, as if in greeting. "This officer wants to search my things," he said in quick Yiddish.

The man indicated he understood with a nod.

"You know him?" the orderly asked.

"No."

They reached the far exit, walked out the door and down three wooden steps to a small patch of grass in front of the next building in the row. Zalman's new friend, the man, raced by on the road. Zalman slowly crossed the grass and then plodded up identical steps. He fake-fumbled with the knob to gain a minute before turning it and yielding to the orderly, who trod on.

They were met with angry shouts and waving fists. The orderly, a big bear of a man, shrunk back, a teddy bear in reality. Someone grabbed Zalman and pulled him through the mob. It was the man he had waved to.

"Go. We'll hold him."

Zalman sprinted out the opposite door. He arrived at his own barracks breathing hard, quickly donned his two sweaters and an overcoat, and checked his pockets for his gloves and the good Russian hat he had liberated days ago. He rifled through his wooden locker, gathering up a sewing kit, a sharp pocketknife, a sturdy pair of scissors and some extra clothes. He put them in a canvas bag. He had another bag full of food tins. He threw both bags on his shoulder and surveyed his little part of the world.

It was just a bed, the locker, and some junk. He had no pictures of family or friends, no sentimental belongings like a *siddur*, the Jewish prayer book, or any other kind of book. He had nothing worth stealing, save what was already over his shoulders. He knew there was nothing for him in Roszowice, either. There was nothing; he had nothing; he was nothing. A low mood began to close in on him.

"Is everything all right?" a bunkmate asked.

Zalman waggled like a dog coming out of a river. Well, he thought, I have to be somewhere. It could as easily be Roszowice as here.

"Yes. I'm going home. Help yourself to what's left. I won't be back."

13

Gitta's belly grumbled. For a day and a half, the farmer had not brought food to the root cellar. He had not come to see her mother, not even to do what they did when they made Gitta face the corner. It was good he had not come. Her mother had stopped moving. In the clammy obscurity of the bunker, Gitta lay under a flimsy blanket, next to her mother's cooling body. She knew her mother had gone away. She knew what it meant when a person didn't breathe. It meant she was with The Name, in The World to Come.

Gitta jumped when the door crashed open, letting in bright daylight, blinding her. The farmer stomped down the stairs, carrying the tin with a white cloth over it and a bucket of water, and he halted at the foot of the pallet. He wore a soft cap with a brim and his sagging jowls were covered in whiskers.

He coughed and cursed.

"Now I'll have to bury her," he groused.

Gitta stirred under the blanket and brushed a strand of dirty hair from her eyes. Her hunger fought with her fear. Generally, he scared her, but the tin and bucket made her stomach hurt. She passed her dry tongue over cracked lips as her eyes darted from the farmer to the food and back again.

"Oh, eat," he said, dropping the tin and the bucket on the floor next to the pallet.

Some of the water sloshed out of the bucket. She scampered out from under the blanket and drank to her fill. She scooped the lukewarm potatoes into her mouth. He searched the boxes storing their meager possessions.

"Hah! I knew she had more!"

Gitta caught sight of a pair of earrings and some coins in his hands. When he scowled at her, she went back to eating.

"Finished? Come put on your coat, girly," the farmer instructed. "Time to go for a walk."

He waited, holding her coat.

She wiped her lips with the back of her hand. He had thrown the edges of the blankets over her mother's face, covering up the lifeless body.

"No!" Gitta dove on the pallet and tore through the blankets, creating disarray out of his neat package.

"What are you doing!?"

She searched through the bedding and found Dolly just as he yanked her off the pallet. He forced her into her coat.

"Are you well, sweetness?" She rocked the doll. "Are you well? You aren't hurt?"

"You must go." the farmer demanded. "There is no more reason to hide now, and I can't feed you anymore."

Go where? she asked herself, becoming fearful.

"Well come on, take what you want and get going."

Gitta inspected her home, the crude cellar with its rough floor that gave her splinters. Her mother's dead body lay partially wrapped in blankets on a wooden pallet, their bed all this time. The lower part of Gitta's forearms stuck out of the sleeves of a coat so small she could not button it. Dolly was the only possession that concerned her. She hugged Dolly close.

"Don't look at me!" he barked. "You have to go. Up and out! Hurry!"

Gitta did not move. The farmer snorted in disgust and turned his attention to their things. He grabbed a blanket and an old blouse. He tore the blouse into strips, picked up a few items and rolled them in the blanket. He tied the roll with strips of ripped blouse and even fashioned a carrying strap. He hung the bedroll off one of her shoulders.

"There," he said, in a soft tone.

Gitta knew he was faking it, was faking sounding kind.

"Now you have to go. We can't feed you anymore."

She forced her feet into her tight shoes. The farmer took her hand and led her up the steps into a magnificently bright and crisp day. The brilliant blue sky surprised Gitta. Veins of blown snow ran through brown fields stretching to a dormant tree line.

"You just walk that way." He gestured in the direction of the trees. "Town is not far. Someone will help you there."

She stood there, too scared to move. Her bare forearms and legs suffered the bite of a late autumn breeze.

"Go already!" He stomped a foot and then shoved her. "Are you stupid?"

She stumbled, recovered and started walking, her shoulders hunched to protect Dolly, expecting the farmer to hit her.

"Don't worry, Dolly. We will be fine." Gitta edged away from the farm, afraid to go forward, afraid to look back. "Are you cold, Dolly? Here, let me hold you close." Her feet began to hurt, scrunched up as they were in shoes she had outgrown.

"Don't worry, Dolly. Don't worry."

14

As night fell in Roszowice, Poland, Jan Pulturzycki came down to supper in the Shapiros' old dining room on a wave of anticipation; his mother had obtained a topside roast. The wonderful odor of slow-cooked beef with potatoes, cabbage and onions had floated through the house all afternoon. There would be horseradish sauce. As he grasped the Shapiros' silver, a knife in one hand and fork in the other, his stomach rumbled impatiently. Jan's father, Hipolit, and his Uncle Boleslaus joked at the table and his aunt and mother fussed in the kitchen and Jan laughed out loud, for no reason at all.

His father smiled at him.

Someone knocked on the door.

Jan's mother and aunt appeared from the kitchen. All five of them exchanged nervous glances. With the war over, the Soviets were starting to make their presence felt. Pro-Soviet Poles, supported by Moscow, were fighting hard for supremacy. Rumors of atrocities abounded. A knock on the door on a cold night had been the stuff of nightmares. It was becoming so again.

"Well, at least it's early," Hipolit said.

He rose to his great height and walked to the front door. Boleslaus filed out next. Curiosity got the better of Jan, and he followed as well. He caught up to see Hipolit facing one of the town constables.

"Mr. Pulturzycki, this Jew has a complaint," the constable said.

Yitzie Strasen, the mean-faced little Jew, bruises fading from his last beating, stood on the stoop.

"You should just know Yankel Shapiro has written. He is coming back," Yitzie said. "All of you need to get out!"

The embarrassed constable smiled. "He's been waiting at the commissariat all day. The sergeant finally had me walk him over here."

Hipolit nodded sympathetically and they shared a small laugh.

"Get them out!" Yitzie hollered at the constable.

"What can you do?" Hipolit shrugged.

"Come," the constable said, taking Yitzie's arm. "Let's leave these good people be."

Yitzie wrenched himself out of the constable's grip. "If you won't get them out, I will!" he shouted, walking to the front door, as if to go in the house.

Hipolit, at his height and girth, filled the doorway, and he instinctively pushed Yitzie with both hands. Yitzie fell backward, landing on his bottom.

"I see you know how to take care of this, Mr. Pulturzycki," the young constable observed. "Handle it quickly. I don't want to have to come back here tonight."

"Yes, of course," Hipolit replied.

The constable walked away, the heels of his brand-new Soviet jackboots clicking on the cobblestones.

Jan, Hipolit, and Boleslaus looked at one another. Jan did not know what was happening.

"*Nu?*" Yitzie said with resignation. "Let it start already."

Hipolit's expression firmed up. Yitzie scrambled to his feet. Hipolit lunged for him, followed closely by Boleslaus, and grabbed Yitzie by his shoulders, who lashed out in a flurry of wild blows, some of which connected with Hipolit's mid-section. Hipolit yanked Yitzie off balance, causing him to squirm and twist and almost get away before Boleslaus, gaining a better angle, punched Yitzie in the face.

Boleslaus beamed triumphantly but made the mistake of getting too close. Yitzie, relying on Hipolit to stay upright, kicked out at Jan's uncle and scored a direct hit on his solar plexus. Boleslaus slowly, silently crumpled to the street.

Hipolit managed to spin Yitzie down to all fours, then he wound up a kick that nailed Yitzie in the ribs, causing an explosive exhale; it sounded like the wind. Jan wished he could punt a football as hard. Yitzie fell over onto his side. Hipolit kicked again and again, persisting until blood streamed from Yitzie's mouth.

"Pop, no! No more!" Jan yelled, pulling at Hipolit to get him to stop. Jan had seen brutality in his short life, but the immediacy of this beating, right here, in front of his own home, by his own father, horrified him.

Hipolit shook his son off and, breathing hard, rested balled-up fists on his hips. Boleslaus whimpered. None of their neighbors had come out to investigate. A large slice of light from their—the Shapiros'—open front door illuminated the deserted cobblestone street.

"This I have for Yankel Shapiro. Give it to him if you see him," Hipolit's boot ricocheted off the top of Yitzie's head with enough force to turn him one hundred and eighty degrees.

"No more," Jan said.

"No," Hipolit agreed tiredly, as he bent down to help Boleslaus stand up. "No more. Let's go in."

15

In a warm garage in southern Nuremberg, Germany, not far from the Ludwig Canal, Volkmar Baur rubbed the paste wax off the black Maybach Zeppelin's left rear fender, then he gave the metal one last caress and paused to admire the grand sedan. The aristocratic nose of the car shot forward from a generous cabin. Graceful lines drew the eye to the tapered yet functional trunk. He had no idea where the old girl had been hidden away. She had come to him pristine, so he had to admit it was he who had violated—er, *modified*—her. The material change to the car appeared at the rear.

They were in a utilitarian commercial structure made of rotting wood that managed to keep out most of the weather. Square posts held up the roof. There was plenty of room for it to be used as a warehouse, but there were no loading docks or yard ramps, so Baur thought of it as a garage. They could drive directly onto a large concrete pad with space for six Panzers.

Baur jumped at a sharp clap of thunder that rattled the windows. It had been raining before, but now the rain came down in sheets. Wind howled. A bright flash pierced the gray, and he twitched at a second crack.

"Our artificer still thinks he's in the east!" Anders Lundgren's voice echoed throughout the mostly empty space. "Hey Baur, the war is over! It's thunder you hear, not Bolshie artillery. No reason for nerves."

Lundgren and the other three men grinned. They were in their headquarters, as Baur thought of it. He had joined them, working here since he and Herr Schmidt had arrived and living here as well, sleeping on a cot amongst the vehicles. The officers all had apartments. The others never discussed the war or their various parts in it, but he recognized officers when he saw them.

Claus Wolfe, Dominik Goda and Ley Kempten were playing cards. Lundgren inspected a variety of shoulder weapons he had laid out on a simple wooden table. Baur's tepid wave showed he took no offense at the joke. Or that he was fine. He did not know which.

His nerves were bad even though he knew the war had run its course. He went over the vehicles again to occupy his mind. A forlorn Opel Blitz one-and-a-half-ton truck sagged in its parking spot near the opposite wall. Rust stained the faded *feldgrau* paint. Baur had poured his life into that beat-up truck. Schmidt, now traveling in Berlin, had made it clear that he wanted the Opel ready for the road immediately.

Unlike the Maybach, this one had required a miracle, and he had delivered. When he had it running right, he'd taken it out for a test drive. It did fine on the streets of the town, so Baur gave it the gas on Marthweg. At first, he had been wary, waiting for a burning smell or strange vibration or that terrible grinding sound, but none came. He had relaxed, enjoying the speed and the rumble of the engine.

All was well until there was a loud pop and the sound of slapping. A belt had ripped and the water pump was leaking. He'd tried to nurse the truck home, but the engine had seized, and Lundgren had helped him tow it back. Now the Opel sagged at the rear, the cargo box resting directly on the wheels. Herr Schmidt would be disappointed.

"Herr Schmidt speaks so highly of your skill as a mechanic," Lundgren said at the time. "What will he do now that you have broken his little darling? To the east, I wager!"

Baur liked the men of his new unit. They were all obviously racially pure. Purest Lundgren, with his strong cheekbones, blue eyes and desired physique, possessed a generally jovial attitude. Herr Kempten and Herr

Goda were lean with harsh expressions but both blue-eyed and blond, naturally. They were good comrades who put the Cause above all else. Herr Wolfe, a tall stocky brown-haired exception to the preferred racial characteristics, had also made the team. His family had an exceptional Germanic pedigree. These men's deference to Herr Schmidt matched Baur's own, and he felt at home fixing vehicles for them in what he had come to proudly believe was their cause.

The door of the garage slammed open, helped along by a bitter gust of autumn wind and a liter of rain.

"Ach! I am drenched!" Schmidt yelled, doffing his wet hat. "It's sleeting!" He swung his arms, spraying ice and meltwater high and wide off his black overcoat. "However, altogether better than the east, don't you think?"

The men walked over to the door.

"Herr Schmidt," Lundgren said, "Baur has something to tell you."

Bastard, thought Baur.

"Yes?"

"Herr Schmidt...the—" Baur stammered.

"Truck," Lundgren inserted.

"My truck?" Schmidt spun until he saw it. "The Opel! Baur?"

"Sir!" He snapped to attention.

"What have you done to my truck?" Schmidt's newly calm tone didn't hide an unspoken threat. "It sags in the ass like an American bubblegum soldier, forced to walk."

"Sir, it, I, the—"

Laughter interrupted him. All the men were smiling. Lundgren slapped his back.

"Show him the automobile, Baur," Lundgren prompted.

"Yes, Herr Lundgren. Please sir, here is the sedan."

"My Maybach! Is this some joke?"

"Joke, sir?"

"Yes Baur, a joke. An amusing or ridiculous incident or situation, a joke. Look at it, with its ass in the air, ready for penetration. Like a Frenchman."

"Herr Schmidt, I—"

"Baur worked on the truck like a dog," Lundgren reported. "The truck itself is the discipline problem. When it failed to cooperate by throwing out its back or having a seizure or a fit or something, Baur here figured out the next best thing."

"Baur?" Schmidt asked.

"Sir, I prepared the sedan for the mission. I made sure it ran perfectly. I improved the suspension. I adjusted the hydraulics and cut new spring stock from the Opel. That is why they have the asses. The sedan can now carry the weight."

"All the men, too?"

"Yes, Herr Schmidt."

"And do we have to drive all over the Reich with our ass in the air? Although, come to think of it, it will make things more convenient for the Jew Bolshevik."

"Yes, Herr Schmidt. No, Herr Schmidt. It will come down when fully loaded. I have modified the liftgate as well."

Schmidt considered the situation. Frowning, he circled the Maybach while stroking his chin and eventually displayed a small smile.

"Ironic, don't you think? In this very city where the Allies are starting their show trials, we are continuing the fight right under their noses. Very well, Baur, pack your kit. You will come with us."

"Yes, Herr Schmidt!"

16

Corporal Fredrick Montgomery of the US Army rifled through the sections of the clerk's field box for an eraser. The olive drab box, constructed out of plywood, was two and a half feet long and the same wide, with a foot and a half of depth. It had a large chamber designed to hold a typewriter and smaller compartments for paper, forms, carbons, all the little things necessary for a bureaucracy on the administrative move.

Fred had dragged the damn box across Europe, from England, up Utah Beach two days after the landings, to Austria and down here to Munich, Germany. It did have its uses, but right now he wanted to shoot it to pieces because he couldn't find his hard rubber eraser. Damn erasers did not grow on trees.

In the villa commandeered as staff headquarters, in the room reserved for the US Army's Criminal Investigation Division detachment, Fred had propped open the clerk box at one end of a dining room table. In camp, when positioned on the narrow side, resting on detachable legs, the lid dropped down to become a work surface. Now, the typewriter sat center stage on a hunk of polished, finished wood that suggested the flight deck of an aircraft carrier, mocking him.

"*Damnificador*," Fred muttered in Spanish. He had screwed up the typing again and needed his hard rubber eraser.

Like the box, he was small and wide. He had the barbers leave enough of his brown hair to part in the middle, which he did over a strong forehead. Intelligent black eyes were set deep below a pronounced brow. His broad nose and mouth cleaved an expansive face. A powerful neck connected his head, which resembled a boulder, to his muscular shoulders. Fred's build came from teenage years of significant manual labor.

"Hey there," Walter said, "watch your language, Corporal."

Fred had been with Master Sergeant Walter Gonzalez somewhat longer than the box had been with Fred. Walter, older and with sheriff's office experience from before the war, was very much the senior. He was six foot, two inches tall, blond, a fair-skinned Anglo Texan without any meaningful Spanish capability, hence the joke about language. He had picked Fred out of his military police company and elevated him to the hallowed ranks of the Criminal Investigation Division.

It made Fred laugh to think about it. He had changed his name to something Anglo after crossing the border to join the US Army, which would not accept obvious Mexicans as volunteers. He'd chosen Montgomery long before he'd heard of the British general. Now here stood his boss with a Spanish label, no more a "son of Gonsalo" than Winston Churchill, and no more Iberian blood in him than Winston, either, as far as Fred could tell.

At first, Fred did not know what to make of Walter. Walter's itty-bitty head perched precariously over slim shoulders on a slight neck, some distance over wide hips and his natural posture was to lean forward. He also had a high nasal voice. Add wire-rimmed circular glasses and a wispy blond mustache and you had, well, Walter.

Not that he wasn't all man. Walter had switched out his semi-automatic M1 Garand for a bolt action Springfield 1903A3, with which he was an excellent marksman. During the Bulge, the German flood had cut the two of them off from the rest of the detachment. Fred had his pistol and the damn box and not much else. Walter had carried his Springfield, a sidearm and some ammunition, but he showed no stress whatsoever as they tramped through the woods, avoiding *Heer* patrols. When they came across some dead Americans, he had collected up their dog tags and a Browning Automatic Rifle, giving his Springfield to Fred.

At one point, as they probed the lines for a way back to the detachment,

Walter had become tense with crackling energy and had acted as if Fred wasn't even there, walking like he was hunting. Then he had opened up with the Browning, shocking the hell out of Fred, swinging the heavy weapon like it weighed nothing more than a broom. He ran with a grace Fred had not noticed before and in short order had killed five German soldiers. Nope, all man, Walter Gonzalez was. Fred had put him in for a Silver Star, but they hadn't heard back yet.

Fred's thoughts returned to the magnificent room they worked in. It shamed any accommodations he had ever previously experienced. He had grown up in Monterrey, Nuevo Laredo, Mexico, with parents who had jobs north of the border. Sensing the opportunities the war would bring, he had crossed over and enlisted just after his twentieth birthday. With his new name and in spite of an accent, he had convinced a recruiter that he was an American who had "lost" his papers.

"What you working on there, Freddy?" Walter asked.

"I'm reporting on this letter from the Gaufering Displaced Persons Camp. The anonymous one."

Fred's mom spoke English well and his dad had some, too. They both made sure all their kids learned. Other than a marked Spanish accent, Fred got on okay. Typing, though, that was another story. He couldn't type to save his life.

"Yes, the black-market complaint." Walter leaned back in his chair and closed his eyes. "Who is the administrator of Gaufering?"

"The complaint says Technical Sergeant Barry Rosen."

"Right. Our Sergeant Rosen." Walter straightened up. "What does the army say about who it is?"

"They ain't saying. I called couple-a times. Gaufering seemed to confuse them, almost like they never heard of it. They said they'd get back to me."

"Typical. Did you pull this Rosen's file?"

"I got the request out, but so far...."

"I think we are going to find that it's a little thick."

"You know him?" Fred was used to Walter's encyclopedic knowledge of their active cases.

"Not really. I've just heard the name here and there. There was a Canadian soldier working some angles in the UK in forty-one and two with that name, but he broke out of a civilian English jail and disappeared, definitely with outside help. They pulled down a wall. You remember the case in Zell Am See over the summer?"

"The rapes?"

"Nope, the angle with the locals and missing supplies. Who was right in the middle of it? A *Lieutenant* Barry Rosen. Of the American army. Shortly thereafter, that Rosen voluntarily accepted a demotion to technical sergeant in a division re-org. I lost track when we came here."

"The same man?"

"I poked around. This Rosen was with the 101st at the time, but came from the First Special Service Force when they disbanded." Walter clasped his hands across his abdomen. "It was all-volunteer, a joint deal, us and the Canucks. I understand some rough characters signed up. Say it's the same guy and he starts the war in the Canadian Army. His buddies are in a hurry to die so they all put their hands up. They bust him out of jail to volunteer with them. He fights with the FSSF and ends up here. It would account for something else, too."

"Oh?" Fred knew Walter needed a prod.

"Yup. The first entry in his two-oh-one file is routine, and he's already at the FSSF. Maybe he's a Canuck?"

"I don't know."

"Me neither. If he was through-and-through Canuck, why would he be in the US Army now? Anyways, keep going with the report."

Fred returned to digging for an eraser. He had to smile; he knew the expression on Walter's face. It meant that Walter was after something so hard, even five German soldiers wouldn't be able to stop him from getting it.

17

Leoshan, Manny and Elya were back at the Gaufering DP Camp. This time word had gone out: They had black market goods and were willing to extend credit. Displaced persons came out in droves on the cold, misty night for a chance at some inventory. Manny handed out items culled from stolen care packages and US Army supply shipments. Elya recorded the recipients and what they had obtained in yet another ledger. Mrs. Levenson supervised from a position next to him, providing supplementary information regarding each DP, and the happy nascent retailers walked away with canned food, clothes and tools to sell in town or in Munich. Elya wrote furiously.

Barry hid in a shadow formed by the protruding edge of a nearby barracks. He knew he should not be visible, but the camp population had evidently not received the same training. He was not fooling anyone. As DPs departed, they investigated the area and, in some cases, eyeballed him directly. Every so often, one of them nodded.

He had to admit Rivka had been right. He did not know why he had taken such an instant and violent dislike to Mrs. Levenson, but he had. Swallowing a shipload of pride, he had let Rivka nag him into talking to Levenson. The broad had made him bleed a bit at first, rubbing it in, making it seem like a plea for help. Then, just before he walked away, she had softened. They had been getting along famously ever since. Rivka had the knack, Barry thought.

"You see, I told you it would work."

The statement had come out of nowhere and he leapt like a cat. Even with the suicide flap over his pistol, he had the weapon half out of the holster upon landing. He faced whomever the sneak was, ready to fight.

"Jeeze, you want to scare me to death or what?" Barry holstered up and re-fastened the flap. "You learn that in the resistance?"

"No, playing with my brothers. See?"

"Yeah, I see. So far, so good. Hey, you can't come out here without a coat. You'll catch a cold."

She wore a thin sweater over her usual dress and the excess material of the sleeves drooped over her hands. She held it closed with both arms, hugging herself. Barry took off his field jacket and draped it over Rivka's shoulders.

"I've seen enough. Let's go." The two of them started walking. "I've got a question for you, you're pretty interested in the religious stuff, right?"

"Yes."

"Well, on one hand, you hang all over *Zaydeh*—"

"Rav Hirsch."

"Yeah, Rav Hirsch, and listen to him and all. On the other hand, you seem to like it when I push the other rabbis around or make everyone work. What gives?"

Rivka didn't say anything for a moment.

"I do believe in Torah," she affirmed quietly. "I believe in rabbis, too. But I think we needed to fight the Nazis when they came. We needed to fight them. Not enough of them fight. Rav is old. Not him. But the others, they did not fight. You fought. You are Jewish. They needed to be like you. We all should have fought. But we all must have Torah, too. So I like it when you read and discuss Torah with the rav. And I like it when you not let them golden brick."

"Yeah, gold brick." Barry laughed nervously. "Say, um...after all this, you know, everything in the war and all, how can you believe in God?"

"Hmm. It is hard to say," Rivka mused. "For the first reason, I am alive, so I am thankful to be alive even now."

"Yeah, but God allowed these things, you know, to happen?"

"I know. Rav Hirsch says we cannot know the plans of the Holy One, Blessed is He. We cannot know."

He started to say something, but she kept talking.

"Also, it was not all bad people. There was this woman. I told you of this Polish woman. She saved many Jewish people, mostly children. She help me. In Lodz she was even with me. She got away by the bare skin. There were good people. I think what happened can only be blamed on people. Not think it, I mean feel it. I feel to blame people, not God."

They stopped in front of Rivka's barracks. The mist had turned to rain. She gave him his jacket back.

"I don't know," Barry pondered.

"I do. I believe in God. So should you."

Before he could reply, she entered the building and softly closed the door behind her.

He drove to town.

Barry had settled into a comfortable routine. He would wake and exercise. At the camp, he learned a little first thing and worked the rest of the day. He spent most nights at the club. Tonight would be no different.

His rudimentary learning occurred when Pinchas and Shimshon were out on their rounds. He, Rivka and the rav were at it again in the morning.

"Rav says 'back to the Ten Statements,'" Rivka translated. "He also wants you to know the statement against murder, which made you so uncomfortable yesterday, does not refer to killing during a war."

He sat next to her at the rav's large table in the camp administration office. Barry had received a basic education as a child, so he had heard this before. At first, he had agreed to the learning because sitting with Rivka, who smelled soapy clean, energized him like he was a high school kid.

To get away with the immodest proximity, he had sold Rav Hirsch on his need for interpretation. He had argued he could not understand the length and breadth of the rav's sophisticated Yiddish commentary, which quickly became true.

It hadn't taken long, however, for Barry to become legitimately interested in the lessons. It was so much more than the rote memorization he remembered from his Jewish education in Newark. The rav brought Torah to life for him.

Barry nodded. The killing he had done in combat did not worry him; it was God's view of other stuff that concerned him now. The potential consequences of his past actions were forcing their way into his mind, distracting him from Rivka's breasts and fragrance.

Rav Hirsch spoke.

"Today, Rav wants to discuss stealing," she explained in English, grinning ironically at Barry.

Okay, he got it, but he couldn't help but notice how much Rivka enjoyed listening to the old man. She smiled more in these short sessions than she did all day.

"The statement forbidding stealing means stealing person," she translated, her forehead wrinkled in concentration, "but it includes all stealing, all kinds, the way the entire Torah is included in all the statements."

"Steal a person? Kidnapping? Um, how could it be kidnapping when it clearly says 'stealing?' The old boy doesn't make sense," Barry said.

Rivka shared his question and then engaged in a fast give-and-take with the rav.

"This is his teaching," she clarified. "The statement in the Torah itself means kidnapping. Through study, the Sages realized it also forbids taking the property of another, too."

Barry concluded that neither kidnapping nor theft was good, but that kidnapping was worse. He knew this already, of course, but he was glad stealing was not as bad as it could have been. At least he wasn't kidnapping anyone.

Rav Hirsch focused on Barry before continuing.

"According to Rav Hirsch," Rivka said, "The Holy One, blessed is He, thinks stealing is so evil, he also forbids it in *Parashas Kedoshim*, where he says 'You shall not steal.' There it is theft."

Swell, Barry thought, just swell. His network stole across southern Germany and into Austria all day and night, feeding his black-market operations and the club.

Rav Hirsch's rheumy old eyes bored into Barry and he had more to say, but they heard the two younger rabbis gabbing as they mounted the stairs.

Rivka scampered back to her place, blushing. Barry hopped up to stand in the middle of the room, hands in his pockets. The old man read intently from the text on the table.

Pinchas and Shimshon's conversation advanced into a habitual argument. The subject was the permissibility of Orthodox Jewish immigration to Palestine, because clearly any future independent country there would be a socialist republic instead of a Torah-based theocracy.

They argued in fluid Yiddish. Barry missed most of it, but it didn't matter. The pair chewed on this topic all the time, and after multiple hearings, he knew Pinchas wanted to stay in Europe, or maybe go to England. Shimshon was ready to leave for Palestine if Rav Hirsch so decided.

The two men stopped talking as they came in and dropped their ledgers on Barry's desk. They glanced at him shyly and then joined Rav Hirsch. Barry thought he might peruse the day's entries, but before he could sit down, the boss arrived.

The ambassador mumbled something Barry couldn't hear and glared at everyone as he stomped across the floor to his corner office. The door slammed shut behind him.

Barry forgot the ledgers. He had some business with Resnick this morning. He contemplated putting it off, considering Resnick's temperament, but decided Resnick's foul mood was someone else's *tsoris*. He retrieved a common envelope from the jacket draped over his chair and knocked on the office door.

"Ambassador, sir?"

"Come."

Barry closed the door as he went in. Resnick's desk filled the tiny space. The matching desk accessories, including a pair of ink pens in a decorative stand, a blotter and in- and out- boxes, all hardwood and polished brass, appeared out of place in an office one step above a storage crate.

Jeremy Resnick also presented a contrasting picture. He wore a midnight blue wool suit and a silk necktie as he sagged in his chair, his overcoat bunched up at his waist, scowling. His hair shot out in all directions over his red eyes, and he had neglected to shave. His necktie dangled loose from an unfastened shirt collar.

"Good morning, sir," Barry said.

"What do you want? I'm busy."

"Overdo it last night?" Barry stood in the cramped space between the front of the ambassador's desk and the wall. Two folding chairs barely fit, arranged as they were, like in a big man's office on Broad Street overlooking the Passaic River in Newark.

Resnick squinted up at him.

"Dropped over a thousand dollars at the new roulette table," Barry recounted. "I bet you felt like you drank a thousand worth of whiskey, too. Drinks and food on your tab. Quite a night, sir."

Resnick's slump deepened. An animal wariness came over his face. "What are you on to, Technical Sergeant?"

"Ulrich is a little worried. He don't think you're good for it."

"Who in the hell is Ulrich?"

"One of the owners. You're in there a lot, ain't you?"

"So are you. What's all this to you, anyway?"

"Not much, but you was in there last night, with a young girl, putting a lot of script down on the wheel and a lot of booze down your throat, sir."

"Watch how you talk to me." The college man attempted a menace he couldn't pull off. "I'm an ambassador."

"No, you're not."

"Pardon me?" Resnick asked, full of righteous indignation.

"You were some kind of consular guy. Spent the whole war in the back of our embassy in London is what I heard."

There was that petulant scowl again.

"I'm thinking of calling the Criminal Investigation Division." Resnick's eyes darted from side to side as he made his threat. "It seems a black-market problem has developed in this camp."

Resnick bluffed badly. Barry paused anyway. If CID were to show up, they would get in everybody's business and nobody enjoyed being judged by pinheads. Still and all, the empty threat was a positive development, a sign of Resnick's ignorance of how the world worked.

Also, he had not come out and made the accusation straightaway. These college types were unable to hold on to juicy information, in Barry's experience. If Resnick had him for sure, he would have spilled the beans.

"Mind if I sit down?" Barry adjusted a chair so his knees would not hit the desk.

"Why are you smiling, Technical Sergeant? Does CID amuse you?"

"No, sir. I don't like them guys much. They got this habit. They get into everything and inspect everything and stuff. Calling them may be…what do officers say? Premature?"

"What are you insinuating?"

"Could be somebody's main bang is a kid."

"What? What did you say?"

"Could be somebody's favorite honey was a fifteen-year-old. Germans don't care right now, they all got combat fatigue from being bombed to heck, but I bet CID would." Barry crossed his legs and picked some imaginary fluff off his trousers.

Resnick's gaze floated to the space above Barry's head, eyebrows knit in confusion. "She told me she was twenty."

Barry pretended not to hear.

"Ulrich wanted me to ask you something for him."

"Yes," Resnick snapped.

"Ulrich thinks the army will be doing a lot of business in this area. What he was wondering was if you could help him get some of it."

"Why don't you help him? You're in the army."

"Who, me? Naw, I don't think so. I'm a little technical sergeant. He needs a big guy, a diplomat guy. He's mostly interested in hearing about upcoming business opportunities, you know, hearing first, if you catch my drift." He slid the envelope across the desktop. "Whatever you decide, he hopes to keep seeing you at the club."

Resnick picked up the envelope and thumbed the bills. "There must be a hundred dollars' worth of script in here."

"And your marker for eight hundred. From last night's action. Ulrich thinks your advice is worth it. On a monthly basis, you understand." Barry feigned disinterest.

Resnick folded over the top of the envelope. He squared his shoulders and pursed his lips, nearly motionless as the envelope made its way into the inside pocket of his jacket. He smoothed the lapels with his long fingers, looking everywhere except at Barry.

"I'm sorry if I did not make myself clear before," Resnick said. "I was asking you if you thought I should call CID."

"Mr. Ambassador, I think the problem is mostly under control. For example, I recently persuaded the supply foreman to stop selling stuff out his back door. I think CID might show up, sure, but what they would find is none of the army's business. You know coppers."

"Perhaps not as well as you, Technical Sergeant. At any rate, I'll make the decision, although right now I am not especially in favor of calling."

"Yessir." Barry rose to his feet. "Sir, the staff is on top of things here. If you're a little under the weather, maybe you should think of sick call today."

"Pardon?"

"Go home and sleep it off. We can handle it here."

"Thank you, Sergeant, I just may. You're dismissed."

"Yes, sir." Out in the common area, he smiled at Rivka as she put on her coat. "Time for the mail, I see. Mind if I walk with you?"

She nodded.

Barry had been accompanying her to get the mail for several days now and word had spread that Rivka had a boy. Once outside, they felt the cold air coming down from the mountains. Thick clouds intermittently blocked the sun. They were on the receiving end of much good-humored attention as they strolled.

"Rav thinks you are very smart," Rivka said.

"I think you are very smart."

She bowed her head forward. Her thick curls obstructed most of her face. "He thinks you could make up for time you have lost."

"What time?"

"Learning. He thinks you have a mind for *Gemara*."

"What do you think?"

They had reached the steps to the supply building. Rivka took two at once and turned, so she could look Barry in the eye.

"I do not think you know why *Hashem* left you alive," she said seriously. "But I do not think *Hashem* left you alive to boss a saloon or to sell on the black market." She disappeared inside.

Saloon running and selling stolen goods wasn't so bad, he thought. The money cascaded in like water over Niagara, counting his operations in Austria and now here.

Then the meaning of her comments penetrated his defenses. Why had he survived the war, and even before the war, when everyone else he knew was dead?

Rivka came out with a pile of correspondence for the administration. As their habit had become, Barry put out his arms to cradle the pile as she flipped through it, checking the address of each piece. As she neared the end, she slowed, until she stopped at the last envelope and took it all back. They walked to their office, Rivka's mood somber.

"Anything?" He knew she yearned for contact from anyone in her family who may have survived.

"Nothing. I hope something might come of my letter to Roszowice, but...."

She had sent an open letter to the village she was from in Poland, hoping some of her relatives may have already made it back.

"Why did God leave you alive?" Barry asked, resuming their conversation.

She stopped walking and brushed some curls out of her eyes with a free hand. "To follow the 613 *mitzvot*, to pray and to learn Torah." She put her head down again and walked on.

He knew practicing Jews followed the 613 divine precepts, or *mitzvot*, prayed and reviewed the holy texts of Judaism religiously. Rivka had answered by rote. He wanted a real answer. It was something he needed to know, now, despite never having given it a thought.

"Hold it." He took her arm and stopped her on the side of the dirt road. "Give it up, sister. Why do you think?"

She studied him from under her black curls. Barry thought she was measuring him against a standard of which he had no knowledge.

"I don't know," she said.

"That's it? You don't know?"

"Rav Hirsch says we cannot know what *Hashem* has in mind for us. We have to do the best we can."

"What?"

"We do not know what path *Hashem* wants us to walk. Rav Hirsch says it could be short, but our actions make it longer. It could be long, but our sins make it shorter. But the set length, we do not know how long. He says *Hashem* has a plan and men have free will. He says it is best not to think too much about such questions."

They continued on their way but Barry, unable to leave it alone, persisted.

"But you just asked me why I thought I survived. Now I'm asking you."

Rivka paused for a minute. "I think I was left alive to live as a Jew, to be a witness and to not forget. I think I was left alive to keep going."

"But the Nazis, why would God let the Nazis do what they did?"

"Rav Hirsch says they were men. They had free will. They did what they decided to do."

"But God let them."

"Yes," she agreed. "*Hashem* let them. Barry, come to *shul* tonight. It's *Shabbos*."

She had been after him to go for some time, and all he had planned was yet another night at the club. What the hell, he could stick around and go to the club later.

"Okay," he said, smiling.

Rivka returned his smile with a radiant version of her own.

"It is late, I am going to get ready." She handed him the mail and fairly skipped away in the direction of her barracks.

Mid-afternoon on a Friday, still too early to call it quits, he thought, mounting the stairs to the office. The rabbis and Resnick were gone.

His conversation with Rivka bothered him. He could buy the idea that people can't know what is going on with the path they want to walk, like their destiny, and that people can do what they want. What he couldn't understand was why God would let it happen. All the innocent people and the bad things that happened to them. How could that happen? How could it happen on such a scale?

He worked the question until near-horizontal rays of light streamed into the office. Barry listened to the silence. The staff downstairs had left. Even non-religious Jews took the opportunity to knock off early on a Friday.

Sundown Friday. He had received a rudimentary education in New Jersey, a million years ago, and his family had celebrated his *bar mitzvah*, but it had been a long, long time since he had seen the inside of a synagogue.

"What the hell," he said out loud, deciding it was now or never.

Barry made sure his ribbons and badges were secure, tucked in his shirt and corrected his gig line. The knot of his tie felt taut. He slipped on his tanker jacket and overseas cap and stepped out of the deserted office into a bracing, darkening afternoon. He shyly entered the building the former inmates had reserved for their synagogue.

Men prayed in a single long room encompassing half the former barracks. Two warped tables with chairs on either side dominated the crowded space. An improvised scrap-wood wall, four feet in height, divided the room lengthwise, creating a smaller parallel section on the western margin. The congregation, all male, wore collared shirts, trousers and hats or skullcaps. Most were in their late twenties to early thirties, with some older and younger men present, but not many.

There were no children.

The dutiful prayed from memory with the leader, a diminutive gray-haired man with a booming voice, chanting the service out loud. It sounded unfamiliar to Barry, whose nervousness grew into embarrassment. Congregants noticed him. Some nodded a greeting. Others ignored him. One grasped his left elbow.

"This is *mincha*, afternoon prayers," Shimshon Gutkin said in Yiddish. "Come, sit by the rav."

Gutkin shouldered his way through the swaying supplicants. They reached Rav Hirsch at the easternmost end of the southern table.

"Crowded," Barry observed.

"Not really. This is the sole minyan in the camp."

"So?"

"So, of all the men in the camp, this is the one group that gathers for prayer on *Shabbos*."

They prayed together in a low murmur. Barry began to remember snippets of the liturgy flying by him. It started to sound like his childhood from before the bad times, from before his father gave up the synagogue for the bar and his mother became bugs.

He felt a shoulder-tap. A short balding older man, maybe fifty or so, smiled sadly, displaying gaps where teeth had been. He held out a small, battered book. Barry demurred with a nod and smile of his own. The little man canted his head to the left and offered the volume again.

Barry took it and thanked the man, who resumed praying. The leather of the stained, torqued covers had worn through at the edges. The pages were swollen and wavy. The book had lost its spine. He reverently opened it, mindful of its fragility, and deciphered the Hebrew writing. It was a *siddur*. He found the afternoon *Ashrei* prayer and started working on the foreign words.

Everyone stood, faced east, and prayed in complete silence. Barry remembered this was the *Shemoneh Esrei*, so named because it was originally made up of eighteen blessings. It was recited standing, which led to another name: the *Amidah*. After the silent recitation, the congregation repeated the *Amidah* aloud, in unison, and he joined in, closing his eyes, the prayer coming back to him now.

A strange but warm feeling grew in Barry's chest and spread throughout his upper body. This started to feel right, like praying was the most natural thing to be doing. He felt embraced by goodness, embraced and supported concurrently.

Rustling broke his concentration. The men were seated. They had gone on without him, finished the afternoon worship and moved on to prayers welcoming the Sabbath. The same man who had loaned him the prayer book indicated that he should sit down, too.

Rav Hirsch took up a position at the front of the room behind a two-foot square box covered by faded blue felt. He rested his hands on either side of it. Memories of well-built, decorated synagogues in their home countries must stand in horrid contrast to where they prayed now, Barry thought.

Rav Hirsch cleared his throat. "This week's portion," he held forth in clear strong Yiddish, "is called 'The Life of Sarah,' but it deals entirely with events occurring after the death of Sarah our Mother. So why is it called 'The Life of Sarah' if it relates only events occurring after the death of Sarah our Mother? I'll tell you.

"The death of Sarah our Mother dealt a major blow to Abraham our Teacher. This had been Abraham's helper, his partner, the person honored by the Divine Presence, the Mother of the Jewish people. They had been together throughout their lives and survived much. They taught Torah, they moved to different places, they made a family, they experienced persecution and war. And after all of that, what happened? The Holy One, may He be blessed, saw fit to separate them. And by his actions in this portion, what does Abraham teach us? I'll tell you.

"He teaches us how to go on. First, he arranges for the dead, a very great commandment. Next, he arranges for Isaac's marriage. He instructs his trusted servant as to what qualities make a suitable bride—something for all of us to remember—and sends him off. And then, as painful as we all know it must have been, Abraham remarries. He marries Keturah. Many of us now know this pain.

"Here, Abraham teaches us directly what The Name expects of us. This portion is a message for us in our times. We need only pay attention to see the way. And what is the way? So, I'll tell you. Now we must arrange for the dead, if it is possible. We must arrange for the suitable marriages of our young. And we must arrange for the suitable marriages for ourselves. Good Sabbath. Oh, and let me tell you one last thing. Let me ask you this: who brought us here? Brought us to this point?"

"The Name," a weak spectral voice emanated from the synagogue crowd.

"Yes, of course. The Name did bring us here. But He made his will known in this world through men. Tonight, Sergeant Rosen—"

Pinchas Shammi jumped up from his seat and whispered in Rav Hirsch's ear.

"Of course, I'm sorry. Tonight, Technical Sergeant Rosen has joined us in prayer. We must not forget him and the others like him who have done what The Holy One, blessed is He, asked of them at great sacrifice and risk to bring us here."

Barry's ears burned.

Rav Hirsch remained standing. Pinchas rose again, and the rest followed until men across the room were on their feet in silence.

Barry felt drawn to stand. With so many eyes on him, all he could think to do was wave and sit down in a hurry.

Rav Hirsch started shuffling toward his own seat, and the men took it as a sign, lowering as one. After the rav was comfortably situated, a tall thin man with a deeply lined face made his way to the front.

"Now you are in for a treat," Shimshon whispered. "Reb Noach Gesser will lead us. He's wonderful."

Gesser kicked off the evening Sabbath prayer by blessing the Lord in a clear melodious voice. Barry took up with the congregation and prayed along through the key phrases he remembered and listened to the ones he did not. Soon they were done.

Confusion ensued. The women scurried in to set the tables for the Sabbath meal. The men, who were standing again, muddled about, getting in the way. After what seemed like an inordinate period of bumping into one another, the women finished and the men found their seats.

Shimshon maneuvered Barry to a seat but one from Rav Hirsch, across from Gesser and the older care-worn and subdued men of the group. Shimshon and Pinchas were on Barry's right and left.

Rav Hirsch chanted the blessing over wine and each person sipped some, then they all rose for the ritual washing of their hands. Approaching a chipped basin, Barry used a cup to pour separate streams over each hand. He joined the file back to the seats and faced the head of the table.

Rav Hirsch picked up a knife and finessed the white cloth embroidered with Hebrew writing to the side, exposing the challah, the two loaves of braided yellow bread resting on a cutting board. He said a quick blessing, sliced one of the loaves and salted the slices. The rav took one and bit into it. Pinchas plucked a piece from the pile for himself and put the rest on a plate. He passed the plate to Barry, who took a slice and sent it on. All the men across from him were looking at him. He nodded and smiled. They nodded and smiled. Gesser mimed Barry should eat the bread.

He did.

"We don't speak after the blessing, until the eating, out of respect," Gesser, who reminded Barry of Abraham Lincoln, apologized in Yiddish.

Barry nodded again.

Gesser coughed politely and continued: "So, Commandant—"

"Barry is good."

"So?" Gesser said to the others. "This is the difference between the Germans and the Americans. Barry." Gesser chuckled, "So, Barry, did you see much fighting?"

"Not with the Canadian Army, but things got hot when I joined up with the Americans."

"For you, one army isn't enough? You were in the Canadian army, also?"

"Yeah."

"So why two?"

"It seemed like a good idea at the time." Barry explained everything, their interest an intoxicant that made his lips loose. He spoke of England, the First Special Service Force and Italy, *Monte la Difensa* and the four bitch mountain sisters.

Anzio.

Île du Port-Cros during that Operation Dragoon. Port crock of shit it was.

"Sergeant Barry?" someone asked, pulling him out of a reverie.

A bowl of soup steamed in front of him. He started to thank the server and saw Rivka placing her next bowl in front of Pinchas. She gave Barry a quick glance and small smile and she was gone. He brought his narrative to a close with his transfer to the 101st and V-E Day. A plate of roast chicken covered in paprika, boiled potatoes and some kind of green vegetable appeared.

"Oh, hey," he said in English, picking up his fork.

Gesser gazed at Barry sympathetically and slowly reached up and scratched a scar on his cheek. This made Barry's own scar, the one on his jaw, itch as well. He scratched it and the two of them shrugged in acknowledgment of common experiences.

After the meal, they chanted Psalm 126, A Song of Ascents. Rav Hirsch nominated Barry to make the invitation in preparation for the grace after meals. He remembered something of this, but fumbled the words, until Shimshon came to his rescue, whispering the words in his ear.

The meal broke up and after some pleasantries, Barry waited outside in the dirt lane until Rivka joined him. She wore a new white-trimmed purple shift with puff sleeves and a modest V-neck. She had cinched it around her narrow waist with a belt of the same material. He wondered where she had gotten it. He would have to get her a coat from somewhere, he thought.

"How did you like it?" Rivka asked.

"It was very nice. I liked it. You look lovely. Where did you get that dress?"

"This old thing?" Rivka said shyly. "Why, somewhere, I guess."

"What are you going to do now?"

"I'm tired. I'm going to go to bed."

"Can I walk you to your barracks?"

Their footfalls made a crunching sound on the dirt that reverberated in the crisp quiet night air. Barry decided he didn't want to spoil their companionable silence with conversation, and neither did Rivka, apparently.

All good things come to an end, however, and Rivka entered her barracks and Barry moved on. He slid behind the wheel of his Jeep and hummed the tune of the Grace After Meals as he started the engine. He drove to his apartment, where he changed into a gray suit, the warm feeling from the camp still with him.

At the club, Barry joined Ulrich at the bar.

"Kurt wants to see us," Ulrich said.

They strode into the gambling room, which smelled of fresh paint and cigarette smoke. The craps and roulette tables were doing brisk business. The lively crowd made a din. Kurt was playing blackjack again and had two hands going. The older man from Kurt's retinue, the one with the prehistoric head, occupied the next position.

The tall, blond, broad-shouldered muscle did not play; instead, he stared at Barry and tactically backed away until stopped by the wall. A waitress brought drinks and Ulrich dismissed the dealer with a nod. After they had exchanged pleasantries, Kurt got down to it.

"I have a job for you, and you will like it so much, *you* will pay *me*," he said.

"I doubt it. Anyway, I don't need any more work," Barry said.

"What you think, Ulrich? You think he will want this job?" Kurt asked.

Ulrich grinned.

"What are you guys on to?"

"Some Jew gold is coming through town," Kurt smiled broadly now. "I, um—"

Kurt asked a question in German.

"Propose," Ulrich said.

"I propose you take it from them," Kurt finished.

"From who?" Barry wanted to know.

"From the people who have it. It is now with some of Ulrich's old comrades. They will be driving it to Italy for deposit. I say we can deposit it just as easy."

"We'll get to the banking in a minute. What's 'Jew' gold?"

"The rumor is Nazis melted gold from, um..." Again Kurt spoke in German.

"For the sick teeth," Ulrich interpreted, pointing at his jaw. "You know?"

"Fillings? Gold fillings?" Barry asked.

"Yes, the fillings," Kurt said. "Melted the gold from the fillings of the dead Jews into Reich bricks. I think maybe some, yes? But also their jewelry and maybe coins? Anyway, lots of bricks are coming through town. You should take it."

"And give it to you?"

"I thought you would never ask." Kurt tried for an innocent expression, but the ugly troll came off as an ugly troll with raised eyebrows. "Yes, some. But not all. Maybe a share? Like I there, but I not be there?"

"A full share for information? You got to be kidding."

The Germans laughed idiotically.

"What now?"

"Tell him the best part," Ulrich suggested.

"No, you do it," Kurt encouraged.

"It was your idea."

"But you—"

"Come on!" Barry interjected. "Spill it."

"I can get into the truck that will transport the gold," Ulrich said proudly. "I can be driving the truck."

With Ulrich driving, they could plan the place and time of the job. He would stop where and when they wanted him to. With Ulrich's intelligence, they could control the situation. With enough firepower, no one would get hurt. They could be away with the loot in minutes. This first blush sounded good.

Like barnacles on a ship, uncertainties soon attached themselves to Barry's reasoning. The complications pushed themselves to the forefront. And there were an awful lot of moving parts to their rackets already. They were doing very well with the club. The black market operation showed promise. Even with plowing cash into the club, there was money to spend. This gold heist would be big, but was it really necessary?

On the other hand, in addition to the job being spoon-fed to them by circumstances, Kurt had called the loot "Jew" gold. Perhaps Barry should leap at a chance to get back some of what had been theirs.

"Ulrich, your friend does not the joy feel," Kurt said. "I wonder if he is a serious man."

"This is big, Barry," Ulrich said, waving vaguely to indicate an immensity. "Why are you not happy?"

"Kurt, thanks for the opportunity. We'll let you know," Barry said, leaving a befuddled Kurt behind on their way out.

"Why does this not excite you?" Ulrich asked at the bar, over two more whiskeys.

"Do we really need it?"

"What do you mean? It is gold. Doesn't everyone need gold?"

"Don't we have enough money coming in?" Barry wet his dry mouth with a gulp. It burned all the way down. "Money is coming in from Austria, the club is doing well, and we are starting to make big profit through the DPs. Why do we need this job? People get killed over gold."

"You do not understand." Ulrich's humor fled. He wiped his lips with the back of his hand. "Kurt wants very much for us to do the job. He set it up. He is getting strong. If we not do it, he might put us out of business."

"Us?"

"You do not understand. Kurt is getting strong."

"He's a little turd."

"Barry, listen, he found out about the job...and he's aware of a connection I have with some—" Ulrich shrugged. "Old friends of mine."

"Old friends?"

"Old friends who may be connected to this type of gold."

"So?"

"So now we do it. We do it with Kurt. He is big. There is no telling what he might do if we do not cooperate."

"I get it. Another short kraut lunatic. Great."

Elya and Manny lingered at a table with their favorite girls amidst empty glasses and soiled dinner plates.

"Why don't you grab a bottle," Barry suggested. "I'll get the boys, and we'll go to the warehouse and talk it through."

He gathered up his little gang with a subtle wave, and they left the bar and trooped over to their hideout. Barry turned on the two bare bulbs hanging from the ceiling.

Even with a trainload of black-market inventory stacked on one side there was plenty of room. One of the large army trucks Leoshan drove, the Jeep from the camp, and a car, a 1938 Hudson coupe, were all parked inside. Barry had come across the Hudson, in good condition, in Austria. He had helped himself, and now it waited for him right here under a khaki tarp.

The four of them arranged themselves comfortably on the boxes and bags of supplies. They drank from the shared bottle, passed hand-to-hand. Barry described the job to the Safek brothers, emphasizing the drawbacks and dangers.

"What do they think?" Ulrich, whiskey dripping down his sophisticated chin, handed the bottle to Elya.

"They think it's just swell." Barry watched Elya drink and hand the liquor to Manny before continuing in Yiddish, "You know, gold always comes at a price. These ignoramuses won't give it away without a fight. One of us could get killed."

The brothers seemed to communicate silently for a moment.

"You don't have to scare us, we are with you," Elya said, then he frowned.

"What is it?" Barry asked, noticing Elya's disquiet. "Spill it."

"This gold," he spoke to the floor in Yiddish, "it came from our people. It is our gold. They should not get to keep it. Those monsters, they don't get to live long good lives with the teeth of our people paying for it, for their drinks and fancy women. Not men who ruined everything." He squinted up at Barry. "This gold should not exist, but it does, and it should be ours."

Barry understood. He compressed his lips grimly.

Manny walked over and stuck out his right hand. Barry took it, and they shook. "I hear what you are saying," Manny declared. "I'm not afraid. Besides, I plan to live to one hundred and twenty! You always say it takes money to live in America. So, like by Elya. Let's get some and go to America! Seriously, Boss, I will go anywhere for you. Don't worry."

Swell, Barry thought. He did not want anyone thinking this operation was for him. The bottle ended up in his hand and he raised it to his lips for a long swig. Ulrich, Elya and Manny waited expectantly.

Barry could see they wanted it. He was not sure he did. The secret to life was getting by with a few extras, which took money. The club and the black-market gig were both generating revenue. He had a place to live out of the weather and enough to eat. He saw Rivka every morning. He liked listening to the old man, Rav Hirsch. And to add revenge, well, Big Meyer would say it's bad for business.

The thing with the man in town, the Nazi, was strictly a one-time deal. He wasn't going to run all over Europe settling the score. He'd end up broke or dead or both. Overall, why mess up what they had going now?

He wanted to decline the robbery.

The crew's desire for the gold burned behind their eyes. Barry wondered if he could lose the gang if he did not go along with this. The idea frightened him.

He put the debate in his mind aside.

"Okay, we'll do it."

Ulrich fell back in relief. Elya and Manny laughed like schoolboys.

"I gangster American!" Manny shouted in English as he jumped to his feet. He held his hands out, one in front of the other, thumbs up, index fingers pointing and other fingers curled. "Ratatat, ratatat, ratatat," he mimicked, spraying his friends with imaginary tommy-gun fire.

Wonderful, Barry thought dryly.

The party broke up. Barry headed for home. The warm feeling he had taken with him out of the camp was gone. The gold job worried him. Somehow, he would have to get Ulrich, the load of gold, and the bad guys onto a particular street at a particular time. Once there, he would have to convince the bad guys to give up the goods, preferably without firing a shot.

"I don't know," he said out loud, as he entered his building.

All the way up the stairs, he screened different versions of the potential action in the cinema of his imagination, working his way through the variables, and at the end of each one, he and the gang ended up dead in a hail of gunfire.

Out of nowhere, thoughts of his sessions with Rav Hirsch came to mind. Wasn't theft forbidden by the Torah? But did Torah forbid the theft of gold someone already stole? What would Rav Hirsch think? At the top of his stairs, his head swam. He was drunker than he thought.

Barry had arranged a sign with Elspeth, the girl downstairs, the landlady's daughter. If she was in, she would hang something on the doorknob and leave the foyer light on. He came out of the stairs and there it was, a fatigue belt dangling right where she must have left it.

Inside, an inky shadowed stillness beckoned from the rear. He turned off the front fixture, plunging all into darkness. With a spinning head and tired from the whiskey, he aimed for the second chamber, thankful she was out cold. Barry shed clothing on the way and was about to tumble into bed when he heard movement behind him.

"I'm sorry, I—" He wanted to apologize for waking the girl, but there was a "click" and sudden brightness.

Elspeth intended to be up.

She had come out of the bedroom and was leaning against the wall, a smile flashing on-and-off. Her sole garment, a new silk robe, was gathered around her shoulders. The skin of her neck, shoulders and smooth upper chest glowed. A bent knee, followed by a bare leg, pushed through a slit in the shimmering material. Her hair fell in shiny blonde waves, and her makeup had been done with a gentle refined touch. There was amusement, as well as nerves, in her eyes.

"Bitte," Elspeth whispered.

He discovered himself standing in front of her. The hell with gold, he thought. The hell with the gold, the camp, everything. Barry used his fingertips to caress the pearly skin of her chest. She closed her eyes and licked her lips. His other hand found the narrowness of her waist.

He stroked her cheek and kissed her. He meant to graze her lips, but she leaned in for it. She wrapped her arms around his neck and hugged him.

Barry broke their kiss. Her mouth was open and her eyelids heavy. He slid the luminescent fabric off her shoulders with his fingertips. She lowered her arms, and it fell to the floor. She had also managed to procure silk knickers, all she wore under the robe. He put one hand on her waist, just above the flare of her hips, and with the other he touched her breast. He ran his palm over a jutting upturned nipple, and she shivered. She took him by the hands and led him into the dark bedroom.

18

"You do not commit adultery," Rivka translated for Rav Hirsch on Monday morning, in the Gaufering administrative office, mimicking his grave tone.

How interesting, Barry thought. Sitting next to Rivka after his recent night with Elspeth, the landlady's daughter, he felt an indigestible pit of guilt in his stomach. Probably exactly what an adulterer feels the morning after.

"You should know," Rav Hirsch intoned through the translating, "the Torah defines adultery as knowing a married woman."

At least he was okay on that score. He couldn't imagine Elspeth was married. And he wasn't anyway. He rubbed his hands together, ready to leave the whole confusing situation behind.

"The rabbis extended this bad thing to mean a married man could not know any other woman." Rav Hirsch was in his element, lecturing steadily. "This is like the second statement, because someone who would not be faithful to his wife would also not be faithful to The Name, like with idols."

Wonderful, Barry thought.

He had slept in after a long, lush farewell to the weekend with Elspeth and had passed on his exercises to avoid being late. Sunday night with Elspeth had left him deliciously run down. He had enjoyed the morning-after glow, at least until he saw Rivka. It all came back to him: Friday's praying, the meal, and his other activities. Irrational guilt overwhelmed any other feeling and extinguished the pleasure of the memories.

The lesson dragged on. He and Rivka finally broke away from the rav for their customary expedition to pick up the mail. They did not say much to one another on their walk and Barry enjoyed the clear air. As had become their habit, he waited outside.

They loitered in the cold while she rifled the mismatched envelopes for a communication from someone she might have known from before the war. With his mind set on a future cup of hot tea, Barry did not immediately notice a shaking Rivka holding a letter in both hands.

"What have you got there?" he asked.

"It's from Yitzie Strasen, from Roszowice!" Rivka tore at it.

She read for a moment, then she held the pages to her chest and blessed the good news in Hebrew.

"Yankel is alive!" Her eyes sparkled. She read on.

Oh, great, Barry thought, probably an old sweetheart from the neighborhood. Why didn't Yankel have the decency to die like everyone else?

She closed her eyes tightly, bowed her head and sobbed once, and sank to the ground.

Barry was not a large man, but he was strong and fast. He caught the falling mail in one hand and scooped Rivka up under an arm with the other, preventing her from completely collapsing.

"Come on, sugar," he encouraged while lifting, "stand up. Stand up now, you don't want to get all dirty."

"They are all dead," she cried, regaining her balance on shaky legs. "All of them."

"Your family?"

"Everyone! There were hundreds of Jews in Roszowice. Now Yitzie writes there are only four left. Him, my brother Yankel, a boy named Zalman and me. He knows of no one else."

"Come on, let's walk," Barry said, his mood much improved. A brother was okay.

"Thank the Holy One, blessed is He, for Yankel," Rivka stated, using the Hebrew for the incantation. Then she muttered, "Blessed are You, Lord our God, king of the universe, who is good and does good."

"Amen," Barry responded.

"Blessed are You, Lord our God, king of the universe, the true judge."

"Amen."

"For the bad news," Rivka said.

"I know.

"Yitzie says the Poles do not want the Jews to come back. He says they have beaten him."

"What about the coppers?"

"The what? What you say?"

"The police? They have them in Poland?"

A wave of misery crossed Rivka's face.

Back at the office, Rav Hirsch put aside his book. Barry managed to heat some water on the hotplate and make some tea. He decided he should bring in a bottle of brandy, for medicinal purposes only, as they say. The two men hovered over Rivka, who appeared very small in her chair.

"There were forty-one people in my family when the Nazis came," she said, "between the aunts and uncles and cousins. I have counted them in my memory a thousand times. Now they are all gone. For true. It is just Yankel and me." She put her face in her hands.

Barry had heard the story before, of course, but the enormity of it churned up shock, horror and rage inside his heart yet again. His inability to do anything with those feelings rooted him in place. Rav Hirsch stood by quietly, appearing more tired and sad than usual. Barry wanted to rest his hand on her shoulder but didn't, afraid he would say something stupid.

Rivka straightened up.

"Well, enough." She forced a smile, wiped her face and blew her nose. "Of course, I will go to him."

He exchanged a worried glance with the rabbi.

"I don't think that's a good idea," Barry said.

Rav Hirsch could not speak English, but he must have guessed the meaning of their words, because he nodded in agreement.

"He is my brother, my last living relative and he is ill." Rivka picked up several of the papers from her desk. "Yitzie says he is at Monowitz, a work camp connected to Auschwitz, in the infirmary. I have to go to him."

She changed the order of the few sheets in her hands.

"Look sugar," Barry said kindly, "just getting across the frontier would be a problem. Do you have documents? And how are you going to get there? Bus? Do you have a car?"

"The Holy One, blessed is He," Rivka chanted in Hebrew, at first, before finishing with, "will provide a way."

"Swell, I'm sure he'll come through for you, but I've got a better idea. Write to your brother," Barry suggested, "and I'll give you some money to send to him. Tell him to come here. We'll take care of him here."

She slammed down her papers. "He is sick!" she leaned forward, her face screwed up in anger. "He is weak, and I am all he has! I'm going!"

Rivka stormed out of the office.

Barry took a deep breath, filled his cheeks with air and exhaled loudly.

"*Yiddishe tochters.*" The rav said, shrugging.

Jewish daughters.

Barry scratched the scar on his jaw. "I'm going to take a walk," he told Rav Hirsch.

He strolled the camp with his hands clasped behind his back, like he had seen the English officers do, and laughed over the memory of Lieutenant Mac being driven crazy by their aristocratic airs. He felt the late autumn cold through his tanker jacket. Regretfully, he realized he would have to give up the tanker jacket for his regulation great coat. The great coat was warmer, but not nearly as smooth.

Barry did not like the idea of Rivka traveling alone. It was still pretty wild outside the gates of the DP camp. How many countries would she have to pass through to get to Poland? Three, he figured. Start off in Germany, motor through Czechoslovakia and on to Poland. Two-and-a-half of those countries in Soviet hands as well. No lark for a girl by herself, even if she had been in the Resistance.

A notion came to him. He could take her. They could drive together, across Czechoslovakia and all. She would not be alone and he could handle the problems that were sure to arise. Truthfully, he had been making a lot of money since the end of the war. He could spend a little on this, reuniting Rivka with her sick brother. He could tell Resnick he had loads of leave on the books. Surely the pansy would let him go, and if not, who cared? How long could it take, anyway? He would need maps. Barry liked the plan and wanted to tell her right away.

"Sergeant Rosen?" a woman's voice asked in Yiddish.

The matron who had hit Manny with the oversized handbag on the first night of the black-market operation spoke. She led two men, a little behind and on either side of her. They came to a halt with the precision of three Coldstream Guards. She had bushy salt and pepper hair, a wide forehead and thin eyebrows over weak eyes. A large bent nose hooked over a craggy line of a mouth.

A pushy broad for sure, Barry thought.

"Sergeant Rosen, we want to talk to you. And who are you to charge so much for your goods?" She criticized him directly and without hesitation.

"What goods?"

"Everyone knows you are the man behind the black-market operation in this camp."

"Every operation," the man on her right piped up.

Barry and the woman faced the man on her right with identically blank expressions.

"Sorry," he mumbled, suddenly interested in his toes.

"A man would lower his prices," the woman opined. "There is no reason why you need to charge so much."

"Lady, I don't know what you are talking about."

"Like by an ignoramus," the woman said sarcastically. "You should know some people want to call the American see-eye-dee on you."

"*Who?*" he growled in English as he advanced aggressively.

The woman retreated a bit, fear flashing across her features. Her expression firmed up. She planted her feet, squared her shoulders and lifted her chin slightly in defiance.

"Some people," she declared.

Barry thought it would be easy to kill her right here, luxuriating in the idea before reluctantly dismissing it.

"Lady, you play a dangerous game," he said in English, walking away.

Army CID, were they advertising around here? he wondered. Maybe it was a sign, like he needed to get out of town or something. He should call off the gold job. If Ulrich didn't like it, he could lump it. He and Elya and Manny could disappear for a bit. Or maybe even permanently.

Barry did not want to leave Rivka.

And the money here was good. He had thousands socked away; he, Elya and Manny could even go straight. He had taken a radio repair course in England. They could fix radios. Not that he had ever fixed any radios. Even with the course under his belt, he had spent the entire war in the infantry.

However, the gold would be worth a lot of bucks, too. He wouldn't have to worry about making a living after a job like that, now would he?

As Barry reached for the door to the administration building, he had an idea. He could use the trip with Rivka to both get out of the gold job and lay low. He could run the sister to Poland and back, and the gold job and the CID business would have blown over by then.

He entered and a din came from the office. He attacked the stairs, two at a time. Pinchas and Shimshon formed a huddle with Rav Hirsch and Resnick in the center of the room. Several of the female workers from downstairs held their own discussion group in a corner.

Rivka had come back. Standing hunched over her desk, with a memo in one hand and a pencil in the other, she worked furiously. The men pretended to ignore her as they told each other, in authoritative tones, what Rivka's brother was going through at Monowitz and how ludicrous it would be to travel to him. The women, too, pontificated, ostensibly to each other, but Barry saw they, like the men, intended their performance for an audience of one.

Barry approached Rivka as she flipped through and annotated papers, stacking the finished sheaves in her outbox.

"If you leave, there won't be anyone to take those out of the box," he said, smiling.

She glared at him before turning her attention to the form in her hand.

"So you boys will have to figure it out yourselves for a chance."

"Change. For a change."

Rivka, clearly angry, held her tongue.

"Say, I was wondering, would you like a little company on your trip?" Barry asked, unsure how this would go. "I could run you on over to Poland and bring both of you back. If you want. Want company, that is."

Rivka fell into her seat. She rested her elbows on the desk and leaned forward into her hands, which she used to shield her face from view. She sobbed once and wiped her eyes with her fingers.

"Would you help me? Please?"

Her tentative request silenced everyone in the room.

"You know I will," he assured her earnestly. "I'll take you, or I can go myself and fetch him."

"You're cockamamie, the two of you," Resnick scoffed. "How are you going to get there? And how will you cross the frontier?"

"We'll drive." Barry smiled at Rivka.

She smiled back, open and honest.

"It must be five hundred miles, and it's winter," Resnick observed.

"It is less than seven hundred kilometers," Rivka responded.

"You can't take the Jeep. We need it here."

Barry wanted to dive into Rivka's black eyes. They erased any compulsion he may have had to remind Resnick that nobody else used the Jeep, and, by the way, Resnick could go to hell.

"I won't authorize the leave," the "ambassador" pouted.

"I'll keep that in mind, sir."

"Even if you take the jeep, you'll have problems in Czechoslovakia. The Reds are there, if you haven't noticed."

"I've noticed." Barry, still gazing at Rivka, said, "I've got a car. It will be fine. Do you have any papers?"

"Only my displaced persons papers."

"Why don't you visit the guy who takes pictures in camp?" Barry dug into a pocket and pulled out a roll of cash. "Get me two or three passport-sized photographs of yourself." He counted his way past the script, down to the American bills and peeled off three fives, handing them to her. "Tell him you need them tonight. I'll be back later to collect them."

"But what if he will not do them tonight?"

"Tell him I'm coming back for them, a special trip back."

"Okey-dokey," she said, smiling again.

"You should go find him now."

"I am going!" She grabbed her purse and sweater on her way out.

She flew down the stairs. Barry thought he could get used to seeing her smile.

The sudden turn of events silenced the peanut gallery.

"Bye, youse guys." He waved as he began his own descent.

"Sergeant Rosen!" Resnick shouted. "If you are planning to commit passport fraud, I'll—"

Barry didn't stop. Resnick's nagging faded as he walked to his jeep. He started it up, released the brake and shifted into gear, heading for the camp exit and town. Energized, he decided to catch up on his physical training, and he worked out in combat trousers and a sweatshirt before driving to Gaufering for the photos. Once again at his apartment, he cleaned up, changed into a suit and hastened to the club through an autumn mist to deliver the bad news.

He slid onto a barstool next to Ulrich

"You look like death warmed over," Barry said.

Red eyes burned out of a puffy face and Ulrich's hair spiked out in complete disarray. His bow tie dangled loose from his collar.

"Barry," he said seriously, "the gold job."

"Let's converse." Barry thanked the bartender for a whiskey. "Something has come up. You remember I mentioned a broad with great tits? Out at the camp? Well, her brother is alive in some DP camp near Auschwitz in the country of Poland. I told her I'd drive her out. I think we need to put off the gold thing." He sipped his liquor and raised his eyebrows to appear innocent. "Oh yeah, I've got to get her a coat, too."

"No, that is not possible."

"Why, they don't make coats any more?"

"You do not understand." Ulrich's hands rested on the bar, one on either side of his untouched drink. "I was going to say to you that the time to start has come." He balled up his fists and released them. He balled them up again and forced a laugh. "You don't know Kurt. He is a raptor. He will not leave me be."

"Tell him he has to." Barry's expression became serious. This was business.

"It's not so easy. He has men."

"So do we. Let's grease them tonight."

"No! I mean, no. It is not like that. You do not know him."

"What does the ugly midget got on you?"

Ulrich drained his drink in one shot. He forced another laugh. "It is from before the war, some things from before the war. They really do not concern you. You can say I owe him some money. He has said if we do this job for him, and give him a share, we will be, how do you Americans say it, square."

"How much do you owe him? Maybe we have enough to pay him off without the gold job."

"It is not exactly all money. Kurt wants to hurt the people holding the gold. So should you. They are the ones—"

"Uh-uh. Don't *you* tell me how I should handle those people."

"No, no. Please to forgive, do not take it—I, well, I owe Kurt." Ulrich wiped some imaginary crumbs off the bar. "Barry, will you help me?"

He sipped his drink. They'd been partners since a month or so before the end of the war and they'd earned a lot together. The German's always been nothing but straight with him, Barry thought.

He took another sip of whiskey as he felt his reluctance to do the gold job weaken. The money would be nice, he thought. He and Rivka could leave for Poland right after.

"We'll do it."

Ulrich said something in German as he leaned back on his stool and raised his fists in the air. "Thank you, thank you!" he continued in English, reaching to shake hands. "You do not know how keen this will be."

"Never mind. When does the balloon go up?"

"They want me to drive with them the last leg, so I can tell them I will do it. I think I have to be in Stuttgart to meet my contact before some days. Do you have a plan, a plan for this job? Your plans are the cat's calling."

"Do you mean 'meow?'"

"Yes, a meow. A Cat's *miau*. What is the plan?" Ulrich fit a cigarette to his holder.

"I don't know yet. Go to Munich and see our friend. We're all going to need new papers. Also, I want a Canadian passport for her." Barry slid an envelope over.

Ulrich lit his cigarette with a shaky hand. His teeth clamped down on the enamel with an audible click and he inhaled. Tension faded from his face. With steadier hands, he picked up the envelope and opened it.

"Very nice girl, if not somewhat thin, what? A Jewess?"

"Yes, from the camp." Barry tried to sound nonchalant, but a warm wave of tenderness washed over him. "Canadian, got it?"

"Yes, of course. And the Red Cross documentation?"

"Everything we're getting."

"I see. And the name?"

"It's all in there. Rebecca Mackenzie."

"Sister?"

"Wife."

"Oh, I see."

"Enough leering and get your mind out of the gutter. Is that sausage? Get us a couple of plates of the stuff."

"As you wish."

"Before we eat, you ought to run a comb."

Ulrich's eyes rolled up, trying to see his own mane, then he checked the state of disarray by touch. "I see. I will return presently." He came back, smooth as usual, his hair slicked back and his bow tie perfectly tight.

They ate German sausages and stolen American canned green beans at the bar. By the end of the meal, Ulrich had returned to his effervescent self.

"How much gold?" Barry asked.

"We hear they transport ten to fifteen London Good Delivery bars at a time."

"What? We going to London?"

"You know, gold bars. The kind of bars of the gold. They are called London Good Delivery. They weigh some twelve kilos each, maybe...um, twenty-five pounds? Thirty pounds?"

"Swell. How much is gold selling for these days?"

"Thirty-seven US dollars and twenty-five cents an ounce."

"Really swell." Barry did the math. "Could be as much as sixteen thousand per bar. Wait a minute, ain't there something funny with those ounces?"

"Yes, troy ounces. It is something I have heard, but I do not understand it fully. I only know it is a lot of gold."

"And how! Hey, what do they drive it in?"

"We don't know for sure, but it is either a small truck or large car."

"Where are they jumping off from?"

"I do not know."

"What is the name of the Old Man in the Moon?"

"I don't know, but he is not driving."

"Come and see me as soon as you get back from Munich," Barry ordered. "Try to have all the details: how many there are, the vehicle, the route, how much gold and anything else you can think of. I'll have a rough plan for you then. By the way, you're paying tonight."

"Thank you for this," Ulrich agreed as he lit another cigarette with the smoldering stub of the old.

"Yeah." On his way out, Barry avoided Elya and Manny, sitting at a table for four with their regular whores.

What the hell, he thought, he ought to be kind and call them girls. It could be circumstances—maybe the war made them cheap. Before the war, they probably had been straight. By next winter, they might be so again.

Barry walked to his flat, uncomfortable in the cold. He could live elsewhere, he thought, even New Jersey; they got winter in New Jersey too, though.

Going home was out of the question anyway. No doubt the G-men were waiting for him to set foot on a quay in New York so they could pick him up for the 1939 shootings, case closed.

He came to a halt in the middle of a wet windswept street. 1939. It'd been a long war, he thought with a sigh. He started walking again.

Elspeth came to mind. He liked the girl plenty, but now he felt a strong sense of loyalty to Rivka. Guilt filled his gut. He had to cut it off with the landlord's daughter.

Cowardice froze him at the front door. He stomped his cold feet on the colder concrete. He didn't want to see Elspeth tonight.

He thought it was too early to count on being able to tip-toe undetected by the girl's apartment. Even if he could, it wouldn't help if she was already waiting for him. There must be something he could be doing elsewhere.

He could plan out the gold job.

A stiff gust blew down the street from the north, chilling him to the bone. He had to think of something. He was willing to try infiltrating past Elspeth, but he wondered if there was some way to confirm she was in his flat. Barry examined the building. Some of the apartments were lit up, some not.

A truck drove by, belching fumes.

He determined the position of his flat and sure enough, she had it bright like the intersection of Broad and Market back in Newark.

Damn, he thought. After some indecision, he decided to get started on the gold job. He would go to the warehouse and plan it there. At least he would be out of the wind.

After a lonely walk, he situated himself on two stacked boxes of institutional-sized cans of peaches in syrup. An irregular piece of plywood across two columns of boxed combat rations acted as his desk. He found a tablet of lined paper and wrote with his fountain pen. Barry wore his hat and snuggled into his coat.

The blank page stared up at him. He pulled out his Nazi cigar holder. Both of the serviceable tubes were empty; he was out of cigars.

"Damn."

He poured some whiskey into a kidney-shaped steel canteen cup, took a shot and got to work. As the army had taught him, he framed the parameters of the mission. He wanted to stop a car or small truck full of armed ex-SS *gonifs* and gold, take the gold and send the *gonifs* on their way.

Maybe if he asked nicely.

All his reservations closed in on him in the murky iciness of the warehouse. The lowest kind of murderous sons-of-bitches would be in the car. Men used to killing. There was no way they were going to give up the gold without a fight. Barry opened a carton of Luckies and lit up, using his Zippo with the US airborne wings soldered on the front.

While he smoked, he ran his thumb over the metal parachute insignia. He had not settled well into army life with the Canadians. After the excitement of the wartime trans-Atlantic crossing, routine training had been boring in England.

The situation changed when Mac, angry that their unit would miss the Dieppe Raid and at the overall lack of meaningful activity, took those fellas he liked with him, back to Canada, into the Canadian Airborne. Mac had gone to the trouble of busting Barry out of a cell in the town jail, he remembered fondly.

Mac had heard about a special unit forming up, the First Special Service Force, and figured it would get them in the war faster. With Mac's mission accomplished, Barry had enjoyed the unorthodox training and the guys were great. It had been almost like a home.

It all went to crap in Italy. Operation after operation and, before long, everyone was dead or wounded enough to go home. The dummies, the slightly injured, returned to the unit until they got it, too. The replacements were untrained green bullet-catchers. They never lasted more than a few operations.

Barry scratched the scar on his jaw. Now it came to this, he thought. A suicide mission over the gold pulled out of the teeth of the victims of industrial murder, gassed to death on a massive scale. What the hell, maybe he would get killed and it would all be over. He rubbed out the stub of his cigarette on the plywood.

"Let's assume they're armed," he said out loud.

We'll need a quiet place to engage them, he thought. Also assume Ulrich (already in position to be behind the wheel of the vehicle carrying the gold) won't be able to merely drive them there. He'd need a reason or excuse. Barry knew of a suitable small street west of the river.

How would he get them there? How do you make someone go somewhere? Jam the roads up somehow? Pile some rubble in the street? Which streets—all over? Even a few piles would be a lot of work for his crew and draw attention while hard manual labor wasted their available time. Get the route from Ulrich and have him stick to it? Yeah, that would be important. Back to blocking, could they blast rubble into the road?

Kind of alert everyone they were there, wouldn't it?

Barry quaffed another mouthful of whiskey and lit another cigarette.

So physical roadblocks are out. How else? Checkpoints? He wanted to keep the team together for the job itself. He and the three of them, Leoshan, Manny and Elya, could man one checkpoint at best anyway. What was the point of just one?

To do checkpoints, he would need more men. Could he get some of Staff Sergeant Washington's men? Hmm. Would the targets even listen to uniformed US soldiers? What if he used Washington's men in police uniforms? In all these months, he had never seen a colored person in a German uniform of any kind. Would the targets even obey Negroes at all? Too bad he didn't have any paid German coppers.

Whiskey. Cigarette.

"Wait a minute, just one damn minute!" he shouted in the empty warehouse.

He's paying Kurt and Kurt got coppers. Let Kurt earn his gold, Barry thought.

Planning went fast after that. As long as Ulrich kept the gold on route and timetable, it could work. He was comfortable with four at the assault location.

He wrote another page and a half of notes and had his plan. He went over the elements one last time, playing the "what if" game to account for contingencies. He lit a cigarette and nursed the rest of his drink. Finally satisfied, he let the cigarette dangle between his lips and used his lighter to ignite the notes. He watched them burn to ash in the cold, then ground out his smoke and went home content, but not happy.

19

"Here they are." Ulrich placed a quarto-sized envelope of rough brown paper on the bar next to Barry's drink.

"About time," he said. "I been stalling Rivka for days. This thing better happen. She's nagging the shit outta me."

Barry reached for his glass. As he brought it to his lips, ice tinkled in the cheap whiskey. The cubes were a new development at *Der Kellar*. Staff Sergeant Washington had organized the ice machine, "liberating" it from a US Army Air Force officers' club. The name of the place, *Der Kellar*, had developed all by itself.

"How many of those have you had?" Ulrich asked.

The two men had reversed roles from their last meeting. This time, Barry was off-center.

"Many. Where you been?" Barry's loud query cut through the din. He put one hand on the bar for support.

"I am sorry, it has taken longer than I thought." Ulrich motioned for his own drink, declining the ice. "However, I leave tonight. It will be my job to take them through the city and through the mountains, a new route for them. Your plan—it is masterful. Start looking for me day after tomorrow. By the way, you are able to make the Jewess wait?"

"Yeah. Been making her get an official Polish passport. The embassy bastards won't even talk to her." The envelope contained Canadian passports and Red Cross papers. "Are these any good?"

"Very, very good. His best work, I assure you. He elevated the price a lot for the girl, last minute and all, but it is good work."

"Okay. I'll cover the price hike."

Ulrich waved the comment away.

"So what time are you leaving?" Barry asked.

"Momentarily. It will be a long ride tonight, but they are impatient to start."

"Well then, this is it."

"Yes."

"No turning back now."

"No."

"Too late for second thoughts."

"And for thirds! Come," Ulrich laughed and slapped Barry on the back, "your plan is the greatest. What can possibly go wrong?"

"The number one thing is—"

"You were not supposed to answer. There is enough time for me to walk you home, I should think." He helped Barry off his stool.

Ulrich saw him to the door of his building, where Barry managed the stairs on his own. The door to his flat, on the other hand, stopped him cold. No matter how carefully he tried, he could not line the key up with the lock. Then, strangely, the door opened by itself, revealing a slender female mid-section sheathed in shimmering white.

Bent at the waist, hat on the back of his head, he sent his eyes upward. They traveled over young breasts, a plunging neckline revealing pearl skin and Elspeth's smiling face. Her lips were bright red and her hair had been done in wavy tresses, like something a pin-up might wear.

"Whoa, sister." Barry straightened up and adjusted his fedora.

Elspeth pulled him in and stretched, trying to kiss him. He put his hands on her silky hips and gently directed her backward. She laughed. He pushed harder. She hung on. He gave her a mild shove, breaking her embrace. She ended up against the wall.

"It ain't you. I got this other dame on my mind. I can't be with you.

Makes me feel terrible. Why don't you stay, and we can eat. But after, you have to—"

Elspeth figured out the brush-off. Her confusion evolved into ire, and she let loose with a rapid string of furious German. She smacked him and dumped more mad German on him.

"Now sister, don't be that way. Let's eat, and we can—"

She straightened up her robe, swung at him again and stormed out of the apartment, slamming the door behind her.

"And there you have it, folks, another satisfied customer," Barry said out loud, with a theatrical wave of his arm in the general direction of Elspeth's departure.

The next morning, he woke parched and with a headache. He put on sneakers, combat trousers and two sweatshirts, then trotted down the gray street, the cold turning his breath to white vapor. He stopped at a park for calisthenics before his daily run. Afterward, he cleaned up and dressed in his usual uniform, proud of himself in a sanctimonious way because he had not slept with Elspeth.

On the other hand, it made him feel bad to have upset her. The jabbering little voice in his mind wasn't helping. "You should have banged the blonde. The brunette would never have known," it said, over and over. He parked the Jeep next to the camp administration building.

Once upstairs, Barry gave in to the impulse to be a hero on the cheap. He showed Rivka her new Canadian passport and identity as Rebecca Mackenzie, wife to his own novel personage, Ian Mackenzie. The forged passport impressed the younger rabbis all out of proportion to the accomplishment. Rav watched quietly from behind his volume.

"This is remarkable," she said. "You have no idea what such a thing could have meant in 1939. Thank you."

"It's nothing." Barry preened in the glow of her gratitude.

"When do we go?"

"We need approval for my leave, which should come, oh, three days from now," he lied. He had no intention of asking anyone for permission to travel.

"This day would be the Sabbath," the rav said in Yiddish.

Barry knew honoring the Sabbath was in the Ten Statements, but their observance really got on his nerves. Rivka would not do anything on Saturdays, other than pray, eat and take a walk. He could not get the rabbis to come into the office for even a half day. He had seen this behavior growing up, to be sure, but lately the strict Sabbath observance of others thwarted every one of his plans.

"I cannot travel on that day," she told him.

"The next day, then?" He lied again, because he planned to grab her the morning after the gold job and hit the bricks, no matter what anyone else thought or what day that turned out to be.

Rivka smiled. "That day fine," she said, holding the passport with two hands.

After work, Barry skipped the club altogether and went to his warehouse instead, wearing a stained fatigue uniform. In the shadows cast by a naked bulb, he contemplated a low, long wooden box that had been nailed shut. A pry bar lay across his thighs. Having to open it made him feel blue because in his current mood, he didn't want to do the gold job.

He walked over to where he had left a tumbler filled with whiskey and a pack of cigarettes. Cigars had become scarce. Barry sipped from his glass and lit a cigarette, the acrid smoke scorching his lungs. Damn, he thought. He really didn't want to open the box, and he didn't want to do the job.

Pry bar in hand, he thought of Ulrich, who was expecting them. To quit now, to run with Rivka to Poland, say, would be dirty pool. He and Ulrich were partners. He could no more run from this than run from combat. It wasn't in him. Elya and Manny, too, were counting on him. They wanted this job bad. Maybe for them it was getting something back for what the Nazis had done. Deep down, Barry craved revenge, too, but hunting down every Nazi survivor of the war was out of the question. No profit in it. The fucking box reminded him of a casket.

He knelt and fit the flat end of his tool into the small gap between the lid and side and forced the lid up. He worked his way from nail to nail, sliding them out of the wood, until the lid had separated completely, exposing three rifles resting in brackets.

The largest, the Browning Automatic Rifle, looked like an industrial age death machine, all utilitarian angles without the grace of a hunting rifle. A long barrel over a shorter, thicker gas tube, both protected by a square wooden hand guard, made up the fore end. The receiver, in the middle, was a huge piece of stamped steel. A wooden stock anchored the weapon. The hand guard, stock and metal parts were scratched, gouged and scarred, but free of rust.

An M1 Garand lay next to the big weapon, sleeker, but still sporting a business-before-pleasure design. The last service weapon, a compact M1 Carbine, was the gun most reminiscent of a hunting rifle. Extra magazines were there as well, thick containers for the Browning and streamlined rectangles for the carbine. Barry stripped the oil off each weapon, cleaned them thoroughly and checked their operation.

The warehouse did not hold heat very well and he hadn't brought a jacket, so he was hungry and cold when he finished. He rummaged through his collection of combat rations, settling on a box of beans and baby dicks, or franks and beans to civilians. He sorted through the tins until he identified the biggest can, the franks and beans themselves. He sat on some boxes and ate the food cold, with a spoon.

Reviewing his arsenal, he thought he would assign Manny the Browning and Elya the Garand. Neither man knew how to use a rifle nor was there time to teach them. Barry hoped the mere appearance of superior firepower would carry the day. He felt vaguely uneasy. He knew no good would come out of his coffin of weapons.

20

Volkmar Baur woke in the trench with a start. A great pressure pinned him and something covered his mouth. He wanted to strike out, but both his arms were immovable. The Soviets must have broken through. He choked on the bile as he thrashed, he would not go without a fight.

"Baur? Volkie? You were yelling in your sleep. It's just us. You're in our garage in Nuremberg. Calm down and I'll let you up."

A flashlight came on. Claus Wolfe loomed over him, a ceiling beyond.

He was not in a trench at the front. He was inside the garage.

"Volkie, I'll let you up if you're quiet, yes?" Wolfe's massive hand covered Baur's mouth.

He tried to nod but couldn't.

"Oh. Sorry," the big man said sheepishly. He released Baur and leaned back.

The men of the unit were assembled by his cot in the warehouse. They were already dressed.

"What time is it?" Baur asked.

"Zero three hundred and the day is wasting away," Herr Lundgren joked.

Baur had cotton mouth from too much black-market vodka. Last night he could not sleep. Marta had stayed in his mind all night, so he had sat on a running board and drank instead.

The men had prepared for a trip all of yesterday, but despite what Schmidt had said about coming along, nobody had told Baur to get ready. He had moved his cot near the Maybach, just in case. He did not want to miss out.

Anyway, every time he closed his eyes, Marta came to him, wanting to know why he was not taking her with him. So he'd drunk, and now pre-puke irritated his dry throat and his head ached. He also needed to piss.

Baur sat up, bent forward at the waist and spit on the floor.

The ring of men parted, allowing Schmidt through.

"Very nice." He knelt by the cot.

"Sorry, Herr Schmidt."

"We have something of a problem."

"Yes, Herr Schmidt?"

"It seems our mission has been compromised."

Baur shot to his feet, causing a sharp pain in his head. "Herr Schmidt, I, you don't—"

"Relax Volkmar. No, I don't think you are to blame. But we need to relocate our headquarters. Originally, I wanted to leave you here with another transportation project to occupy your time. Unfortunately, we are abandoning these fine accommodations."

"Yes, Herr Schmidt."

"As usual, we do not have enough men. Can I count on you to do your part?"

"Of course, Herr Schmidt."

"There will be some disagreeable activity this morning, after which we will depart. I want you to come with us. You will be armed, yes?"

"I would be honored."

"Volkmar, I believe you have figured out by now what we are doing concerns the entire Reich? Not merely us?"

"Yes, Herr Schmidt."

His manner had become fake-relaxed, the comportment of the superior officer when sharing sensitive information.

"We are going to transport something of value to those of our mind set, those interested in continuing the struggle. You will be coming with me. Bring all your tools, understood?"

Baur straightened to the position of attention. The men formed up in a half-circle, Schmidt in the middle.

"Yes, sir!" Baur said.

Schmidt reached out and Lundgren produced a Schmeisser submachine gun and supporting black leather gear. "You are familiar with this, I trust? Very good. Get your things ready, and the car. We'll be leaving after breakfast." Baur received the weapon, belt, suspenders and equipment pouches in both arms.

Schmidt addressed the group. "First section will leave after we eat. Second section will clean up and load out this place, down to the sterilization level, after the first section leaves. The rule will be that we were never here. Baur will concern himself with the car and his personal belongings only, understood?"

"Yes, Herr Schmidt," the men answered in a ragged early morning chorus as their commander walked away.

"And Baur?"

"Yes, Herr Schmidt?"

"Get dressed."

Each of the men made eye contact with him and nodded or stuck out a hand to shake or performed some other indication of welcome as they wandered off. Soon he stood alone by his cot, holding the weapon by its sling, wearing nothing but undergarments.

The submachine gun had seen better days. Metal had been rubbed bare on its ridges. Rips and stains marred the brown leather sling. The belt gear, used but well-tended, contained two loaded magazines. He could not suppress his smile. He was on a mission for The Struggle, as Herr Schmidt called it.

Baur spent a busy hour and a half getting ready and packing the Maybach, and he finished setting up his combat gear at the same time that the odor of frying sausages filled the garage. He had never carried a Schmeisser in battle, but he had fired the weapon on the range. It was all right. His stomach rumbled.

The loading bay door opened.

"Breakfast!" Herr Kempton hollered from the back.

Cold wind blew a drizzle into the headquarters. Clouds covered the dawn. A Russian board truck with an upright cab, old fashioned snout, large round fenders and a dual axle, a ZIS, Baur thought—backed in. Dominik Goda emerged from the driver side.

Schmidt and most of the men moseyed over.

"How did it go?"

"Like clockwork," Herr Goda said, gesturing with a nod.

Baur followed the gesture and saw a new man, probably in his mid-thirties, a little over six feet tall standing next to the ZIS. The new man had blond hair and brown eyes. Narrow, colorless lips were set in a line under a well-shaped patrician's nose.

"Ulrich Genscher." Schmidt walked up with his hands in the pockets of his black leather jacket. "Glad you could come along on our little drive."

"Would not miss it for the world, Emil." Ulrich offered his right hand. "How are you?"

Herr Wolfe moved swiftly and punched Ulrich in the jaw. He fell and rolled up onto all fours. Schmidt brutally kicked him in the ribs, and he rolled again and tried to crawl away. Herr Wolfe dragged him to Schmidt.

"Fine Ulrich, fine, taking into account the fall of the Reich and all," Schmidt sneered. "You know how it is. And yourself?"

"Not too bad." Ulrich struggled to his feet. "All things considered, until this moment."

"Yes, I see. Do tell us what you have shared with the warm brother down in Furstflarn, please."

"Why Emil, I have no—"

Schmidt's hand came out of his pocket so fast Baur heard the crack of the slap across the new man's face before he registered the swing of Schmidt's arm.

"Your eyes gave you away just then," he said. "I'm ordered to take you on. The Organization thinks that, with your English, you can get us by the Americans, around Munich and through the mountains. Even after what my little efforts at intelligence have uncovered about your new associates and current activities, they think you are essential. I am not so sure. Now, what information have you disclosed?"

"I told him I had to be away to do a favor for a friend."

"A favor for a friend? Ass. You betray our cause and the Organization by merely associating with that pederast defective." Schmidt paced the garage. "Well, we shall see. We shall see if your oath has meaning and we shall see when we spring the trap you two have undeniably set. Our leaders will see and we shall see. Ulrich, if you have taken up with that defective, you will be dealt with."

Ulrich glared at Schmidt.

"We shall see," Schmidt intoned.

"Food is getting cold," Herr Kempton shouted.

The men slunk toward their breakfast.

"Load the damnable car before you eat!" Schmidt roared, his face turning red.

Baur pivoted on his right foot and sprinted for the Maybach. He started the engine and, after it settled into a contented purr, he backed it over to the truck. He felt relieved to see the others complying. They were ready with wooden boxes made of freshly cut pine. Baur opened the trunk, and the boxes were stacked in no time.

Now free, he sat on a running board and ate a hard-boiled egg with his fingers. The new man, this Ulrich fellow, had hobbled off to the other end of the garage. Baur contemplated the significance of the commotion as he chewed and wondered how it boded for the future.

21

The morning of the big day broke cold and clear. Elya, Manny and Barry were in the Jeep, windscreen and canvas up, parked on a short dead-end in a commercial section southeast of the Munich *Hauptbahnhof*, the central rail station. The factories and warehouses of the neighborhood had been bombed into dirty heaps of broken masonry. The hellish cityscape consisted of a corner of a once-useful structure here or a small section of bare brick wall there. No traffic impeded the crossing avenues. No pedestrians traversed the sidewalks between the curb and the piles of damaged stone. Across the street, someone had drawn bug eyes and a large round nose over a single black horizontal line on a remnant of finished façade.

"Kilroy my ass," Barry said.

"Boss?" Elya asked.

"Let's scrub the mission."

In the back, Manny stroked the fore grip of his Browning Automatic Rifle. Elya shifted his Garand and laughed nervously. Barry knew from experience that specific laugh meant Elya had not understood the English.

They wore US Army uniforms, including helmets. Barry had drilled them mercilessly. They could now get out of the Jeep, grab their weapons, chamber a round and take up their stations in an instant. He had loaded the magazines of both firearms but made sure the chambers were empty. No need to risk getting shot by one of his own guys in their fear-fueled rush.

Barry felt warm enough in his great coat. He also wore a helmet, olive drab scarf and bulky gloves. One of his Colt semi-automatics hung off a web belt in a regulation suicide-flap holster on his right hip, outside his coat, and the other lay in the left pocket. He had four extra magazines in canvas pouches. His lucky fighting knife from the First Special Service Force, a long, double-edged dirk, dangled from his belt in its worn leather sheath.

A walkie-talkie, dull green and boxy, with protruding ear and mouth pieces, rested in his lap. The fully extended chrome antenna poked out from under the Jeep's canvas top.

A burst of static squawked over the radio. The men braced themselves, but no further transmissions occurred. Nobody drove onto their street. The quiet returned.

Barry had already been by the two police checkpoints. Kurt had provided older officers who had asked no questions and were happy to do nothing all day. Their story would be that the roads were blocked for the demolition of unsafe structures. If Ulrich stuck to the route, the detours would lead them right here.

Early morning grew into late morning. It did not get any warmer. Clouds rolled in. The breeze out of the north freshened, the air became damp, and their urine steamed when they relieved themselves on the dusty detritus. As the weather deteriorated, so did Barry's tolerance for the job. He wanted to wrap it up now, more to get out of the cold than for any other reason.

The click of a keying mike, followed by static, came over the radio.

"Look sharp," he snapped. "Something's up."

A US Army Jeep with two soldiers in the front seats appeared, heading for them. Elya and Manny reached for their weapons, nerves crackling with dangerous energy.

"*Calm,*" Barry soothed in easy Yiddish as he patted Elya's arm.

They had parked facing the intersection, passenger side against the curb. Barry left the relative comfort of their Jeep to meet the oncoming vehicle. It stopped next to him.

"The nigger said you were the boss," the driver, a military police private, all peach fuzz, pimples and drawl, stated.

The MP's eyes bounced from Barry's face to his technical sergeant stripes and back to his face.

"That's right, Private," he replied, his tone comprised of patience and contempt, in even parts, that experienced non-comms reserved for the young and uninitiated. "What can we do for you?"

The MP's demeanor matured from cocksure to tentative. He checked with his partner for guidance. None came.

"Um, what are you doing here?" the private asked.

"We're waiting for a shipment."

"A shipment of what?"

Barry bent forward for a better view of the passenger seat and focused his attention on the hard-eyed, whiskered corporal he found there.

"A shipment we are going to take to the Brits up north. It's coming over from Vienna and, Corporal, that's all you need to know. Am I right?"

They measured each other.

"Yes, Sergeant," the corporal said. "Sorry to bother you. Okay. Take care." He elbowed the private and pointed down the road.

The private shot a furtive glance at Barry. "But I think—"

"Do as you're told," the corporal scolded. "Just one time. Can't you do as you're told without back-talk just once?"

The private glared as he put the Jeep in reverse and sped away. Leoshan, bundled up in every piece of regulation cold-weather gear the army had ever issued him and with Barry's M1 Carbine slung over his shoulder, walked up, bringing a freezing mist with him.

"The kid MP give you a hard time?" Barry asked.

"No, but he sure was pushy." Leoshan smiled. "I see you shined him on."

"Come on, I'll buy you lunch."

At the Jeep, Barry jerked his thumb and Elya moved to the back with his brother. Barry, now in the passenger seat, produced some combat ration cans.

"Got ham and limas, pork'n rice, mystery meat stew and beef'n boulders. What you want?"

"Oh, Mr. Barry, you all pick. I gots what's left." Leoshan's good humor remained intact, despite the MP's conduct, the cold, and his standing outside in the street.

"Nope. You go first."

Leoshan picked the beef and potatoes. He held the box in both hands while ruminating over the empty front seat.

"Well, you gonna get soaked to the bone out there or get under the cover or what?" Barry joshed.

He sat behind the wheel with a grin. The others chose their meals and left Barry with the pork. Elya and Manny devoured theirs. The soldiers ate their entrées but packed away the balance of the rations in their various pockets.

Barry pulled his collar closer and said, in English, "I'm thinking of scrubbing the mission."

"Oh, Mr. Barry, all that gold. And there's Mr. Ulrich to consider."

"What about him?"

Barry would sooner shoot himself than abandon a comrade in a jam, so he had no idea where these thoughts were coming from. Who knew what Ulrich was going through right now in his effort to get the carload of gold onto this street on this day? Who knew what would happen to him if they were not there to at least get him out of the car?

Even so, the urge to walk away rattled about his brain.

"You don't mean you'd leave him with those krauts?" Leoshan seemed legitimately concerned.

"You know what I think he was," Barry said, half-acting as the devil's advocate.

"I think he was one of them hard-core Nazis, too, but that was before," Leoshan said. "He's with us now. Why, they might kill him up good. If it be the waiting that's worrying you, well, he'll be along shortly, I believe."

Barry felt Leoshan's optimism thaw his somewhat icy perspective. "We'll wait it out. At least for the rest of the day."

"I best be getting back to the truck. Thank you for the lunch. You think on waiting tomorrow, too."

"Yeah, hey, since you're so motivated and all, why don't you go see if them coppers are at their posts."

"Will do, Mr. Barry." Leoshan ambled off.

Barry knew in his heart that Leoshan was right. He shouldn't be concerned with second thoughts now. He needed to see the heist through to the end. One of his gang depended on it.

Baur rode in the back of the Maybach with Herr Goda in the middle position and Herr Kempton on the far side. The day had started quite nice, but a layer of thick low clouds had come along. Even so, they made good time to Munich, and he enjoyed the fast gentle ride down the autobahn, feeling great personal pride at the outcome of his work. The weight of the men, their equipment, and whatever was in the wooden boxes had the exact effect he had calculated on the suspension; the old girl rode marvelously.

Not so marvelous was the temperature in the car. The Maybach had excellent climate control. Schmidt had put his overcoat in the trunk at the beginning of the trip, but no one had caught the significance. Baur and the others had left theirs on. The heat was unbearable. His undergarments were drenched, but his fear of Schmidt, who had set the level for his own comfort, kept him sweating in silence.

The new man, this Ulrich Genscher, drove. Herr Schmidt occupied the front passenger seat. Baur's sub-machine gun rested between his legs, barrel up. He had put the magazine into the well but had not charged the weapon. It consoled him, as the heat and the rocking of the car relaxed him, and before too long, he drifted off to a dreamless sleep.

Back at the Jeep, downtime turned minutes into hours. A front brought frosty air and steady rain. Barry became more and more apprehensive and not because of the elements, although he had come to hate cold and wet. His doubts grew like weeds. Every time he thought of the payday, he imagined Rav Hirsch's face with his sad, sad eyes. Barry saw the rav's eyes and a dead Ulrich.

"Get us out of this district!"

Schmidt's yelling woke Baur. They were in a city, in an urban valley defined by mounds of gray debris. Nerves tightened his gut and his mouth was dry. Clenching the receiver of his weapon made him feel better.

"What's going on?" Baur whispered to his neighbor.

"We have just passed through two checkpoints," Herr Goda said softly. "They were detours to take traffic around operations to clear rubble. Herr Schmidt is furious."

"Why?"

"The new man was supposed to get us through the mountains without attracting any attention. Now we have been seen by two police detachments. They were oldsters to be sure, but anyway..." Herr Goda shrugged away the sentence.

"Turn here!" Schmidt yelled again.

"I know a way," Ulrich Genscher said, driving straight.

Schmidt struck him in the face. Baur noticed the driver had positioned his head oddly. He must have been getting hit a lot.

The Maybach screeched to a stop.

"Emil," Genscher said quietly, "I will take care of us. I grew up here. I know my way."

"Fine, drive us to meet your deviant friend. We will know how to greet him."

"And yet another matter I wish to discuss with you. I am for the cause. I'm doing business with Kurt. That's all. There's not much opportunity at the moment, you know. We can't choose our comrades to work with nowadays. Now, if you question my loyalty again, I'll kill you."

"Just so, Ulrich. As you say. But if you lie, you will yourself pay the price. As for the rest of you, prime yourselves. There may be some action yet!" Schmidt yelled.

They started moving again. Herr Goda drew his pistol. Baur saw something shocking: Herr Kempton held a wire with two handles at either end. He crossed his arms so the fine wire dangled by his knees in a loose loop. A garrote! Herr Kempton watched the driver's head intently.

Baur became nervous. He did not know what to do. Herr Kempton's eyes flicked to Herr Schmidt and then to the driver's head. Schmidt could have the driver strangled at any moment!

The car bounded through a rut and the Schmeisser's front sight scratched Baur's face. The sharp pain smoothed out his thoughts and helped him focus. He managed to find the bolt by touch and cycled the weapon. The loud metal-on-metal crashing sound caught everyone's attention.

"Baur is ready," Herr Kempton remarked drily.

"Aw, crumb," Barry griped for no apparent reason as he pulled a fudge disk left over from lunch out of his pocket.

Elya, next to Barry once more, gazed at him with puppy-dog eyes.

"What?"

Elya stared at the chocolate.

"Oh no, my friend," Barry teased in English, "you ate yours. This is mine."

He made a show of stripping the foil off the confection, sniffed at it, luxuriating in its "fine" bouquet, as if it were a cigar. Then he shoved the whole thing deeply into his mouth. "Mmmmmm," he voiced, chewing theatrically.

Manny laughed from the back. He slapped his knee, and his eyes danced with mirth.

"What the hell is that?" Schmidt demanded.

Out the rain-streaked windscreen, Baur saw an American lorry parked in the middle of the right-of-way, leaving no room betwixt itself and fragments of bricks piled up like plowed snow. They lurched their way through a hard left turn.

Barry heard the robust engine before he saw the car. He hopped out of the Jeep, dropped the radio on the seat and flung off his gloves. He tried to call out to the others, but his mouth was full. He spat out the chocolate.

"This is it!" he yelled.

Static erupted out of the radio. A large black sedan with a chrome grill made up of level spars parallel to the ground executed a high-speed turn onto their street. The driver locked up the wheels and it slid to a stop on the wet pavement.

He heard a deuce-and-a-half's diesel revving up. The plan was for Manny to provide cover from the front of the car with the Browning Automatic Rifle while Barry and Elya approached the driver side. Elya knew some German. Leoshan was to close off the road with his truck.

As usual, the plan failed to survive first contact with the enemy.

Baur saw a US Army Jeep parked on the left. Armed men scrambled out of it into the street. He did not know if he should do anything. He decided to wait for instructions from Herr Schmidt.

Barry saw Ulrich behind the wheel, his hair in disarray. The rain on the windshield made it difficult to see more.

The front passenger punched Ulrich in the face.

"You traitorous bastard!" Schmidt yelled, hitting the driver again. "Do him! The rest of you, attack!"

Thank God Herr Schmidt was with them, Baur thought, swallowing hard. He appreciated the presence of a real leader.

Barry heard gears grind. The sedan's rear tires whirled maniacally, slipping on the wet road. The car started backward, fishtailing slightly as the tires bit, picking up speed. He hoped Ulrich was buying time and not trying to run.

"Where the hell is Leo?" he yelled, pulling his pistols. The one from the holster, the right one, came clear. The one in his pocket snagged its hammer during the draw.

Leoshan's big drab deuce-and-a-half, trailing a cloud of purple exhaust, roared through the intersection and slammed into the left rear quarter panel of the sedan, knocking the car off-center and bringing it to a stop. Leoshan slipped down from the cab and hurried to Barry, carbine at the shoulder.

Barry finally freed his second pistol. With both of his arms out straight, he trained his right pistol on the man in the seat behind the driver and the other at the front passenger. He thumbed back two hammers simultaneously, their dual snick audible in the post-crash hush. Frozen rain pelted his face.

The team was off its plan. Elya, centered on the hood ornament, pointed his M1 Garand at the Germans over the car's long snout. Manny crouched on the passenger side, Browning at the ready, in a perfect crossfire situation with Leoshan. Barry caught Manny's eye.

"Move over next to Elya," Barry ordered.

Manny, laughing, a big kid at play, didn't budge.

The crash came out of nowhere, Baur thought, disoriented. Herr Kempton and the driver were fighting over the garrote! Outside the Maybach, the tall man adjacent to Baur had the features of a Jew Bolshevik. He remembered everything, the *Führer*, the Soviet occupation and Marta, and it made him mad. Can't they leave the Fatherland alone?

The Jew took his eyes off the car, his attention moving to something on the other side of the road, and he laughed! Who was this Jew to laugh? Who did he think he was?

Baur held the submachine gun horizontally out and away from him, across his stomach and aimed by instinct. He pulled the trigger and kept it pulled. The Schmeisser bucked like a truck driven fast over a rutted field as it pumped out round after round, shooting through the door.

The bbrrraaaappppp of the shots and the distinctive loose rattling of the Schmeisser's action made Barry flinch. He saw the impact of multiple nine-millimeter rounds on Manny's torso. The hits walked up from his lower belly to his chest and his expression veered from joyous excitement to pained confusion. He sank to the pavement without even charging the BAR.

"*Menachem!*" Elya yelled, dropping his Garand and running to his brother.

Barry and Leoshan started firing. Leoshan covered the rear, so Barry lined up his sights on the front passenger. Emotional pain welled up inside him at the thought of Manny's wounds. He compartmentalized and concentrated on protecting Ulrich.

After firing four rounds from each pistol, he wedged his left-hand Colt behind his belt and opened the driver's side door. Blood saturated the cockpit. The riders were all motionless, save one.

The passenger closest to Manny, the one with a Schmeisser in his lap, waved a hand vaguely in the air, the thumb and two of his fingers glazed red. Barry shot him in the head; blood and bone sprayed the pillar and window. The hand fell.

He grabbed Ulrich's shoulder and pulled. Barry laughed in relief as Ulrich struggled out the door.

"Are you hit? What's this?" Barry undid the wire from around Ulrich's neck.

"*Nein.*" Ulrich had taken some serious blows to his face and his right ear, surrounded by dry scabbing, had been twisted until torn half off. The ragged cut across his throat did not reach deep enough to hurt anything important.

"*Noooo!*" Elya wailed.

Barry and Leoshan looped around the car to where Elya cradled

Manny, who pressed his arms against his torso as if he were keeping everything inside. Blood thick as spilled paint coated his lips and chin. A spasm wracked him. He closed his eyes and grimaced.

"Let's get him out of the rain," Barry said.

Barry had not even thought to locate a stretcher or bring a poncho. He unhooked his web belt and tugged off his great coat. Leoshan, Elya and Barry slid Manny onto the coat and used it to carry him, screaming, to the bed of the truck. Leoshan dropped the gate and they pushed and pulled him onto the cold metal bed. Barry walked around the deuce-and-a-half to the rear of the sedan and clipped his belt on.

"Mr. Barry, shouldn't I get that boy the first aid kit from the Jeep?" Leoshan asked.

"With those hits? Manny'll be dead before we pull outta here," Barry whispered. "It'd just be a waste of morphine."

"But—"

Barry grabbed Leoshan's upper arm firmly. "See here, I liked the guy too, but he lost his focus. He took his eyes off his target and his target got him. He stopped paying attention and he got it good—you hear me? You can't do that in war."

"We ain't in the war no more."

"Think like that and you'll get dead, too. The truck's in the way, but help me get in the trunk."

"But—"

"God damn it, Leo! I didn't even want to do this stupid job!"

"Okay, it's okay. I know it," Leoshan said in soothing tones. "I know you didn't want this job. Here, let me help you."

Chrome handles secured the trunk lid, one on each side. Barry yanked on the right one.

"Goddamned thing won't give."

Leoshan went to the cockpit.

"Got the keys," he said.

"Are they keyed? Sure are."

"Here you go." Leoshan wiped the bloody keys on his leg and handed them over.

Barry tried to line one up on the notch in the cylinder. He suddenly became very conscious of the passing of time and felt anxious to get the gold and get away. His hands quavered.

"Crumb, I'm scratching the hell out of the chrome."

"I don't think no one will mind," Leoshan said, "considering."

Barry examined the sedan as if seeing it for the first time. "I guess you're right."

"Can't get into it that way, old boy," a composed Ulrich told them. His head stayed cocked at a slight angle. "Here, allow me."

He reached into the cockpit, groaning with effort, and jerked on something. The trunk popped open slightly. Leoshan forced his fingers under the lid and tried to raise it farther. It gave a little more, stopping amid the sounds of abrading metal.

"Won't go no more, Mr. Barry. The crash must have jammed the fender into the trunk."

"It's coming up right now." Barry moved next to Leoshan and grabbed on with both hands.

The two of them lifted. After more metal-on-metal noise, the lid flew up. Barry dove in, throwing a leather overcoat and a *feldgrau* canvas tool bag to the street.

"Oh, boy," Leoshan said.

Four wooden boxes were precisely arranged in the center of the trunk.

"Five bars each, my friends," Ulrich said. "Congratulations."

"Yeah, well, we ain't out of this yet. Leo, got a pry bar?"

"Sure thing, Mr. Barry." He peeled off toward the deuce-and-a-half.

Ulrich gave them all a shaky smile. Leoshan came back with a pry bar painted army green.

Barry inquired about Manny.

Leoshan swiveled his head sadly.

"All right. Give it to him," Barry ordered, pointing to Ulrich. "Open one." He stepped back, pulling Leoshan with him.

"What is the matter with you?" Ulrich asked, confused.

"If it were my gold, I'd rig it up so if someone opened it, it'd go 'boom.'"

"You do not trust me?"

Barry shrugged. "Open the box."

"You do not trust me, then I do not trust you now." Ulrich held out the pry bar. "You do it."

Barry reached down to the holster at his side. "Manny is dying or dead and you are three quarters of a day late. Open the box."

"Okay. Okay, you cowboy!" Ulrich forced the flat end between the lid and body of the wooden box second from left and shoved.

They separated with a minimum of effort, and he flipped the lid off to the side.

"Boom," he said at his most urbane.

Five shiny rectangles glinted, even in the low light, on a bed of straw. Barry slowly reached out and touched one. Cool and velvety.

"Oh, would you look at that." Leoshan ogled the gold over Barry's shoulder.

Barry worked a hand underneath one of them and brought it out. "It's heavy."

"Fifteen kilos, more or less," Ulrich replied. "Maybe thirty pounds? They are London Good Delivery, negotiable anywhere in Europe."

"Not with this on it they're not." Barry held the bar with two hands and displayed the front for the team.

Someone had stamped the *Reichsadler*, the Nazi spread-winged eagle grasping a swastika, on it a third of the way up, followed by three rows of numbers.

A wave of hate surged through Barry with the inevitability of the tide. He found it inconceivable that these bars had been struck out of the fillings and jewelry of his people, but the hate was there, nonetheless.

Ulrich grinned through his bruises with the satisfaction of a job well done, until he registered Barry's displeasure. Ulrich's countenance became serious.

The freezing rain came down steadily. Barry took control of his murderous mood.

"Leoshan, let's get these into the truck." Barry returned the bar and replaced the cover.

He and Leoshan lifted the box by its rope handles and carried it over. The gate hung down. Elya knelt by Manny in the middle of the truck's bed.

They swung the box up into the deuce-and-a-half and slid it in, scraping along the metal floor.

"How is he?" Barry asked in Yiddish.

"He's breathing but unconscious," Elya informed him.

They made short work of loading their consignment. Barry had forgotten to put his gloves back on and the 150 pounds of gold lugged in each trip imprinted the hemp fibers of the handles on his palms. With the fourth box loaded, they closed and secured the gate.

"We've been here too long," Barry said. "Let's get going. If I see a good spot to pull off and bury Manny, I'll do it, otherwise, it's back to Furstflarn."

"He ain't dead yet, Mr. Barry," Leoshan said.

"Yes, he is. He just don't know it. Let's go."

Barry waved Ulrich over to the Jeep. He limped to the leather overcoat that lay in the street on the way and scooped it up.

"You will be cold." Ulrich handed the coat to Barry.

"Shit," he mumbled, glowering. He slipped it on. "I'm swimming in this thing."

Leoshan climbed into the truck's cab. Barry gunned the Jeep's little engine and jumped the curb onto the sidewalk to avoid the wrecked sedan. He stopped at the intersection.

Leo tried backing away, but the sedan had hooked on somehow and he dragged it along. The truck's diesel roared, black smoke poured out of its stack, and then it bounced up onto the sidewalk, shaking the bumpers loose. Shifting gears, Leoshan changed directions, smashing into the sedan again and bouncing it out of the way. In next to no time, the two army vehicles were hurtling out of Munich in the freezing rain.

They sped on through the cold afternoon as the day dwindled into early evening. Barry's feet and fingertips went numb, as numb as his heart. He felt anesthetized to the successful score and Manny's being hit. Manny's having been shot became a mere problem. His friend had become a problem to be solved. That was all.

Fields lined both sides of the pavement. He wanted to find earth with a line of trees or shrubs blocking the view to shield their work. Kilometer after kilometer passed in the growing gloom, failing to reveal anything he liked. He slowed anyway.

"What is the matter?" Ulrich asked as they came to a halt in the middle of the deserted road.

"I want to see what is going on in the truck," Barry said.

In the fading daylight, Leoshan pulled up behind. Barry dashed through the rain to where Elya hovered over Manny.

"How is he?" Barry asked, in Yiddish.

"Still breathing," Elya confirmed.

"Does he need morphine?"

"He's sleeping."

Barry walked back to the Jeep.

"How's he doing?" Leoshan called down from the cab of the big truck.

"Still with us but out cold." Barry hopped onto the running board. "I'm not going to look for a place to bury him anymore. Let's run on back to the warehouse. Got it?"

"Got it."

They drove to Furstflarn through the frigid rain. Ulrich slept all the way, waking at the warehouse. The deuce-and-a-half barely cleared the entrance. Barry squeezed the Jeep in behind.

Ulrich murmured something in German. Barry and Leoshan, ignoring him, pulled the restraining pins on the gate and lowered it onto the hood of the Jeep. They both climbed up into the bed.

Elya looked at them sadly. "*Niftar.*"

"Oh my," Leoshan said, not needing a translation, as he removed his knit cap.

Barry exhaled sharply.

The three of them descended and gathered under a single bare bulb. Ulrich rubbed his neck.

Leoshan broke the silence. "We got to take care of him tonight, Mr. Barry."

"I know it. Should we run on out and bury him? Now?"

"Mr. Barry, the gold makes me nervous, too."

"Criminy."

"If I might say, we should load up the gold and the dead boy and I'll take care of them both."

"Leo, you want to load up, drive out, bury a body and drive on to Switzerland?"

"I want to stick with the plan."

"You'll be driving all night, through the rain."

"We was with General Patton," Leoshan said with tired pride. "We drove up to the Bulge. Three days and two nights, all snow and cold. I can drive anywhere, anytime. The burying is a sad thing, but it needs to be done."

"I help," Elya said.

"See, Mr. Barry? The two of us can do it."

Barry considered one man, then the other, gauging what they had left.

"Okay then. Let's get started," he said.

They brought the boxes containing the gold bars down from the bed of the truck. Leoshan opened each one. The precious metal reflected the dim glow and grabbed the men, rendering them immovable.

"There are twenty," Barry said, breaking the spell. He decided to change the agreed-upon split. "Six goes into twenty—"

"Six!" Ulrich exclaimed. "What is six? There are four of us!"

"Six shares. Me and Leoshan, Manny and Elya, and you and Kurt."

"I forgot about Kurt. But Manny? He's dead."

"Elya gets his share."

"Why?"

"He was in the gang. He went on the job. He died. His family gets his share. Elya is his brother, the only family he has left."

The conversation troubled him because he knew gangs often broke up when deciding the issue of the split, sometimes fatally. Big Meyer warned him greed can trump friendship.

"That is not smart," Ulrich said. "We could divide by five. Each of us would be a bar ahead."

"It's not the way my gang operates." Barry, certain of his position, calmly waited out the tired and whipped Ulrich.

"That is not smart," the German repeated, breaking eye contact and turning away. "Anyway, you rabid dog, I would not want you to kill me over Jew filth."

Barry kicked Ulrich in the back of his left knee and as he fell, grabbed him behind the neck and slammed his face into the edge of the jeep's windshield. Ulrich howled in pain. Barry pulled him backward and threw him to the floor, pouncing on him and pinning him to the cold concrete with a knee on his right shoulder.

Barry reached for his fighting knife. He shoved the sharp tip into the sleeve of Ulrich's wool overcoat at the armpit, stopping before he penetrated skin. He tore some of the sleeve and did the same to the shirt underneath.

"You crazy American hooligan, what are you doing?"

"You know what I'm doing," Barry said, conversationally, sheathing his knife.

He pulled the clothing apart. Scarred flesh, maroon and ragged, the size of a US fifty-cent piece, marred the yellow skin on the inside of Ulrich's upper arm.

"No! No, it is not what you are thinking, really," he babbled.

Barry unfastened the flap of his leather holster and drew his .45. Thumbing the hammer back, he rested the muzzle against Ulrich's forehead.

"I figured. I guessed it," he muttered. Then he spoke up. "I always knew what you were. Where is the blood group tattoo? As a former SS man, you ought not give me any excuses to kill you."

"No!" Ulrich shouted, then calmed down, his voice shaky. "I will not do so, Herr Rosen. I must have not been thinking. It has been a long day and I am much fatigued. Please to forgive me."

"What do you guys think?"

Elya wore a firm stony expression. Leoshan' head slowly rotated from side to side, once right, once left.

Barry wanted to off Ulrich, then he didn't. He lowered the hammer.

"This is the way it is going to be," Barry said. "You, me and Leoshan will get the value of three-and-a-half bars. Elya will get twice that, the extra for Manny's share, leaving two and a half bars for the armchair commandos. Staff Sergeant Washington gets the value of one bar. I decided to add him. Good for business.

"Kurt gets one and a half bars. To make it easy, I'm going to give him two gold bars—I'll make the half up out of my end—and he can do whatever he wants with them. Otto is waiting for Leo in Switzerland. Otto will fence the rest, take a cut and put the francs in our accounts, like always. You got a problem *boychik*, you come and see me, *capiche*?"

"I 'got' it," Ulrich said.

"Good. Get your kraut backside outta here. I'm tired of looking at you."

Ulrich rose to his feet and shuffled toward the door. He paused and turned slightly, perhaps to say something, but thought better of it and disappeared into the cold night instead, leaving Barry with the feeling he would never speak with Ulrich again.

"Let's get to work," Barry said.

22

The war was over and Special Agents Walter Gonzales and Fredrick Montgomery, of the US Army's Criminal Investigative Division, normally worked in civilian clothes. Walter had them in uniform today due to the crappy weather, and their respective ranks were clearly visible.

"Again private, what did you see this morning?" Fred asked the mouthy young military policeman.

They were standing near the damaged Maybach in the dying light of the dreary Munich day. US Army and German police vehicles were parked pell-mell in the intersection. One was the sector military police patrol Jeep.

The rain slackened and the wind stiffened, hunching shoulders and freezing fingers. Ice formed here and there, including in the crannies of the bashed car. The CID agents worked amidst the wrecked vehicle, with its open trunk lid, the lifeless bodies, and the street stained with diluted blood. Walter, all business, would not let anyone move anything as he carefully studied the scene.

"Listen here," the private blurted out, his eyes shifting right and left, making sure no one was close enough to hear. "I'm tired of niggers and wetbacks telling me—"

Suddenly, Walter was there. He smacked the private in the head and sent his helmet flying. The MP corporal, alarmed and unsure what to do, vacillated.

"Do you need an attitude adjustment too?" Walter asked the corporal, turning him to stone.

"No, Master Sergeant."

"Fine. Let's get started. What's your name?"

"McCutcheon, Sergeant."

"Come with me, Corporal McCutcheon. Private, if you make Special Agent Montgomery ask you even one more time, I'm going to take you out to the wood pile. You're out of uniform; pick up your goddamned helmet."

Eventually, Walter and Fred finished their interviews. They were comparing information until the ranking officer on the scene interrupted.

"You're done here, Master Sergeant Gonzales?" The Lieutenant yelled from across the street, making his question sound like an order.

"No, sir. I'm going to take pictures, and Corporal Montgomery is going to collect up the spent shells."

"Well, hurry the hell up. It's cold out."

"Yes, sir!"

Walter indicated they needed to get busy with a nod. Before long, Fred was at the wheel of their four-year-old army-green Nash Ambassador sedan. It had big white stars painted on the front doors, a missing chrome rub rail on the left side and various bumps and bruises that included several bullet holes.

"Did your private's attitude correct itself?" Walter asked, rubbing his hands to warm them.

"Yes, but all he knew was there was a Negro driver who wouldn't move along when instructed to and a technical sergeant who chewed him out for no good reason."

"Nothing else?"

"Nope, nothing."

"What did the Military Police and Jerries get in the neighborhood canvass?"

"Nothing. They didn't even find nobody in the neighborhood to ask anything."

"Well. Well, well, well," Walter began, "I got this. My corporal, the one riding with your private? He remembered all the private remembered, too. He also noted there were two other men in the technical sergeant's jeep. He said that while the Negro and the technical sergeant were ay-okay, there was something about the two other men. They were in uniform, but they struck the corporal as wrong. They had weapons, but the corporal thought they were holding them like boots, but they were too old to be fresh out of boot camp. And he was pretty honest, he said the technical sergeant scared the hell out of him. Now what does that tell us, Fred?"

Fred had no idea what that told them.

"It tells us they were there to do this, my boy. They met the guys in the big Dusie or whatever the heck it was, shot 'em to pieces and took off."

That made sense. Fred said as much.

"What was in the trunk?" Walter asked.

"The trunk?"

"Yes, you know, the storage compartment at the rear of the vehicle." Walter sounded more like a sympathetic teacher than a boss annoyed because the person working for him was a little thick. "It had been pried open after the wreck. Not only pried open, but empty by the time we got there. Ergo, somebody wanted something from the car bad enough to kill for it."

"Someone could have come after and looked inside."

"Maybe. But A, there's all the shot guys; B, if you're right, the so-called army guys waiting would be a coincidence, and I don't care for coincidences at all; and three, keep it simple."

Fred didn't comment.

"Now investigate this," Walter went on. "We have a *technical sergeant* being ratted out at the camp, a *technical sergeant* here in a hunter's blind and a *technical sergeant* setting up angles with locals in Austria. All the same technical sergeant?"

Fred hoped his boss didn't really want him to answer this question, either. He had no idea if it was the same technical sergeant.

"I think it would take a former commando-type, like a vet out of the First Special Service Force, to shake up a seasoned MP corporal." Walter settled into the passenger seat and sighed. "We got us a who-done-it, Freddy boy."

23

Prior to the heist, Barry had made three US Army crates with false bottoms. Elya and Leoshan helped him re-pack the gold bars in the secret compartments, less two for Kurt. They piled engine parts on top of the gold: carburetors, manifolds and any other junk Barry had been able to obtain. They hammered the lids on tight. It took all three of them to lift each crate onto the hood of the jeep and from there into the bed of the deuce-and-a-half, where they ignored Manny's body as they worked.

"We have to get going," Leoshan prompted.

"Okay." Barry put his hand on Elya's arm. "May you know no more sorrows," he said in Hebrew, shrugging.

"By sorrows, I've had enough already," Elya responded in Yiddish with a dismissive wave. The men shook hands.

Desolation washed over Barry. He felt like he would never see Elya again. Elya and Manny were his guys.

"Don't worry," Leoshan offered, "we'll bury the boy good."

Leoshan, too. They were leaving and Barry felt like they would be gone forever. Everything seemed to be coming apart. He should go with them, he thought, to make sure...make sure of what?

To make sure they would be safe.

He wanted to say something, but no words came. He could only nod.

They killed the light and opened the door. For a moment, Barry listened to the ticking of frozen rain on stone, then he rolled out in the Jeep, to get it out of the way, followed closely by Leoshan and Elya in the deuce-and-a-half. The truck backed out and drove off.

Barry pulled back in and closed the door. He had started this job in the early morning hours, changing into his uniform here in the warehouse. His suit and a trench coat lay neatly arranged on some cartons. He placed his pistols next to them and slowly stripped, exhausted from the day's activities. He discarded the leather coat and dressed in his civilian clothes: his suit, the trench coat, and fedora.

At first, he was going to leave his pair of Colts, but the two holsters on his belt shamed him with their emptiness. He knew he would not be able to sleep tonight unless he cleaned them, which he decided to do at the apartment. Out of habit, he topped off all his magazines with stubby fat .45 rounds, all the while asking himself how he got into this situation.

"Why can't you get a real job?" he asked. "Not all these shadow trades, this black marketing, this Operation Judgement and, now, robbery of stolen goods."

The last thing he did was hide Kurt's two gold bars in his canvas-covered civilian sedan by shoving them beneath the driver's seat. He dragged ass to his flat, arriving shortly before midnight. All he wanted to do was clean his heaters, eat a quick meal and fall into bed.

At the top of the stairs, he saw one of his neckties drooping from the doorknob and thanked God Elspeth had decided to come back. He planned to get her started in the kitchen immediately.

"Put your clothes on, sweetie," Barry said as he pushed through the door, "and cook me up something good. I'm famished."

"You will please to excuse, but I am dressed and not a good cook," Kurt replied.

The single lamp left most of the room in shadows. Kurt sat on a chair facing the door, Elspeth a decoration on his lap, gripped firmly by the waist, his right hand under her white blouse.

"Do come inside," he said.

Barry entered the apartment and gently closed the door. Someone had dressed Kurt's squat Neanderthal in a suit. He occupied a chair on Barry's far right. Ulrich lay unconscious at Kurt's feet. Blood trickled out of his ear and nose. His face had been battered some more. Kurt's other muscle, the Aryan god, in a black sweater over some gray field trousers, leaned on the wall to Barry's left, smirking. Barry nodded in return.

Swell, he thought.

The girl whimpered.

Barry carried his overcoat in the crook of his left arm and his keys in his right hand. His hat rested on the back of his head. He broke the silence by telling Kurt to let Elspeth go.

"Oh, I not think so," Kurt said. "We decide to take the gold, not two bars you want to give me, big money man, but all. Think like this, you buy the girl for all the gold, yes?"

Elspeth seemed emotionally put out for sure, but overall, no worse for wear. Except for the little troll's paw on her breast. Ulrich was another story.

Adrenaline chased away Barry's fatigue. He transferred his keys to his left hand.

"You not move!" Kurt said quickly, with a panicked glance to either side. "Buy the girl for all the gold, yes?"

Kurt's shouting made the Neanderthal shift nervously and brought the Aryan god off the wall.

The hell with this little monster, Barry thought. He reached up and moved his hat forward, lowering the brim over his eyes, then let his arm hang straight down.

"No."

Kurt yapped an order in German. The handsome, blond muscle on the left smiled wider.

It was now or never. Barry picked now.

He dropped his keys and his overcoat. With his right hand, he flicked back the side of his suit jacket and drew his pistol. Crouching slightly for balance, he pointed the Colt across his torso, to his left, pressed the trigger, reached over the top of the weapon with his left hand and grabbed the slide, thrusting it to the rear and letting go.

The instant the slide slammed forward, the pistol erupted. Barry continued firing at the handsome man with his large muscles and blond hair. The man was fast—he was already running, but Barry's draw had been fast as well. The first round holed the black sweater, low and to the right, when the man was still two yards away.

Barry adjusted his aim and noted, in passing, the man's expression change from arrogance to confusion and fired three more times before they were close enough to touch.

Barry swept his left arm around and up, catching the wounded man under his right arm and rolled the dying man over his hip. The man crashed to the floor. Barry pivoted to face the Neanderthal, who had risen to his feet, determination etched on his thick features.

Barry started firing. At the same time, he drew his second Colt to blaze away with both weapons. The slide of the pistol in his right hand locked back and he stopped firing the left as well. The Neanderthal had fallen and lay unmoving at the foot of his chair.

Barry's ears rang from all the banging. He whirled to face Kurt. The little monster had not moved. Cordite hung in the air and stung Barry's throat. Elspeth screamed. He cast off the empty firearm and transferred the pistol in his left hand to his right. He had forgotten how many rounds he had fired. Just to be on the safe side, he released the magazine and plunged a fresh one into the handle. He steadied the pistol with both hands.

"Let her go," Barry said.

"Perhaps I was hasty, yes?" Kurt's eyes darted to his dead associates. "Maybe we think about it?" He yipped out a small nervous laugh. "We should get doctor for Ulrich? Yes?"

Barry zeroed in on troll's forehead. "Let her go."

Kurt cowered behind Elspeth. Most of the target vanished. Barry could see one of Kurt's eyes and some of the top of his head.

"Two of the gold, no, one is fine. Just the one. Ulrich needs a doctor," Kurt stammered from his protected position.

"Nuts to that you sawed-off piece of crap."

Barry stepped to his left and fired. Elspeth recoiled from the crack. The new angle had exposed more of Kurt's head, and the bullet plowed a furrow through his scalp before leaving a ragged hole in the wall behind him. Blood stained the white plaster.

"Ahrrgh!" His hands flew to the wound.

Elspeth sprung up. She tried to run but tripped over Ulrich. Barry sighted in on the little man's chest and fired four more times, the body convulsing with each hit. After a moment of noise and smoke, it was over.

Barry coughed.

The better half of Kurt's muscle lay face-down in a pool of his own blood. The uglier half had crumpled in an ass-high heap, his knees and head supporting the rest of him. One of his arms was splayed out, reaching. Kurt was face up in his chair. Ulrich, on his back, still out, continued to breathe. Barry lowered the hammer and holstered his pistol.

He picked up the empty Colt and out of habit, pressed the magazine release. Barry drew a fresh magazine from his belt and jammed it into the weapon. He charged it, the slide crashing forward, and holstered up as he crouched by the crying Elspeth.

"Go on downstairs, honey," he said as calmly as he could.

She sobbed softly as she rested on one hip and both arms, her head down, her hair hiding her face from view.

"Hey, sister, you need to go on downstairs."

Barry lifted her to her feet. He could not find any blood or bruises. She seemed very young as he led her to the door.

"Come on now, go see your momma." He guided her out into the hall.

Elspeth walked away, shoulders high, clearly in shock. The door closed behind her. Barry knelt over Ulrich; he pried open first one swollen eye and then the other. Ulrich's left pupil was large and round, hardly any color visible on its perimeter, while the right was a drop of black engine oil floating on a sea of brown. His rapid but slight respirations barely stirred the air.

Barry slumped to the floor, his eyes clamped shut. He rammed his fingers into his hair, knocking his fedora off, making tight fists and pulling, the resulting pain a lifeline to sanity. If he had any tears left, he'd have started crying and never stopped.

They were all dying.

All he had wanted was something to eat and some sleep. Now he had to clean up three, probably four bodies before sunrise.

"Damn," Barry said.

The deal in Furstflarn had been sweet for him and the boys. The club and the expansion of his already existing black market to the camp had produced far more money than he had imagined they would. And yet, like always, his friends couldn't help getting themselves killed.

Manny was dead. He had liked the big dope. Ulrich would join Manny before sunrise. The guys from Barry's army unit were all gone or badly wounded, especially the Canucks. Those bastards had fought hard and died for their trouble. To his mind's eye came an unbidden memory: Lieutenant Mac, gut shot, falling on their Italian mountaintop battlefield. The gang from Newark, too. The Meyers and the rest, all history. Now he had to run, just like before.

A raspy pitiless sound emanated from Ulrich's throat and he became quiet. His chest stopped moving. The bleeding in his brain had finally killed him.

Barry buried his face in his hands and closed his eyes. He rocked back and forth, kneeling on the floor, next to his dead friend, surrounded by dead enemies. Time passed. He did not know how long.

The mean little voice in his head, the pragmatic survivor, spoke up. It told him to get himself together. It told him to get out of the apartment. It told him to get going.

He listened.

24

"We don't care! We forbid it!" Pinchas Shammi thundered at Rivka Shapiro in Yiddish.

A moment later, he threw a raised-eyebrow, questioning glance at Rav Hirsch.

So much for the thunder, she thought.

Rabbi Hirsch, Shimshon Gutkin and Shammi were in the camp's administration office, at their usual positions in the ambassador's anteroom, wearing second-hand overcoats. They were on the same side of their table, a skirmish line of pessimism facing Rivka.

Under the umbrella of their negativity, they were still who they were: the angry Shammi, the sappy Gutkin and a compassionate, but still unpersuaded, Rav Hirsch. Ambassador Resnick reigned from where he stood at the head of the men's table, his handsome features expressing supercilious pity.

"So that's what you say," Rivka countered. "He's my brother. You think maybe I should let him die? The only one left from my family? Finish the work of the Nazis, maybe?"

"No one is saying that," Resnick said in smooth but Americanized Yiddish. "But think for a moment. It's dangerous to cross borders now. And it is very cold. We can send for him. It would be better for everyone if we had him brought here."

"Like the Nazis brought people." Rivka's heart rejected the idea of merely sending for Yankel, as it had whenever the suggestion arose.

They had been hammering her like this since the sun had set. She had walked out on them to visit with Hannah, but when she came back to finish some work before she left for Poland, they had appeared and resumed their hounding.

Rivka ignored their posturing. She realized her mistake had been to turn on a light. Strict Pinchas Shammi had seen her and rallied all these men. He thought a woman should not undertake such things as a rescue trip to Poland. Clean and cook and type, yes. Rescue a brother, no. As she had a hundred times already, she explained it all to them.

"Yitzie wrote me. He said he had a letter from Yankel, my brother. Yankel wrote asking after me and anyone else from our family. He has recovered his strength and was starting out for Roszowice." She spoke slowly, leaning forward for emphasis. "He will be sick. He will be in danger. We know how it is all over Poland. He needs me there. Not here, where it is...safe."

Rivka wished Barry were next to her. Unlike these men, Barry knew the world and how it was. He would let her go. He would drive her to the train, she was sure. He might even honor his offer to take her, although she did not put much stock in it. She had been disappointed too many times.

"Yes, we know already. Be reasonable. I will send for him." Resnick also leaned forward in his earnestness. He ruined the effect, however, with a peek down her blouse.

The slow swinging of the office door choked off Rivka's reply as it grabbed everyone's attention. A specter emerged from the dark, wearing an overcoat and a fedora. He moved his right arm, as if he were putting something in his pocket.

Barry entered. "There is a lot to be said for safe, sister." He spoke in English. "Late night for everybody."

Barry had been into some trouble, she knew instantly. His brown eyes were alert, but heavy lines bracketed his mouth, and the color had washed out of his pale face. His tan trench coat hung open, showing a rumpled gray suit.

"What's going on?" he asked with an easygoing, tired smile, in his accented Yiddish.

Resnick started to speak, but Rivka cut him off. "Yitzie Strasen wrote me. My brother is not well, but he is traveling to our home in Roszowice. I want to go to him. They will not let me."

"I am taking you." Barry smiled at her. "I told you already."

Her heart leapt. She laughed out loud and hopped slightly in her chair. "Really? Would you do that?"

"Of course. We go. Right now."

"*Wait one minute!*" Resnick shouted in English.

Rivka watched as Barry's mien transformed. He had been smiling at her like a tired little boy. Now he radiated cold menace.

"Come, we go." Barry faced their boss but raised his arm and wiggled his fingertips at her, indicating she should come along.

Rivka knew if she took Barry's hand, he would walk her outside and they would drive away. She wasn't sure if she was ready. This had all happened so fast.

"Don't you do it!" Resnick yelled.

"We forbid it!" Shammi barked.

Rav Hirsch's sad eyes rested on her. She would hate to defy any ruling he might make. He sighed and began to study the top of the table.

She understood Rav Hirsch would not be taking a position on the matter.

Was going to see a close relative before the war this much trouble? She didn't know. Papa had taken them to Latvia, Czechoslovakia, and even as far as France, but she did not remember the details; she had been so little. Although she was fearful, not to go would mean Hitler, may his name be erased, had won after all. Also, she would forever be at the mercy of men who talked to her breasts instead of her face.

"I would like to say goodbye to Hannah Blimah before we go."

"So? I'll meet you in front of your barracks. We leave tonight."

Rivka felt the weight of the moment. She had long thought more action during the war would have saved more lives. Here was her chance to act.

She could conceivably save her brother's life. She caught Resnick slyly ogling her again. Shammi seethed. Sympathy cocked Gutkin's head. Rabbi Hirsch looked sad.

"Okay," she said in English.

She was going to get Yankel! Rivka bolted from the room and skipped down the steps, diving into the icy night.

The rain had stopped. Thick clouds choked off the moonlight. She shivered and pulled her sweater tightly around her shoulders. It did not help much with the frigid wind. She sped to the barracks, impatient to share what had happened at the office. Hannah will love the part where Barry showed up at the last minute!

The dimly lit barracks felt cold. The presence of the women at Hannah's end of the hall made Rivka wary and she slowed to a walk. She knew those women and knew why they would be here at this time of night.

Mrs. Levenson watched from next to the bunk, impressive in her returning girth. Mrs. Adamowski and Mrs. Kugel, two bird-like ladies, fussed over her friend.

"No," Rivka whispered. "No. Not Hannah Blimah."

She knew the small women were part of the camp's Holy Society, volunteers organized to prepare cadavers for burial according to Jewish law. They cleaned the decedent and stayed with the body until the funeral.

"I came to check on her and she was gone," Mrs. Levenson said, mournful in the half-light.

"A miracle really," Mrs. Adamowski added compassionately, as she carefully folded Hannah Blimah's blanket. "So frail, the girl was, no?"

"Another for the Germans," Mrs. Kugel mused to no one in particular, "may they all live to one hundred and twenty." Syrupy sarcasm dripped from her two-faced blessing.

Rivka sniffed loudly, wiped her eyes and gathered up her sorrow. So many of the people she had cared for had died. Then she sealed her sorrow and buried it deep in her heart. Without comment, she slid over to her own sleeping area and began to pack her meager belongings.

"Daughter, where are you going?" Mrs. Levenson asked.

"My brother is on his way to our village," Rivka said in an even monotone. "I'm going to get him. I'm going to bring him over to the American zone."

The small busy ladies of the Holy Society were undressing Hannah Blimah's lifeless body in preparation for her last sponging.

"Why daughter, it is too much for you." Mrs. Levenson feigned sweetness in her voice. "Who is taking you? It's that army cowboy, isn't it?"

"It's Sergeant Rosen who is taking me."

"Yes, I see." Mrs. Levenson's eyes narrowed. She compressed her lips into a thin line. "Now the two of you will end up in the World to Come, instead of just him. What does the hoodlum want from you?"

"Maybe just to help!" Rivka shouted, throwing a dingy nightshirt into a marred and scuffed Gladstone bag.

"Not him, daughter. He wants something, all right."

"It's not always what you say, you know. There are still good people in the world."

"And you are sure your American hoodlum is one of those good people?"

Rivka scowled at Mrs. Levenson in reply and finished packing in a blind rush. She secured the clasp on the Gladstone and sighed. She looked at Hannah Blimah and felt tears coming on as an ocean swell of grief threatened to breach the dykes she had built inside herself. She waited it out. The grief broke against her internal bulwarks. She calmed and felt herself return to what now passed for normal in her life. She picked up her small bag.

She walked over to Hannah Blimah. The women of the Holy Society made room. Rivka leaned over her dead friend's body and kissed Hannah's forehead. After, she strode purposefully out of the former concentration camp barracks that had been her hellish home for so long.

25

Resnick and the rabbis were wrong, at least about the start of their trip. Barry and Rivka's drive through Germany had been as uneventful, so far, as Resnick had predicted it would be dangerous. Maybe before Hitler, may his name be erased, a journey could have been routine like this. She didn't know.

Rivka liked driving with Barry in his sporty car with its swept-back grill and modern lines. He had been solicitous of her comfort. He had even produced a coat for her. He stopped when she asked and let her address the temperature with the controls.

He seemed to know where he was going. Even though he checked the maps he carried in an olive drab canvas folio, and sometimes a complicated green compass, he did so casually. Like he had come this way before. He bartered easily for gas, paying with food and liquor.

Barry wanted a rural border crossing, which he judged best for avoiding Soviets. They drove through the German countryside as the sun set, fields to their left, hilly woods on the right, on a road barely wide enough for a single vehicle. Rivka heard a loud "click" when he switched the headlights on as the gray day gave way to cloudy night. Eventually, a slight grade led up to a taupe clapboard guardhouse.

"Ah, Czechoslovakia." Barry grinned. "I thought I'd lost it."

Pale smoke wafted out of a stacked stone chimney. Illuminated windows made the house cheery in Rivka's mind. Even so, she felt nervous. The house crowded the macadam, which, up ahead, cut through a copse of green pine trees. A red and white striped pole horizontally blocked their way.

They pulled up to the pole and parked next to a small porch. He hit the horn twice, two jaunty blasts of optimism. Barry had told her it was an American car, built before the war. Only an American car could sound like that, so happy. The ratcheting sound of the parking brake mixed with that of the engine winding down.

"It's show time, sister." He opened the door.

Cold air invaded the cockpit. Barry was out and walking toward the house before Rivka could comment, his overcoat flapping in the night. She knew he had a brace of pistols on his belt, hidden under his jacket and coat. She worried for him.

A border guard in his shirtsleeves emerged and froze on the porch. His suspenders hung from his waist and his uniform trousers were bloused in his boots. He retreated into the house, leaving the door ajar.

Barry grinned again, lifted his eyebrows and shrugged.

The guard and two friends filed out of the house in a jumble. All three wore fur hats, green wool tunics and matching trousers. The first guard gave out a startled shout and ducked back in. He returned immediately with a long bolt-action rifle. As they approached, Barry started speaking in English.

The guards retreated slightly and conversed among themselves. Barry winked at Rivka.

The Czech guards finished their consultation. The middle one, the one with the rifle, took charge and motioned sharply.

"He wants you to get out, sweetheart," Barry shouted through the glass.

"I did not know you understood Czech," she said, exiting the car.

"I don't. I understand soldier."

The guards were not menacing. They were boys. But the memory of young Nazis in their uniforms with their rifles, with their power of life and death, proved too fresh for Rivka; she started to tremble. She wanted Barry to give her a sign of assurance.

Barry chuckled at some gesture one of the Czechs made, a waving of his fingers. Barry grazed the outside of his coat, where she knew he wore one of the large pistols he favored, as if to confirm it was there.

The uniformed men laughed, too.

Rivka became afraid Barry might shoot at the guards. If he did, she knew she and Barry would be killed. They always killed, these men in their uniforms. The fear from the camps gripped her chest in a vise. She felt like crying and closed her eyes.

"Honey?" Barry sounded concerned.

"Huh?" She must have fainted. She was in her seat on the passenger side of the car and all four men hovered over her with fretful expressions on their faces.

"Are you okay?"

Rivka forced herself to calm down. She nodded and tried to smile.

"One of these boys speaks Polish. He wants to talk, okay?"

She nodded again and waited for one of the boys to speak.

"Miss, hello," the one on the right, tall and thin, greeted her tentatively in Polish.

"Hello," she muttered in the same language, just as shyly.

"Why are you coming into Czechoslovakia?"

"Refugee business for the Red Cross."

"I do not mean you need a reason, miss. You would be welcome anytime."

Rivka could not be sure, but she thought he was blushing.

Barry signaled for her attention with their passports.

"We have papers," she said.

This caused the boys to posture officiously. They looked at one another seriously. Ultimately, the one in the middle, the rifle slung on his shoulder, took the passports. He opened each with an overplayed air of formality.

"Ask them if they want to search the trunk." Barry's English sounded strange to her.

He started walking to the rear of the car. The boys suddenly became agitated. He stopped. The boy with the rifle fumbled with it in near panic, quickly losing his grip. It slipped down on its sling to the crook of his arm.

He could not hold on to the weapon and the paperwork and the rifle clattered to the ground.

"Tell them everything's okay and they can search the trunk," Barry said calmly, as he raised his hands and stepped away from the car.

Rivka felt the cold fear again in her lower belly. "Search the car. He wants you should search the car!"

The boy with the rifle got it pointed at Barry, who remained in place, hands up, smiling. The three guards darted glances at each other, the travelers, and around the area like chickens in the yard.

"Ask them if I can open the trunk," Barry said.

"Yes." She switched to Polish. "Please search the trunk. He wants to know if it is okay to open the trunk."

"Why, is it a trap?" the tallest guard suddenly turned wild.

Rivka was glad he did not have a weapon. His eyes made her fearful.

She hoped Barry would not get mad. She did not think he knew what young men in uniform were capable of, even if he had been in the war. Even if he wore two pistols like an American gangster.

"Tell him to search the trunk," Barry casually repeated.

The one with the rifle, after checking with his friends, waved at the trunk. Barry and the three guards walked to the back of the car. Rivka left her seat again but stayed next to the passenger's door. She wished they were driving away.

She wished she had never come.

The open trunk lid hid the men. All went quiet. Rivka wanted to run away into the night.

She heard someone laugh. Others joined in.

They came back. Each of the Czech boys held two packs of American cigarettes. The tall boy, the one whose eyes had been wild just a minute ago, also held a bottle of liquor. The apparent leader joked with Barry as he returned their papers. In no time, Barry and Rivka motored through the gate and into the Czech countryside.

"Easy peasy, Japanesey." He smiled at her.

She burst into tears.

"Hey sister, what's this about now?"

"You joke, but you do not know," Rivka said as she sobbed. "They could have killed us, shot us dead."

Barry's cavalier attitude in the face of men just like the ones who had kept her in the camps and murdered so easily scared her.

"Don't you worry, daughter," he said, switching to Yiddish. "This I know. They would not have shot you." He had become very serious, almost solemn.

Rivka chose to believe him.

26

Ernst tumbled through frigid Polish woods. Heavy clouds made the air thick with the promise of snow. He noticed a thinning of the trees ahead and at first assumed he approached a meadow, but soon he realized a road cut through the forest, perpendicular to his direction of travel. He stopped at the unexpected byway and questioned his course. Then he heard terrifying sounds, heart-stopping sounds.

He heard men speaking Russian.

Fear froze him stiff and held him upright. He could not see them. Their conversation came at him from the left. He had picked up some Russian during the fighting and in camp, but he could not make out what they said. The air, pregnant with moisture, muffled their words. Ernst pressed himself to a tree. He assumed they were soldiers. Who else would be out just before a snowstorm? He wondered if they were chasing him specifically.

Please God, he silently prayed, I do not want to go back to the prison camp. I will die. Either they will kill me, or I will die from lack of strength. Please God, make them go away.

He could not think of a course of action, so he played the statue. No, he thought, too heroic. The rabbit, hunter's prey.

How many of his own victims, since now he thought of them as such, had said similar prayers? How could he have been party to this kind of monstrosity? Where had his heart been then? He had no answers, and misery took hold of him.

A great ache grew in his chest. In his anguish at both his past and present, he opened his mouth to wail, until he remembered his predicament. He choked off his sobbing by rubbing his face on the rough brown bark. The pain helped. His soul cried out in sorrow, but his body maintained its quiet.

Ernst did his rabbit imitation for what felt like forever. A truck engine coughed and came to life; there was shouting, a gate clanged shut and then the engine accelerated. In no time, he was alone with his regrets and *Frau Perchta*, who froze his guts as she sat in judgement and spun out the length of the rest of his life.

He pushed off the tree and hurried across the road, plunging through a line of elderberry bushes to get under the tall pines. After skirting the southern shore of an iced-over pond, he entered a stand of oak, the bare boughs of the trees reaching up to God in supplication. Minute flakes started falling. From childhood, Ernst had loved to watch it snow.

He realized he had stopped to look up. Cold seeped into him, through his coat and right into his bones. To restart, he concentrated on moving one foot forward at a time, knowing the way home was step-by-step in a westerly direction. His newly regained momentum came to a halt when he blundered over a log and hit the frozen terrain hard.

Pain wrapped him up like layers of blankets, one on top of another. Pain from keen hunger came first. Painful, penetrating cold followed. The numbness fell away from his aching feet. Pain from his fall covered it all like a quilt. Fatigue pressed him into the loam. He wanted to give in and let the tiredness take him, even as he thought of Jesus's last walk through Jerusalem, of His falling and His pain. Thoughts of sin and repentance stopped up his mind. Ernst decided to pray on his knees before lying down and giving up.

"Dear Father," he said as he struggled to get up, "I did this to others, so it is right it be done to me. I confess my sins against people, those of the old covenant—starving them, murdering them." Finally on his knees, he paused to catch his breath. "If you accept my confession and allow me to live, I will work for the peace of Jesus Christ. I commit body and soul to see to it that your children do not murder this way again. I shall become a prisoner of Christ Jesus."

Ernst's ragged breathing slowed, and his strength improved. He no longer needed to lie down. With all his might, he rose up from the earth and gained his footing, slowly moving off in the direction he hoped was west.

White slivers the consistency of confectioners' sugar dusted the toppled trees and the dead brown leaves of the forest floor. Falling snow made the woods quiet, save for his own struggling footfalls and labored breaths.

Until there was another sound. He stopped. He watched the flakes, listening to what he thought could have been a small animal. He wanted to make sure it was not another patrol before moving again. What initially may have been a woodland rodent sounded more and more substantial as it drew closer. It did not strike him as soldiers or even a person. Ernst's heart thumped hard. He did not know whether to run or persist in impersonating Mr. Rabbit.

The decision was made for him.

A girl of six or seven with matted, dirty brown hair came stumbling out of the underbrush. He thought she must be cold with her coat unfastened like that. The sleeves came down to her mid-forearm. A worn dress ended well above her raw red knees. Her uneven gate took her right into a tree. She bounced off the trunk and staggered a few more steps. She stopped and gawked and found Ernst and met his gaze. She squinted, as if she were reluctant to believe what she saw. Evidently she believed, because she screamed.

"Hush, hush," he hissed urgently. He did not want the girl to attract any official attention.

She screamed and screamed.

Ernst reached out to the child, palms up and fingers extended. "I won't hurt you."

At the sound of his voice, she ceased screaming and her eyes grew large. He relaxed, as she was clearly one of the *volk*. He started walking toward her and spread his arms. She backed away. Just as he moved close enough to scoop up the little miss, she dodged his embrace and scurried away in the direction she had come.

Ernst shouted as she vanished in a swirl of snow. He dropped his arms to his sides, feeling very sad. The sound of her flight faded. A thick silence descended on the woods.

The fading day was so cold. There was nothing he could do. She had come and gone so fast. He was unsure if he could even chase her.

The route before him stretched out to the west. He did not have the strength to help the girl. He had not had the strength to help the ones in the camps, either. The truth was, he had not even thought to. Another moral failure, he realized. But tonight, he knew he had to turn to the west. He knew it instinctively, as a matter of survival. He had to start walking west right now, or die.

Ernst resumed praying out loud. "Dear Father, please forgive me for this additional failure. I had not the strength. Please forgive me yet again."

And so, he consciously willed a foot up, forward and down, to continue his long walk.

27

When the bad man in the woods started talking, Gitta knew he was bad. The gray coat had made her suspicious, but hearing his talk, she knew for sure. She dashed away fast. Her lungs hurt. Her muscles ached. She slowed, exhaustion trumping her fear of the bad man. She thought she had left him far behind.

When she checked over her shoulder for the bad man, she tripped and fell near the unrooted trunk of a large tree. She crawled to the trunk, rested on it and pulled her coat close, wrapping her doll inside. Only the doll's head poked out. Gitta's ears, hands and feet felt like sharp things were sticking them and she shook all over and Gitta did not want Dolly to feel the same way.

As she caught her breath and calmed down, the slowly falling snow captivated her. All the walking had made Gitta very tired. She had not eaten for a long, long time. The cold hurt. Hunger, a constant companion, announced itself now with a new vigor. Even cold and hungry, she mostly thought about her mother and felt very lonely. She wanted to cry, but tried not to so Dolly would not be afraid.

She thought she might take a little nap. The cold was not so bad anymore. The bad man was far away now. Gitta's eyes were heavy. She yawned.

A voice called out to her. "Gitta, Gitta!"

Gitta sought the origin of the voice, a little scared.

"Here I am," she said.

She rubbed her eyes and saw a house. It was Grandmother's small wooden house! Bright pure light streamed out of the windows and the open front door. The Germans had come and burned it a long time ago, but Gitta was sure it was the same house. The rays pouring out of the house caused the surrounding woods to disappear in shadows.

People were inside. The house felt welcoming and drew her in. Once at the door, she sensed the light streaming past her. Rich odors of roasting chicken and fresh warm bread enveloped her.

"Come in, come in child." Grandmother beckoned her into the front room.

The candlesticks were arranged for the Sabbath on the large cabinet, as they had always been before the Germans had come. The large table had been set for the Friday night meal, with a white linen tablecloth, china and gleaming silver. Light danced through crystal goblets.

"We are ready to light, Daughter," Grandmother said, smiling. "Come quick."

Gitta was in the dining room. Her heart soared with joy when she saw her mother standing behind Bubbeh. Momma did not look at all like she had in the cellar. Healthy and well rested, she wore her beautiful Sabbath dress, the one made from green velvet. Her mother smiled. Tears were in her eyes.

The start of the Sabbath shamed Gitta, in her dirty old coat and too-small dress, and in front of her mother and grandmother no less. She would be in trouble for sure. As she tried to brush her coat with her hands, to get some of the dirt off, it felt strange.

The coat and clothes were gone! She wore a smaller version of her mother's wonderful dress, in blue, her favorite color. Lace decorated the collar. For the first time in months, she was warm.

"Come, it is time." Grandmother reached for a small silver box of matches.

Gitta broke into a grin and ran up to the table. Her sisters were there, behind their mother. The luminosity made it hard for Gitta to see them exactly, but she knew it was them. She was so happy to be with her family again. Not just happy, but filled with a great sense of contented joy in her heart. She wanted to say as much but instead asked a question.

"Where's Papa and the boys?"

"Singing praises to The Name," Grandmother replied, striking her match.

Her Grandmother beamed and put the match to the first candle. The flame caught. The wick began to burn brightly. She moved the match to the other candles, and they flared up in turn.

"Blessed are You, Lord our—" the old lady intoned, reciting the ancient blessing, waving her hands over the flickering flames in the traditional way. The others joined her.

Gitta copied them as she had done on Friday nights before the Germans had come. With her hands over her eyes, she mouthed the blessings, quiet because tonight only Grandmother spoke out loud.

The light embraced her, entered her and passed through her.

She was not alone anymore.

28

The black evening chased the leaden afternoon as Zalman walked behind Yankel in the direction of Roszowice. They traveled down a narrow road. Harvested fields of brown stalks stretched out on either side. The air smelled fresh, not like at camp, fresher than even a clean camp. He knew it was cold out, but he felt snug bundled tightly in the thick Russian clothing.

Zalman worried about Yankel. They had been lucky with rides, but for many kilometers now, they had been walking. For the last several, he had been unable to walk in a straight line.

"Let's stop for the night already," Zalman said. "You are going to collapse any second."

Yankel lurched on. A few steps later, he spoke. "We are almost there."

"You have no strength left. Let's rest."

"No."

Zalman wracked his brain to come up with some reasoning Yankel would find appealing. The winter gloom deepened as he advanced unevenly down the road. Zalman followed slowly, waiting for Yankel to drop dead.

"What's that?" Zalman asked, hearing a sound.

The sound became distinct.

"It's a truck!" he shouted before catching himself. "It's a truck," he whispered.

Fear preceded the approaching vehicle. He didn't want to try for a ride this time. In the distance, a tree line of spruce and oak absorbed the road. The fields offered precious few hiding places. The revving engine grew louder. He instinctively felt the urge to run out into the fallow rows and lie flat until the truck passed.

"Let's go!" Zalman grabbed Yankel's shoulder. "We have to hide!"

"No!" He pulled free with more strength than Zalman would have thought he possessed.

"Come on! We have to!"

"No!" Yankel shouted at the boy. "The war is over! We have nothing to fear! We are men! Men, I say!"

They glared at one another.

"I will not hide. I am a man."

They had wasted too much time. An army truck, a ZIS, had cleared the trees and bore down on them with awful inevitability.

"Too late now." Zalman's heart sank. No good will come of this, he thought.

Yankel stood firm in the middle of the road, braced as if prepared to stop the truck by impact. Zalman moved to the shoulder.

The driver decided not to run Yankel over at the last instant. The ZIS hopped on locked up brakes, stopping a meter away. Zalman could see the two men in the cab leaning forward in a questioning posture. The passenger snapped an order and the rear gate crashed open. Soldiers appeared and positioned themselves on either side of the bonnet.

Zalman relaxed. They were Russian, not Polish. He had heard in the camp that White and Red Polish armies were fighting each other and killing the returning Jewish survivors in their spare time. He hoped the Russians were too tired from the war to kill him and Yankel.

Three of the soldiers were his age and their downy pink faces were visible between the high collars of their great coats and the bottoms of their thick fur hats. They carried long bolt-action rifles that they fingered obsessively. Their eyes darted from Yankel to Zalman and then each other.

Two bewhiskered older infantrymen hung back, beside the cab of the truck. They cradled *papashas*, short submachine guns with drum magazines, across their chests. They lit cigarettes, scanned the fields and sighed.

One of the younger men shouted. The Russian came too fast for Zalman to catch. To be on the safe side, he slowly raised his hands. Raising his hands had worked with the Nazis.

"No! I am a Man!" Yankel yelled in Yiddish.

The young soldiers eyed each other. They pointed their rifles at Yankel. One of the older veterans grinned. The soldier who had spoken previously shouted squarely at Yankel, who screamed "No! You get out of *my* way!" back.

Ridiculous. Number one, he couldn't speak Russian. Number two, after years in the death camps, he should have learned not to yell at men carrying guns.

They were not getting off to a good start.

The soldier said something yet again, waving his free arm in a slow broad arc.

"No!" Yankel yelled, spittle flying. "You get out of my way!"

The Russian repeated his statement, accompanied with a short chop in the direction of the field.

"No!" Yankel countered, stamping his foot.

The young man charged Yankel with his rifle raised over his shoulder horizontally, oriented backward. Zalman thought the young man wanted to smash the butt plate into Yankel's face.

One of the tired old soldiers, moving faster than Zalman would have thought possible, grabbed the barrel and pulled the young man back until he fell onto the hard road. The young man spun on his backside and yelled as he tried to aim at the older soldier, who knocked the rifle out of the way and smacked the boy's head with the stock of his *papasha*. The boy dropped his weapon and collapsed, clutching his head with both hands.

Another young soldier thought to bring his own rifle to bear. The second old soldier ended up right next to the helper, ramming the barrel of his *papasha* into the boy's soft cheek.

A sharp yell from behind caught everyone's attention. The youngsters faced their officer. The oldsters kept their eyes on what was going on in the road. After a long, shouted command, the veteran retreated, and the boy scrambled to his feet. The three young soldiers shuffled off to the back of the truck.

The two weary infantrymen walked toward Yankel and Zalman. The closer one pointed silently to the right while the second picked up the abandoned rifle. Yankel started to say something. Zalman moved to take Yankel's arm, to calm him.

The barrels of both *papashas* came up, leveled at their chests.

"Come," Zalman said, "so we'll stand in the dirt. It doesn't mean we aren't men. Come."

"I'm a man," Yankel whined, shaking Zalman off.

"So be a man, only do it in the field," the Russian who had knocked down the youngster said in Yiddish.

A Jewish soldier! Zalman had met a few. They had come by the camp after liberation, offering what help they could. They had generally been impressive. This one seemed steady.

"Yankel, please. Let's get out of the way." Zalman again took him by the arm.

Yankel let himself be moved. The two of them shuffled off the road and Zalman received a fraternal smile from the Jewish soldier. The displaced persons ended up shoulder to shoulder, watching the two Russians stroll to the rear of the ZIS. As they drove away, the soldier shouted something and threw two small brown balls at them. The truck receded in the distance as Zalman scampered back onto the road to see what they had been given.

"Bread!" He raised one of the smalls loaves to his mouth.

"Don't eat that! It can't possibly be kosher!"

"Don't be silly, have one." He held out the second loaf.

Yankel resumed walking down the middle of the road.

"Two for me then." Zalman shrugged at blatant disrespect for food, reeled off a quick blessing and bit into the fresh bread. "We should find a place to rest for the night."

"Very close. Almost there," came the hoarse reply.

The closer they came to Roszowice, the weaker Yankel grew. Zalman continued trying to get Yankel to stop for the night, even after it started snowing.

"Almost there," Yankel said. "Almost there."

They reached the outskirts of Roszowice. Zalman didn't recognize the village of his youth, much less have any affection for it. The dark and the weather added to his apprehension. If they had to travel on foot somewhere, it should have been to the allied zones in Germany, may that name be erased from history.

"We have to find a place to rest," he suggested again. "It's cold and the snow is steady."

Yankel staggered on.

Zalman had survived the death camps by relying on his instincts, and now they told him to go to ground. Fear nibbled at the edges of his consciousness since he had first heard the truck, causing in him a general sense of unease.

"Yankel." He grabbed the sick man by the arm and stopped him. "We need to rest. Tomorrow we can see what has changed here."

"It is my house!" Yankel shouted. "Tonight we sleep in my house!" He added a stern expression for emphasis and tried to twist out of Zalman's grasp.

The most he managed was to trip. He would have fallen if Zalman had not held on and steadied him. Once Yankel had his balance, they momentarily struggled before Zalman let him go.

They had hiked through a stand of trees, passed several widely spaced houses and into a neighborhood of wooden clapboard residences with tile roofs. It looked foreign in the shadows, a strange place. Yankel led Zalman down an alley formed by stables and homes. It was wide enough for a wagon and little else.

"Our road is just over there," Yankel said, "Our house is three up, on the left." He walked off, his lurching from side to side energized by his proximity to home.

Zalman, watchful and wary, followed through the snow.

"Our stables! Where we keep our animals!" Yankel strained against the heavy wooden door, grunting with the exertion.

Zalman joined in and thought of his own street, his own home. Would anyone from his own family be there? His mother?

Ridiculous, he thought. He knew for a fact they were all dead. He went right at *selektion*. His mother and sisters went left. They were gone.

The door opened wide enough for a person to pass through. Zalman stopped helping.

"Come on, push," Yankel grunted and struggled on without effect.

"It's enough already. Let's go in."

He waited for Yankel to go in first. If the *nudnik* wanted to risk getting his brains smashed, so be it. Zalman had survived this long. He did not relish the idea of losing his life sneaking into a stables where he did not belong.

Yankel squeezed through the gap. Zalman glanced up and down the deserted street. Snow fell as the day died. He followed.

"There is a lantern right…over…here it is!"

"Please don't," Zalman said tiredly.

"Why not?"

"People may come; besides, we should sleep now." Continually explaining the obvious drained him. "Tomorrow we can look and see if things are kosher."

"Are you a lunatic? The war is over. No one is going to hurt us. Besides, I have no matches. You do it."

At first, Zalman intended to continue arguing, but didn't. He let the air out from his lungs in an audible rush of surrender.

Zalman unbuttoned his Russian great coat and pulled a match out of his pocket. He struck it. Yankel held the lantern open. He moved the bright flame into the glass enclosure and lit the wick.

"Turn it down, at least."

Yankel did so without comment. There were six stalls, four along the far wall and one on either side of the door. The new owners had stacked hay in the front stalls.

"They take care of it." Zalman fingered fresh wood used to repair some damage to a nearby partition.

"Where are our horses?" Yankel leaned on a vertical beam for support. "And this cow! Whose cow is this?"

"And what, would your animals live to one hundred and twenty?" Zalman sneered, his sense of propriety overcome by his companion's stupidity.

"You shut up!" Yankel screamed, a new and manic energy playing across his face. "Shut it!"

"Let's put out the lamp and go to sleep right now, here on this hay. It's warmer in here than outside, and the cow can give us milk in the morning."

"I need to see the house."

"Tomorrow?" Zalman begged.

"Now."

"Don't go now. I have a feeling like I felt in the camps. Something bad is going to happen. I get it here." He touched his heart. "Let's sleep now. In the morning, we'll go look."

He held Yankel's fevered gaze. Those fanatical orbs told Zalman that Yankel would go to the house and nothing he said would matter. He had seen it in the camps. An inmate would have had enough. He would get the crazy eyes. Before too long, such an inmate would do something to draw attention to himself and the Germans or their helpers would kill him.

Simple.

Yankel had the crazy eyes now.

Zalman, who felt the presence of the Angel of Death, would not go to the house.

29

Vigorous knocking on the front door of their house disturbed normally quiet Roszowice and made Jan wince.

"Who could that be?" he asked.

"Your cretin friend, no?" his father, Hipolit, said. "Answer the door. Get rid of him."

Jan walked by the kitchen. His mother gave him a sympathetic smile. He smiled back nervously. His father's tone had stung. Stefan would not come this late. And he wasn't a cretin, either.

What if it was something else? The war was over, sure, but hard knocking at night was scary. He opened the door.

Jan could not comprehend what he saw. Cold air rushed past him.

"Who is at the door?" his father shouted.

"Yankel Shapiro!" Jan answered.

Yankel's haggard, exhausted expression and thin face seemed a ghostly apparition in the middle of Russian army green.

"We thought you were dead," Jan said. "Come in before you freeze."

"No!" Hipolit roared. His chair scraped the wood floor, and Jan heard his heavy steps as he hurried to the door, moving fast for his size. "It is too late. You may not come in."

He filled the doorway and crossed his arms. The rolled sleeves of his work shirt exposed his large forearms.

"This is my family's house, my house," Yankel glared. "It is you, you who will leave. Now."

The returning survivor swayed slightly as small steady snowflakes fell on his Russian army cap.

"I am a little tired of you Jews telling me whose house this is," Hipolit said. "You left it to rot, for someone else to maintain and now you expect it back. Isn't that like a Jew? We took care of it for years. It is our house now. You go away."

Jan's Uncle Boleslaus walked up to the entranceway where he exchanged a knowing smirk with his father.

"The Germans took us! You know it!" Yankel screamed himself hoarse. "How could you blame me for not being here?" His mouth firmed up and he stopped shifting his weight from foot to foot. He glared intensely at them. "You idiots!"

Jan became frightened.

"You get out," Yankel said softly.

"Pardon me, Jew?" Hipolit asked.

"You get out now." He moved aside and waved them out, as if they would comply. "This house belongs to my family. I will sleep in it tonight. You get out."

Hipolit clenched a heavy fist and struck Yankel so hard his Russian cap flew in an arc through the air as he fell to the walkway. With one step outside, Hipolit, in his shirt sleeves, began kicking the downed man in the side, pounding on his rib cage again and again.

Uncle Boleslaus barging past reassured Jan. His uncle would stop his father and pull him off Yankel Shapiro. Much more of this and his father would kill the man.

To Jan's horror, his uncle ran opposite Hipolit and joined in. Yankel curled up into the fetal position. His father booted his midsection, and his uncle had free access to Yankel's back.

"You filthy dirty Jew bastards," Hipolit screamed. "Throw my family out into the night? I say where I live!"

Hipolit grabbed Yankel by the hair and dragged his victim to the pole holding up the telephone wire.

"Get ropes," Hipolit bellowed.

"There is some in the stables!" Boleslaus barked.

"No!" Jan yelled, but nobody paid attention.

"Better!" Hipolit shouted, hoarse now as well. "We go!"

Jan's father dragged the feeble and moaning Yankel like a half-filled sack between the houses. His current rage surpassed his usual displays of temper, scaring Jan, who could not fathom why his father wanted to tie this person up. He walked behind the older men in the wide trail Hipolit made in the fresh dusting of bright snow.

Jan wished Yankel had never come home.

Someone had lit a lantern at the stables. Boleslaus reached the door first and pushed through the narrow opening, his round stomach hindering him briefly. Inside, events moved swiftly. With a triumphant shout from a stall, Boleslaus held up a coil of rough brown rope.

"Over the beam," Hipolit shouted.

Uncle Boleslaus's thick features displayed a fanatic stupidity as he hustled out of the stall. Hipolit towed Yankel to the center of the structure and kept hold of the beaten man.

"Over the beam," he ordered again.

Boleslaus heaved the line but botched it. He tried once more, missed, and threw it up yet again. The rope finally straddled the beam, just out of Hipolit's grasp.

"Get me the end!"

Boleslaus stretched for it but could not get it. He jumped and failed again. "I can't reach it."

Hipolit cast a hand up in a wide arc that missed by a centimeter. With a sigh of annoyance, he let go of Yankel and made for the dangling rope with both hands.

The beaten Jew took off like a scalded cat, scrambling on all fours toward the door.

Hipolit howled in frustration but snared the line and pulled until the end hung down in front of him. Then he took several steps in pursuit. Boleslaus, also running after their escapee, bashed into Hipolit and bounced off. Boleslaus staggered away, arms windmilling for balance, his expression changing from concern to jester-like alarm.

Jan stifled a laugh.

His father caught Yankel by his coat and dragged him backward and punched him in the neck. Hipolit rolled him over, hit him twice more in the face, and then wrenched him to his feet. Using the rope, he threw a quick loop around Yankel's neck.

"Grab the end!"

"No," someone said.

Jan thought he heard the soft word of protest from his right and, squinting that way, believed he saw hay rustling in the shadows.

"Pull!" Hipolit yelled at Boleslaus. "Pull, you bastard!"

The brothers heaved. Yankel dangled from the beam, toes just off the floor, and clawed at his neck. His lips parted and his tongue stuck out.

"Pull him up!" Hipolit shouted.

The two men put their backs into it. Yankel rose in short quick spurts and spun slowly, his left leg jerking, his face changing color from pallid white to an unnatural red. As he turned, he made eye contact. In his scary red face with garbled grunting, Jan saw him pleading for his life.

"Stiff-necked dirty Jew bastard just won't die," Hipolit muttered. "Boleslaus, let go."

Jan's uncle did as directed. Hipolit also let go, but for the merest of moments before clamping on to the rope again. Yankel fell and jerked to an abrupt stop with a loud powerful grunt.

"Damn," Hipolit said. "Help me."

Now he and Boleslaus hauled their prisoner so far up his head touched the beam. He reached for it weakly, struggling like a pinned bird.

"Let go!" Hipolit shouted.

Yankel plunged two feet. Hipolit seized the line and Jan heard a distinct "crack" as Yankel's descent stopped short.

Yankel Shapiro, quiet now, twisted slowly.

Hipolit tied off on the nearest crossmember and inspected his palms.

"Chewed 'em up, the Jew did." He displayed his palms and smiled with the satisfaction of a job well done.

The speeding rope had torn at Hipolit's thick calluses.

"Should we hide him?" Boleslaus asked, wide eyed and timorous.

"No. Leave him here to warn the next Jew who visits us tonight. We'll take care of him tomorrow. Let's go in."

"You think there are more?"

"No. There aren't any more. Let's go."

Only now did Jan realize that he had been party to a hanging: A hanging just like the Germans had done to so many from the village. He had failed to act while his father and uncle, the two men closest to him in the world, had killed a neighbor.

Yankel's body stopped turning. The legs did not twitch. His arms dangled at his side. He had known this man, and the situation made him feel unmoored.

"Jan," his father called gently from the door.

Jan shuffled out into the cold, cold night.

30

Walter Gonzales of the US Army's Criminal Investigation Division wore a pair of soiled white cotton gloves as he hunched over a brass shell casing on the dining room table in the CID office. The fingerprint powder had revealed partial prints on three of the .45 caliber casings they had picked up at the shooting scene in Munich. He carefully applied the transparent adhesive tape to the last one. Once he was sure the tape held the partial print pattern, he lifted the tape off the brass and smoothed it onto an unmarked clean index card.

His partner burst into the room, fresh from having conducted an interview related to a fraud case at the US prisoner of war camp detaining Germans at Kaserne Garmisch.

"Boss," Fred Montgomery gushed, "I've got the statement from the paymaster. He confessed to the whole thing. Said he spent the cash on booze and whores." Fred shucked his great coat and plopped down in front of the typewriter.

"That paymaster." He concentrated on lifting the prints. "So I guess he wasted the rest?"

"Huh?"

Agent Fredrick Montgomery of the CID amused Walter to no end. Unrelated to the general, hence, one of the jokes: A wetback and a limey with the same family name. As funny as his own surname of Gonzales. He imagined a Latin lover, tall, dark and handsome, no doubt, having grabbed the attention of one of his distant maternal ancestors. Granny could have been a hot tamale herself.

"Nine thousand dollars," Walter mused. "That's a lot of drinking and screwing."

He had guessed Freddy would make a good partner. Something about Fred generates high expectations, and he meets them, even knocks them out of the ballpark. Their experiences during the Bulge had cemented Walter's affection for his partner, who had been as solid as a rock when the two of them were wandering around, cut off, especially the time he broke up a German charge with just his pistol. Walter had nominated Fred for the Bronze Star, but they hadn't heard back.

"What you doing there?" Fred asked.

"These are the casings from the Munich shooting. I lifted a couple partials off a few of them. They don't completely match each other, but in some places they do."

"Oh yeah?"

"Come here. You remember how many shells were on the street at the murder scene in Munich?"

"Not the number—"

"No, not the number, just lots, right?"

"Right."

"Well, the Jerries got two .45 casings off them four dumped bodies, the ones down by Furstflarn. They found them in the clothes. One of the dead fellows had a holstered weapon. It was a small-caliber Walther. Another guy had an empty holster and two had no gun or holster. No forty-fives anywhere on them. I got curious, so I dusted each one of the recovered shells. Look what I got here."

Walter used a magnifier, basically a large camera-type lens on a microscope stand, to show Fred the loops and whorls of the prints he had lifted and transferred to index cards. "So far as what we got is concerned, what we got is one partial off one of the Munich rounds that has a matching section to a partial from a single round from the dumped bodies. It don't tell me much, but I'm having a heavy hunch the gunslinger is the same guy in both locations. Did you see the mail?"

"Not yet."

"First thing is a formal complaint from the director of the Gaufering Displaced Persons Camp. He says his Technical Sergeant Rosen is definitely in the black market in a big way."

"No kidding? Did he also send the first letter? The one with no name on it?"

"Naw, his English was too good. Anyway, Gaufering is just outside of Furstflarn. The four bodies came out of a field off the road between Furstflarn and Munich. Coincidence? Maybe not. The second thing is, well, all you need to know is we're going out to Gaufering to meet with our *Technical Sergeant* Rosen. You might want to bring your handcuffs."

"You going to arrest him, boss?"

"All I'm saying is, y'all might want to bring those bracelets, if you know what I mean."

31

Barry and Rivka made good time to Western Poland with just one night of sleeping in the car. Here it was, the evening of the second day of travel and Roszowice dead ahead. Paying off the border guards had been well within Barry's budget, mere bottles of liquor or American cigarettes; it had been easy. The guards had readily bought the validity of the forged Red Cross papers, and the cover story for Rivka, that she was a new employee of the Red Cross, had held.

"There it is! Our house!" she exclaimed, pointing to a wooden house on the left.

"Okay," Barry answered. "Let me drive around and make sure everything is hunky-dory."

The Hudson, firm-footed in the white dusting of snow, rolled on. Night had fallen. Small flakes fell through the clear beams from the headlights. He made several right turns. All appeared quiet in the neighborhood, and even the snow was not sticking to the windshield.

Back on Rivka's street, Barry parked three properties away to avoid warning the people inside. He liked how Rivka did not question his precautions. He turned off the lights and the engine and exited the car. His overcoat hung free, allowing both the chill in and easy access to his pistols. The brim of his gray fedora fell low; he felt *comme il faut* with it rakishly forward, and the ends of his black scarf stirred in the cold breeze.

Barry looked, listened, and smelled. He saw a still, calm village and sensed the coming snowstorm. He held the door for Rivka.

"It's good, doll-face," he said.

Rivka gave him a nervous grin as she took his hand and stepped out of the car. He liked the way her face protruded out of the big overcoat he had given her, her head wrapped in the pink scarf he had also found. A real cutie.

"That is it," she announced in English, "my family's home."

"Roger—you want me to clear them out?"

"No. We ask after Yankel. We hear what they say. We leave."

"It's your show, doll-face."

Barry felt the energy that sometimes crackled through a battlefield before the shooting started. Ever the combat infantryman, he listened and sniffed audibly again, catching only the pleasing odor of heating fires over coming snow. He accumulated details as he followed her up the short walk to the front entrance. The snow had been disturbed and spoor indicated something had been dragged.

Rivka knocked. No one answered, so Barry banged on the front door sharply. They heard angry steps and it flew open.

A very large man shouted at them in livid Polish.

Barry did not take it as a good sign.

The shouting man filled the doorframe. He wore a work shirt, suspenders, and rough trousers. His straight hair was in disarray. Hatred and resentment emanated from him like heat from a fire. Barry felt more than saw Rivka fall back a step. With all she had been through, she ought not to have to fall back a step for anyone. His ire started to rise.

Except for *"Żyd,"* Barry had caught none of the raging Polish, but he caught the tone all right. A shorter, fatter man glared from behind the giant, and a scared boy, pale and wearing oversized work clothes, hovered in the background.

Barry made eye contact with the big man. He waited out the tirade with no more notice than the spreading of his coat, not far enough to show his heat but to position his hands, thumbs now hooked in the waistband of his trousers. The yelling stopped. Barry saw, by the expression on the man's face, that he was considering a move, until indecision flickered across his features.

"Ask him about Yankel," Barry said.

"*Anglik*?" The big man questioned.

"Ask." Barry maintained eye contact with the man.

Rivka did so, in Polish.

The big man in the doorway of Rivka's house licked his lips. His eyes lost their focus for a heartbeat, then he glared at them. He made a statement Barry did not understand and started closing the door.

Before the door latched, Barry kicked it hard. It exploded inward. Surprise and anger played across the big man's face. Barry began to move inside. Rivka stopped him with a hand on his chest.

"He knows nothing," she said sadly. "Let us go."

"But this is your house."

"We go. This is the way it is here."

Barry did not agree. Something was wrong, but he couldn't put his finger on it. Reluctantly, he did what she wanted. After a last scowl at the men and the boy, he backed out. Everyone moved slowly. The boy came from behind the others, smiled furtively at Rivka and closed the door.

"I want to see the stables," she said in English, her sad eyes focused on the front door of the house. "Yankel might be in there. Out of the winter."

"Okay."

"It is this way."

Again, Barry noticed the tracks in the snow, a bundle dragged, confused footsteps. He did not dwell on them, reflecting instead on what the attitude of the men in the house might signify. Rivka merely accepted their conduct, their squatting in the house, and their overall hostility.

"This one is ours, with the light," she said as they approached the barn. A source inside illuminated a quarter-circle in front of the slightly cracked door.

"No!" Barry yelled, caused by a bursting sense of general caution. "Me first!"

He tried to shoulder her out of the way but bungled it, ending up next to her with his pistol out.

Then he saw the hanged man.

Rivka shut her eyes with enough force to cause her cheeks to meet her brows. Her mouth opened to her molars in a round, silent scream. Barry figured it was Yankel swinging there from the wrong end of the rope. Out of habit, he scanned the area. A boy's face, white as an opossum, darted back into a stall. Rivka doubled over slowly, as if she had been struck in the abdomen. She started to sag.

Barry caught her with one arm before her knees hit the ground. He holstered his pistol, scooped her up and left the barn. All Rivka had wanted was to reunite with her last surviving family member. She wanted so much to find family with which to begin again. She had hoped to start a new life with her brother, maybe in America, maybe in Palestine.

Now this.

This should not happen, he thought. Even in war, this should not happen to a girl like Rivka. To survive untold horrors, to make it home and then to get the business from some Polack squatters was a travesty. She did not deserve to find her brother doing the swing in her own barn.

The scene in the stables triggered a vivid memory of the garage in Newark. He felt an unholy fury explode inside himself like an atomic reaction. The scene where Lieutenant Mac fell, gut shot by a supposedly surrendering Nazi, played on the movie screen in his mind, newsreel style.

Rivka whimpered.

She did not deserve all this and neither did the dead guy. Barry's anger started to drag him to a black place. Perhaps what was needed here was some justice, maybe some of Little Meyer's justice.

Rivka ruptured emotionally and great wracking sobs shook her body. He wanted to carry her forever and protect her from any more ugliness. He swore she would never be this broken again. On the way to the car, he walked in front of her house without a care, silently wishing they would look out so he could shoot them dead.

Barry put the body together with the tracks in the snow, concluding the squatters, led by that fat bastard, had killed Yankel. He must have gone to the door, maybe even within the hour. They had fought right there. The Poles had won and had dragged Yankel to the stables and hanged him dead.

At the car, he placed Rivka on the passenger seat and checked the area. Small flakes drifted down onto an empty street in front of warm glowing homes. They faced an uncomfortable night in the Hudson. This Yankel was coldest of all, hanging from his rafter.

Barry, again in the driver's seat, started the engine and put it in gear. She had curled up facing him. He drove slowly as they cleared the town. What he had witnessed tonight was not right. If life had taught him one thing, it was that a man had to help himself. No police would help, not the army, certainly not neighbors. No one.

Settlement gave way to dormant fields dusted with snow. A deep drainage ditch divided the road from the fields. Trees had been planted in a row, forming a border between the ditch and the croplands. Barry guided the coupe into a gap in the row and crossed a small bridge onto a field. He parked parallel to the trees, killed the headlamps and paused in the idling car.

"You are going back," Rivka said flatly.

"Yes."

He expected an argument. He knew she was religious, even after the camps. The rav had been teaching him the Ten Statements. Don't murder. He expected her to tell him "that's the way it is," and pester him to leave.

"Should I wait here?" she asked.

"Yes." Barry silenced the engine. "If I'm not back by dawn, drive away, all the way to the American zone and forget all this garbage." He held the keys out.

Rivka uncoiled a bit and reached out. He put the keys in her hand.

"I won't be long, not long enough for you to get cold, but if you do, start the car and run the heat."

She coiled back up and closed her eyes.

After he had taken care of Kurt and his boys, he had packed the Hudson to the brim. He had thrown blankets, booze, smokes, food and clothes into the back seat, filling it to the windows. Two gold bricks rested under all that inventory.

Barry rooted through the trunk, chockablock with bulkier items: toolboxes, cans of petrol, mess kits and the like, until his fingertips brushed a leather handle. He grabbed hold and pulled out his viola case, setting it down in the snow. He re-arranged everything, shut the lid and adjusted his fedora low over his eyes, snapping the brim down in front, up in back.

Little Meyer's boys always looked smooth.

He picked up the viola case and walked to town.

32

Zalman had lain immobile under the hay for a long time, only coming out after Rivka and the stranger left. Yankel had survived so much: the camps, the beatings, the work. And so much had been by the skin of his teeth. All that, and here he was. Zalman sighed and extinguished the lantern.

"I told you we should not have come," he murmured to Yankel's body.

Well, at least Rivka was alive. Rivka and Yitzie Strasen and him. Maybe they could go somewhere and start their own village. A Jewish village.

He laughed at the thought. Wherever they went, someone would try to finish the job the Nazis had started. Zalman lay back in the hay. He stayed there, in the muck, yawning, hungry, waiting for he knew not what, too tired to sleep.

The creaking of the stables door startled him. He dove for cover, worming his way into the fodder and against a stall wall. He tried to move quickly and quietly, but he knew he had been too slow and too loud. He cursed his luck and waited.

Someone walked a few paces into the stables and stopped. Zalman did not even breathe.

"So?" A man said in Yiddish. His inflection sounded strange.

Zalman remained quiet.

"So, light on."

Zalman had never heard such ridiculous Yiddish. It must be the stranger who had been with Rivka, he thought.

"Light on now," the man growled.

He decided to risk it. He felt for the lantern until the wire handle met his fingers. He lit it with his last match. It was the stranger in his gray hat, black scarf, flapping coat, and gloves. He carried a viola case.

"What your name?"

"Zalman."

"Who did this?"

The man did make him wary, but not wary enough to stifle his curiosity. What was one stranger compared to years of Nazi hoodlums?

"Where is Rivka?" Zalman asked.

"In the car." The man jerked his head at Yankel's body. "Who did this?"

"Jan's father and uncle."

"Jan?"

"He is the boy in Yankel's house." Zalman waved in that direction. "His family organized the Shapiro's house."

"Org—organized?" The man stumbled over the word.

"Are you English?"

"American."

An American, Zalman marveled. Will wonders ever cease? "They stole it. It's theirs now."

"No."

"No? You will complain to someone? Like the Russians, maybe?"

"Did Jan do this?" the American asked again.

"No, I told you. Jan's father and uncle did."

"You saw it?"

"Yes."

"Get cow out barn."

The American started moving hay with his foot. After three tries, he stammered something in a different language, possibly a curse, and reached for a pitchfork.

"Get the cow out now," he ordered.

Zalman got to work. The recalcitrant animal eventually sauntered to the door as the American spread hay out into the middle of the floor.

"Where should I take the cow?" Zalman called out.

"Quiet. I not care. Let it go street."

He managed to get the animal to the alley. At first it mooed plaintively, but after a few more moos, it wandered away. Back in the stables, he saw the American using hay to make a big X, stretching from corner to corner and crossing in the center.

"What's this for?" Zalman asked.

"This their barn."

He threw the clasps of the viola case and pulled out a very ugly gun. It looked like a metal tube with a handle on the end. A green strap hung from it, fastened at the front and back. Zalman had never seen one like it, but he knew it was a gun. He wondered what the man was going to do with it.

The American opened a trap door on the top of the weapon and operated a small lever on its side. Zalman flinched. In the camps, sounds like that, lubricated metal-on-metal, meant it was time to run. The American took out two magazines made as one with some kind of dirty white cloth around them. He attached the magazine through a receptacle built into the front and closed the trap door.

"Do not worry," the American said, "not for you. The house, it is not Jan's house or his family house." He pointed at Yankel. "This is not right. Rivka is in car crying out eyes. This is not right."

He pulled the wire stock out of the rear of his weapon. It clicked loudly into place. He stuck his right arm and head between the strap and the tube. He whipped out a boxy silver cigarette lighter, flicked the top and lit it, all at the same time. He held the lighter to the hay, where the two arms of the X crossed in the center. A small red flame began to dance.

The American was burning down the stables! But Yankel! Zalman raced forward to save the body, but the man blocked him into a low stall wall.

"This is Yankel's barn and Yankel's house," the American insisted in his horrible Yiddish.

His right hand rested on the pistol grip of the weapon hanging from his shoulder. Fire leapt up behind him.

"Wait for me in alley," he said.

Zalman followed him outside, where the American handed him the viola case. The American steered him to a safe place in the shadows and motioned for him to stay. As the man walked toward the Shapiros' house, Zalman asked him a question.

"Who are you?"

"Barry," came the quiet reply.

33

Barry retraced his steps to the house. He knew what he was going to do and felt nothing, but he did think of Rav Hirsch.

The Torah says not to murder, Hirsch had taught him.

"Too late, old man," Barry mumbled, arriving at the front door of Rivka's family home.

He opened the ejection port dust cover, pointed the gun at the top hinge of the ancient door and fired a short burst. The powerful slugs chewed the old wood and iron to bits. He quickly did the same to the lock and lower hinge. As the shots echoed in the square, he stomped on the door, knocking it flat.

With the collapsible wire stock jammed tight in his shoulder, he surveyed the scene over the top of his weapon. Stairs on the left, kitchen on the right, and darkness straight ahead. Two men, the old fat ones, froze one third of the way down the flight of stairs. The shorter, fatter one occupied the higher position. Barry wanted them exactly there.

He aimed at the shorter man and let fly, firing a longish burst. One after another of the heavy bullets plowed into the man, who yelled out in pain and amazement. He fell and the larger man instinctively caught him. Cordite hung in the air. Barry sighted in on the taller man, the one who had insulted Rivka earlier.

The man, Jan's uncle or father, depending, managed to sneer and look afraid at the same time. He said something indecipherable. Barry paused to see if this sucker would switch to English. He didn't.

"You should have left." Barry pulled the trigger and tore them up, concentrating on the taller, meaner murderer, until he, too, fell down the stairs.

The bolt locked back and, by habit, Barry switched the taped thirty round magazines as the dead men came to rest at the bottom of the staircase.

A woman screamed. Two peasant matrons huddled together, framed by the doorway to the kitchen. One of them started to wail.

He saw the kid outside the kitchen, somewhat in the shadows, brandishing a large chef's knife, blade down, in his right hand. Jan was in the middle of his teenage years, scrawny and scared. Barry could tell immediately by his awkward arm position that he was no expert. Assuming the kid had something to do with Yankel's death, despite what Zalman had said, he figured he should shoot Jan, too, and sighted in squarely on Jan's face.

Both women screamed.

The kid half-heartedly swung the knife and gestured at the dead men.

Barry heard Hirsch say, "Do not murder."

Jan shouted at him in Polish and he assumed it was a good cursing, angry and scared at the same time. Jan waved the edged weapon some more.

According to Zalman, the kid had not been involved in hanging Yankel. The rav had told him not to murder. Pretty basic, the way it was stated in the Torah. Written plain as day. The Torah was supposed to be God's word.

Jan let loose with an anguished cry, pain etched onto his face. He cocked his knife arm, clearly telegraphing his next move, his goal to bury most of the sharp steel in Barry's chest. Jan launched himself forward.

The boy sure had moxie.

Don't murder. Commandment number six.

Barry thrust his weapon sideways and up at Jan's now falling right arm, stopping the blow cold and knocking the knife out of the boy's hand. It spun end-over-end into the confines of the house.

He pulled the submachine gun in tight, butt in his shoulder-pocket, cheek welded to the frigid wire. He leaned forward slightly. Six inches of space separated the business end of the barrel from the kid's face.

Bloodlust coursed through Barry's veins. He wanted to blow Jan's head clean off, but the urge wrestled with something else, something stopping him.

"Don't murder," the old rabbi had taught him. After all the old man had been through, he still believed in God's law.

The boy hadn't had anything to do with Yankel's hanging.

Barry ground his teeth until his jaw hurt.

The women had stopped their wailing. The moment hung thick in the silence, all of them on the precipice.

Someone yelled from outside. A short word in Polish, shouted again and again. It sounded like "oh-gen," with a hard "g." He heard the call repeated down the street.

Barry barked out his war cry and with practiced violence, flipped the weapon sideways, lengthwise, and used the front sight assembly to tear a ragged gash in the boy's cheek; Jan staggered back, hand to face and blood gushed from between his fingers.

"You didn't do a damn thing to stop it, either!" Barry bellowed in English.

He backed up. One woman tried to break away from the other. The second woman locked her terrified eyes on Barry and refused to let the first woman go. Jan fell on his rump. Barry retreated out the door, weapon slowly swinging from the stairs to the women. Once out, he raised the barrel skyward, pivoted on his heel and started striding to the alley.

He slipped out of the sling, closed the ejection port cover, detached the magazines, and collapsed the stock.

Flames completely engulfed the stables and heightened the shadows. Zalman was right where Barry had left him, and he smiled, relieved, happy even. Zalman had not run away.

"Open the case," Barry snapped, in English, by way of greeting.

The youngster did not respond, so Barry pointed.

Zalman opened the case. Barry placed the weapon and magazines inside.

"Do you want to carry it?" he asked, switching to Yiddish.

The youngster shrugged but took the handle without further prodding. They headed down the alley and out of town. Zalman leaned forward and started to speed up, perhaps preparing to run.

"Slow down," Barry said. "Walk calm."

A lone man carrying a bucket ran up to them and shouted at Barry, who picked out the "oh-gen" word from the mass of Polish coming his way.

He made sure he had quick accessibility to his pistols. They altered course just enough to pass by the man with the bucket and walk on. Barry smelled the burning wood all the way out of the village. He turned and walked backward; no one followed them. Down the road, he saw the glow from the fire through the snow.

"Clean away," Barry said. "What did that man want?"

"He said we should help with the fire."

"Fat chance," Barry scoffed in English.

They made it to the fields without further incident, Barry looking smooth, the boy carrying the viola case. Small snowflakes fell. No one followed them.

"Did you kill Jan?" Zalman finally asked.

34

Ernst Hoffmann, former German prisoner of war, lurched out of the forest. With great weariness, he assessed the field for threats. It lay fallow, crop stubble scattered here and there. Accumulating snow left white residue in the depressions. Someone parked a car on his side of a line of trees running in single file along a road some forty meters distant. The air smelled of more snow and the car would be a good place to wait out the storm and rest.

The rough terrain gave Ernst some trouble. Slipping and tripping his way across took all of his concentration. Exhausted, he closed his eyes as he tottered on. Eventually, he crashed into the stationary vehicle, banging his knee. He ended up hanging onto the car, arms athwart the roof, torso on the glass and legs pressed to the metal of the passenger side door.

"Dear God," Ernst said, "I am hungry."

He caught his breath. He could hear the falling snow in the quiet of the countryside. The precipitation spurred him to get out of the weather. He fumbled for the latch, forcing his numb fingers to hold their shape as he pulled and lifted, this way and that.

"Thank you, Jesus," he said when he felt a sharp release.

Ernst rotated so his backside would fall into the seat. He landed on a pile of rags. They moved! The rags started screaming like a woman! He had to laugh. His first opportunity for some real shelter in days and it was already occupied.

The woman elbowed him in the face.

"Ouch!" Ernst said in German. "Miss, miss, calm down. Look, I am leaving."

The woman hit him again while he reached for the roof post. He was struck yet a third time as he tried to pull himself out. Whenever he gained purchase, the flailing woman whacked his arm away and he fell onto her. He saw the humor in his not being able to get very far and, laughing, sought to apologize.

Then Ernst was yanked out by the lapels of his coat, killing his mirth. Before he could find his feet, he was thrown, landing on his back. The fall nearly knocked the wind out of him. As he tried to breathe, a figure wearing a fedora and an unbuttoned overcoat materialized. Ernst began apologizing. As he spoke, the man checked on the woman in the car.

Then the man savagely kicked him. Sharp pain shot out from his ribs up to his neck and down his legs. Ernst marveled at the speed of the attack, appreciating its professionalism.

He rolled up into a protective ball. The man pulled at him and unrolled him. Before he could process the threat, the man knelt by his arm and started cutting away at the inseam of Ernst's upper right sleeve with a fighting knife.

His upper right arm!

He tried to roll away, but the man slapped him hard in the face and pinned his shoulder with a knee. Ernst had no more energy left. He closed his eyes. The field-gray army overcoat had not fooled this hooligan. Once the gangster finished his cutting and saw the blood group tattoo there, something he obviously knew about, all would be over. There would be no explaining anything.

Ernst opened his eyes and watched the snow. Diminutive flakes fell straight at him. Beautiful. He appreciated the crisp air. He wanted to truly experience the last minutes of his precious life.

All his surviving had been for nothing. The painful walking, the agonizing hunger, all for naught. Well, maybe it was his penance. He closed his eyes.

Dear God, Ernst prayed silently, I confess my sins and accede to the wisdom of your judgment. My fate is in your hands. Thank you for the opportunity to repent and to accept the Lord Jesus as my savior. I am unworthy of your mercy but pray for it all the same.

An engine tried, coughed and eventually fired up. He opened his eyes. The headlights came on, illuminating the falling snow. Was he alone? He rolled up on his side, wanting to run away. Before he could bend his legs, someone grabbed him and dragged him to the front of the car.

They were going to run him over to death!

"Oh Father, dear Jesus, Mother Mary," Ernst prayed, burbling out loud now. "Please make it quick. Not like this. Please, please make it quick."

The man was back. He ripped Ernst's coat and the shirt underneath and wrenched his bare arm up into the glare.

"Ess, Ess," the man said. "Schutzstaffel," he continued, matter-of-factly.

The man dropped Ernst's arm, and Ernst chanced a glance. The man held a large pistol out to a young boy whose small frame swam in Red Army winter gear. The boy stepped back, lifting both arms to hold his hands up, palms out and his head swiveled from side to side.

Ernst let his own head fall. He understood clearly that the man was offering up his pistol to the boy so the boy could kill him. Thank you, dear God, he prayed, thank you for making the boy not want to kill me.

What if the man decided to kill Ernst? Only one thing for it—more prayer.

"Hail Mary, full of grace, the Lord is with you. Blessed are you among women and blessed is the fruit of thy womb, Jesus. Holy Mary, Mother of God, pray for us sinners, now and at the hour of our death," he recited softly, over and over.

Curiosity got the better of him, so he took a gander.

The man wearing the fedora lingered over him, aiming the automatic so that Ernst could see the huge soul-absorbing circle of the wide muzzle, a portal to the Devil's hell itself. With both eyes shut again, he repeated his Hail Marys as fast as he could, trying to get in as many as possible before the inevitable.

Ernst did not believe he could have repented completely in the time available since the end of the war. No matter. He would meet Our Father as fully repentant in his heart as possible and with prayers for mercy on his lips.

35

Zalman hoped Barry did not think less of him. He wasn't able to stop himself from throwing up his hands and stepping away from the gun. The idea of it was so...repulsive. The worn, gaunt man, even if he was SS, could not even hurt a fly. The way Barry threw him around, like a doll, it did not seem possible he could have been a Nazi.

His refusal would not help the SS man, though. Barry pointed the huge pistol at the SS man's head. The night had become stagnant as it snowed steadily.

Zalman grew tense waiting for the "bang!" of the weapon. The others kept their positions: Barry, with his pistol in one hand, standing over the SS criminal and the criminal on his back, his lips moving as if in prayer.

He wondered if this Barry would shoot, like he had seen the Nazis shoot so many. Zalman thought he must have shot Jan's father and uncle at Rivka's house.

It did not bother Zalman a whit that Yankel's hangmen were dead or that this man might die in the next second. Just because he didn't care to kill the German didn't mean he gave a whit about the SS man's life.

Zalman was curious to see what Barry would do. Was it kosher to kill the SS man? Zalman wasn't a child. He understood Jan's family had murdered Yankel and would have gotten away with it if the American had not come by. This man, though. They were not sure what he had done or even if he was SS.

Did SS men pray, Zalman wondered as he watched the German's lips moving. The German had his eyes scrunched shut so tight it bared his teeth. Strange how quickly things had changed, he thought. Not long ago, it was Jews cowering, depending on prayer.

What will the American do?

Barry lowered the hammer of the pistol with his thumb, then he used the barrel to move his coat and jacket out of the way and holstered up.

"Get in," Barry ordered.

Zalman, forgetting the viola case, ran to the car and pushed the passenger seat forward, squishing Rivka. She uttered a bleat of protest.

Barry picked the case up and carried it to the trunk. Zalman could not see him anymore.

He shuddered with sudden fear and couldn't catch his breath. Zalman saw in his mind's eye the SS man, this German, with a submachine gun, spraying them with bullets, killing them all, and squeezed his eyes shut in an attempt to block the image.

The liftgate slammed shut, bringing Zalman back to the moment. The German lay on the ground, as before. Barry came into view and took a few steps toward the German. Then Barry threw a blanket at him! The Name be blessed. A minute ago, the American wanted to kill the SS criminal and now, the German gets a blanket.

Life can be confusing, Zalman thought.

Barry half fell into the driver's seat and asked a question in English that Zalman did not understand.

The rear bench seat was filled with things he had to shove aside to get comfortable. Riding on a soft bench in a warm automobile, instead of walking, would be a great treat. Zalman even felt scratchy wool blankets, promising a homey night's sleep for a change. He handled a can. Could it be a food tin?

His hunger made itself known as if it were a living thing gnawing at his insides. It was an old companion. He clutched the large can and jiggled it to test the contents.

Barry put the car in reverse and craned his head to see out the rear window. He caught sight of Zalman examining the can, then stopped, laughed and spoke in English as he reached over the seat.

Zalman reluctantly gave up his prize. Using a folding appliance, Barry severed one end of the can slow enough for Zalman to see how it was done.

"Food," Barry said in Yiddish, handing over the can and the little appliance itself.

Zalman wasted no time. He went at it with his fingers. It was cold, and it turned out to be meat and noodles with an interesting flavor. The car moved backward and stopped again.

Zalman looked up from his dinner. Barry leaned over the wheel, gazing at something out the windscreen.

"Idiot," he mused in Yiddish.

The German sat upright with the blanket balled up in his hands.

Barry yanked the gearshift into neutral, applied the parking brake and stormed over.

Zalman thought Barry would shoot the German after all.

Instead, he snatched the blanket and holding one side, launched it out into the night air. It spread out and fell as gently as the snow. He draped it over the German's shoulders then stamped his way back to the car.

"Damn it," Barry muttered, sitting still. "Should kill bastard."

What now? Zalman thought.

Barry came up with two more cans. He growled something Zalman didn't understand, but it sounded like a command.

He held out the empty can of noodles and meat.

"No," Barry said, annoyed. "Opener."

Zalman had a smaller can in his hand. He quickly opened it and only then gave the device back to Barry. Without even being able to see inside, he pulled at some kind of wrapping. He tore into one of the small packages and jammed a piece of something in his mouth. A taste from before the war. What was it? Caramel! Good, he thought.

Barry strode over to the German. He threw both cans at the man, startling him, and reached out for a hand. The German tried to scamper away, but Barry was too fast for him.

"Opener," Barry yelled, pressing the small metal tool into the man's captured hand.

Back in the car, Barry worked the gearshift lever, let up on the clutch and drove out of the field.

Maybe the killing was over for the night, Zalman thought. He chewed a fruit roll as they motored away from his hometown and he gave no thought whatsoever as to where they might be going.

36

Rivka did not say much on the ride back. Mostly Zalman peppered Barry with questions about America. By Barry, the cities were violent greedy places and the countryside was beautiful. As Rivka listened, she tried to plan out a future, but she could not see beyond their return to the DP camp. She wondered if she should start seeing Barry, or if that was even a choice.

She was not sure she wanted to marry him. He had some nice qualities, she thought. He took care of her, for instance. He was handsome and she knew he found her attractive. He could handle a problem almost as efficiently as a woman and he seemed to be able to make a living. There were other things, though.

He did not seem very dedicated to Torah.

Barry had shown a nascent interest in religion. He had at least paid attention to Rav Hirsch at the camp. On the trip, however, he had let Zalman, a boy brought up observant before the war, eat the American rations, even the spiced pork slices. In fact, Barry had eaten them himself. He smiled when she skipped the meat portions of her own servings. The bottom line was that he had not yet made any commitment to Jewish observance.

Rivka believed. Not because she was alive at the end, but because it felt right. Whatever the suffering had been for, Torah felt right to her.

There was something else. She had no enthusiasm for human relations. She knew it was a *mitzvah*, a commandment, to marry and have children, but she did not feel like it. All of her family was gone. As far as she knew, they had killed Yitzie Strasen, too. She and Zalman were the only Jews left of the Roszowice community. Her life from before was completely obliterated, and she faced a bleak future. Sadness weighed down her every thought and every move.

She rode in the passenger seat and took in the blur of fields and trees that flew by her windows.

They spent a night at an inn and enjoyed hot food.

And then they were back where they had started, at Gaufering, the DP camp. Barry pulled over and stopped the car. It was eleven o'clock at night. The winter wind rocked them to and fro, and Rivka could see thousands of stars in the clear sky. Ahead of them, the camp hulked in the distance.

"What next, sweetness?" he asked in Yiddish.

"Let's go to the camp and sleep." She failed to suppress a yawn.

"Can we eat first? I'm hungry," Zalman added, waking in the back.

"Sweetness, I can't stay," Barry said. "It is time for me to move on."

Rivka had been expecting this. She had come to realize he was finished at Gaufering. He had not mentioned leaving or named a destination, but she knew it in her heart. She acted as if it was news to her.

"Will the army let you go?" she asked innocently, already knowing the answer was immaterial.

"I am done with the army," Barry answered.

"And the camp? Who will run it?"

"Resnick will find another person."

"What will you do?"

"This and that."

"How will you live?"

"The Holy One, blessed is He, has provided."

"Where will you go?"

He grinned at her like a boy. "Where would you like to go?"

Unexpectedly, her heart soared and she smiled back.

"America?" she suggested hopefully.

Barry shook his head. "I cannot go back to America."

She did not ask why. It had been a long war. Unspeakable things had happened, probably everywhere. Even in America. She forced herself to concentrate on the future.

She countered with Palestine.

Rivka watched as he frowned, nodded, and finally shrugged in acceptance.

"Palestine," he agreed. He put the car in gear and they drove down to the camp.

37

Barry unlocked the gate and let the Hudson idle its way forward in first gear to Rivka's barracks. The tires crunched the dirt as they rode between the wooden buildings, up to her door.

"Be ready to go right at dawn, okay?" he said.

Rivka bobbed her head, gathered her jacket and her small bag.

"Where should I find you?" she asked.

"I'll come get you. We will leave early, okay?"

"Oh-kay."

Barry and Zalman made their way to the administration building the same way they had come in, slow and quiet. They took the only sleeping bag for Barry and blankets for Zalman and walked upstairs to the dark office.

Barry rolled his bag out on the floor, behind the desk Howie (the jerky clerk Barry had replaced) had used. He draped his coat and jacket over the chair and his tie and shirt joined them. Both holstered pistols ended up on the seat of the chair and he stripped down to his trousers and undershirt. Once inside the sleeping bag, the floor felt a little firm, but waves of exhaustion washed over him.

Zalman had not moved from where he had stopped after they first entered. He had not even taken off his coat. Not that Barry gave a shit. He closed his eyes, resolving to ignore the boy.

The resolution did not last.

"So?" Barry asked.

"I have to go to the toilet."

"Downstairs."

Zalman didn't reply. His eyes darted from side to side.

"What?" Barry barked.

"Could you show me?"

Crap, he thought. He put his shoes on without socks and led Zalman to the facilities. Once again upstairs, he zipped himself into the sleeping bag. The boy came back fidgety, taking forever to quiet down. Just as Barry began to drift off, someone banged on the downstairs door.

"Who's there?" Zalman asked.

"How the hell do I know?" Barry spat in English as he unzipped the sleeping bag and put on his shoes again.

He took one of the pistols with him. Rivka was at the door, and he let her in. Mrs. Levenson surprised him, trooping in with Mrs. Kugel and the woman who had hit Manny (Manny!) with her purse that day. Some younger women came in as well. They all wore coats over nightshirts. Many used kerchiefs to cover their hair.

"What?" Barry asked Rivka sharply.

"Rivka says you will take her to Palestine," Mrs. Levenson interjected. "Is this true?"

"What the hell business is it of yours?" he argued in English.

She glared at him.

He switched to Yiddish. "It is not your business."

"It is if you don't come get her in the morning or leave her halfway there."

"You said he would have left by now," Rivka mocked, then to Barry, "She said you would leave me."

"I have not left. I am not leaving you. I am leaving *early*. With or without you. Let's all go to sleep."

"We want to go," Mrs. Levenson declared suddenly.

"You do? So go!"

"We want to go with you!"

Before he could answer, the men marched in.

"What now?" Barry slipped his pistol into his waistband.

Rav Hirsch led the way, followed by Shammi and Gutkin. Noach Gesser was there and the leaders of the Zionist groups, both the religious and non-religious, came in as well. All the men were in trousers and coats.

"I suppose you want to go also," Barry posed sarcastically.

"Go where?" Rav Hirsch asked. "Is somebody going somewhere?"

"Never mind. What do you want?"

"Some men came to the camp, asking for you. They were German police. We told them nothing." Rav Hirsch beamed with satisfaction.

Barry grinned back.

"That being said, Sergeant Rosen," Rav Hirsch continued, his melancholy expression returning, "we are somewhat curious as to why they think you are involved."

"Involved in what?"

"He's going to Palestine tomorrow," Mrs. Levenson blurted out.

"With our Rivka," Mrs. Kugel added.

"*Eretz Yisrael*," Rav Hirsch murmured reverently, saying "the Land of Israel" in Hebrew.

"You want to come?" Barry asked.

"How are you going to get there?" Rav Hirsch quizzed. "How are you going to get around the British?"

It was common knowledge the British were not easing their restrictions on Jewish immigration into Mandate Palestine.

"It will be swanky," Barry chuckled. "We are going in high style. So high, no one will stop us. It will be cramped in the car until we can get a bigger one, but I got room for Rivka, Zalman, you and your two guys. What do you say?"

"And the rest of us?" Mrs. Levenson wanted to know.

"I'll come back for you," he lied, mostly to shut her up.

She looked at him doubtfully.

Smart dame, he thought.

Rav Hirsch changed the subject. "Four men were killed in town. The

German police seem to think you know something of these four men. Why do you think that is?"

"And Palestine, Grandfather? Are you coming?"

The rav and his two scholars conversed among themselves.

"How are we going to get our black-market supplies?" Mrs. Levenson asked.

Barry had no idea. In fact, he didn't care. He said the first thing that came to mind. "The Black American soldier will bring them. It will be fine."

Rivka smiled at him.

"So, we will go to *Eretz Yisrael*," Rav Hirsch pronounced.

"Excellent. I'll come get you," Barry checked his watch, "at four in the morning. Now, everybody out. I need to sleep."

38

Corporal Fredrick Montgomery of the US Army's Criminal Investigative Division rode shotgun as Master Sergeant Walter Gonzales drove too fast in a southerly direction out of Munich. Fred usually handled the routine chores but today the boss had claimed the keys to their staff car, which the two men matched nicely in their khaki shirts and trousers, neckties and sidearms.

The flat landscape changed to rolling hills under a blue sky filled with puffy white clouds. The sight of a fairytale farmhouse triggered a stab of great joy in him, at his being alive to see the Bavarian countryside. Eventually, they blew through Furstflarn. As they left the city center, a tan coupe sped by in the opposite direction.

"Was that a Hudson?" Walter asked.

"I think so," Fred said. "I think it was. What's a Hudson doing here?"

"Dunno."

Walter checked the receding Hudson in the rearview mirror as they drove on. He began to chew the inside of his cheek.

"Should we chase them down?" he pondered aloud. "That was him, betcha."

Fred kept quiet.

"Bet that was him fleeing. Bet that son-of-a-bitch guessed we was coming and flew the coop."

"Are we going to get him?"

"Where'd he find a dash-burned Hudson coupe, for God's sake? We should. We should, but I don't want to be late for our appointment. We had to wait long enough for it. What a pompous ass." Walter chewed on his cheek a little more. "Damn!" He hit the wheel with the heel of his hand.

Fred knew the pompous ass was the fake ambassador.

They drove into the camp and parked in front of the administration building. He stepped out and immediately felt a thickness in the cold air. There was some kind of palpable mournful feeling floating around.

"What's up?" Walter asked, looking up and down the camp's main dirt road. "Something's up. What is it?"

"Don't know."

"Might as well go in and find out, I guess." Walter slammed the car door and headed for the entrance.

Fred followed. Once inside, they saw the administration staff grouped together behind their high counter. Some of the women were weeping. They ignored the two CID men. A tap on Fred's shoulder got his attention; his partner pointed to the stairs. At the top, they found a tall, trim man in his mid-thirties, his brown hair disheveled and his face unshaved, rifling through papers.

"Who're you?" he demanded, holding a sloppy pile of onion skins in each hand.

"Master Sergeant Gonzales and Corporal Montgomery of the Military Police," Walter replied. "We have an appointment with Ambassador Resnick. Who're you?"

"Ambassador Resnick. I'm the director of this camp."

"No, you're not."

"Pardon me?"

"You're not an ambassador. You were some kind of embassy staff guy, but not an ambassador. Maybe you're the director here, maybe not. But you're definitely the guy we came to see. We got your letter."

"You idiots!" he screamed, waving the onion skins. "You just missed him! They just left! Him, my secretary and some dumb kid they picked up in Poland. Why the hell didn't you stop him?"

"Why should we?" Walter affected a bored demeanor.

"Why should you? How about because he took over the black market of the camp, hell, the whole town, days after he got here? Because he beat up our supply foreman? Because he runs an illegal club and hires underage girls to work there so he can blackmail his clientele? You should go get him over all that rigmarole! That's why!"

"Well, what of it? Did you tolerate the black-market problem you had here before Sergeant Rosen showed up? And exactly how did you find out there are child whores at the illegal club?"

Resnick let the onion skins fall to the desk, took several dejected steps to a nearby chair, and dropped into it. Fred saw the resignation all over his face.

"Sometimes the State Department awards the title 'ambassador' to men that haven't actually led an embassy," Resnick said.

"But that ain't you, either," Walter stated with finality. "My partner here noticed the camp seems a little out of sorts. I think so, too. What's going on?"

"It's Rav Hirsch."

"What happened to Mr. Hirsch?"

"No, no...it's a title. Rav Hirsch. Rabbi Hirsch, like a Jewish priest. He was the spiritual leader of the Jews in the camp. He died in his sleep last night."

"I'm sorry to hear it. My condolences."

Resnick gave Walter a lopsided smile, nodded his thanks, and waved away the comment. "He was well liked. Everyone respected him, even if they weren't religious—"

"Like the guys going to the whores?"

The question changed Resnick's smile to a grimace.

"Yes, like them," he agreed. "Anyway, Rav Hirsch was a learned man. Before the war, he was a *Rosh Yeshiva*, a head of a religious school in Lithuania. He had hundreds of students, not to mention nine children and even grandchildren before the Germans came. He and two students made it out. His wife, children, everything gone."

Walter frowned.

"Last night," Resnick said, "Rosen and Rivka came back."

"What's a Rivka? Came back from where?"

"What's a...not 'what' but 'who.' Rivka means Rebecca. Rivka Shapiro, my secretary." Resnick explained it slowly, as if Walter was a mental defective. "They said they couldn't find her brother, and then without so much as a pause, they announced they were leaving."

"Leaving? Where are they going? When you say 'came back,' where did they come back from?"

"Poland. He took Rivka to Poland to look for her brother."

"When did they leave for Poland?"

"A week ago yesterday."

"Right after the Munich shooting?"

"What Munich shooting?"

"Never mind. What do you know about the bodies they found on the road?"

"What? Huh? I know the mayor says they were gangsters."

"So then, they were leaving—"

"Who was leaving?" Resnick interrupted, confused.

"Rosen and Rivka. R and R. Like rest and recuperation. Did this Rav Hirsch try to stop them?"

"Huh? Oh, on the contrary," Resnick said, resuming his narrative stride. "Rav Hirsch and his surviving students planned to go with them. They said they were going to Palestine. Couldn't Sergeant Rosen get in trouble for that? Going AWOL or desertion or something?"

"Not really. I wanted to ask you, this Rosen, he was real tall and smooth faced?"

Fred thought that was a great trick, to give the Ambassador the wrong description, to see what would happen.

"No, more like average or even a little short, with a scar on his jaw," Resnick said.

Ah-ha, Fred thought. That's our guy.

"Yeah," Walter said, dragging out the word, "see, that Rosen, he discharged-in-place in Austria. He wasn't in the army anymore. In fact, your camp wasn't supposed to have an army administrator after the last guy. The position was phased out."

"We were never told," Resnick said.

"So what happened then? To the old rav?"

"He died in his sleep, last night. He died. I can't believe it. They went to wake him and he was dead. He looked like he was asleep. Rivka was distraught."

"Was she?"

"Yes. She wanted to stay for the funeral, but Rosen insisted they go. They left minutes ago. Literally. You may have seen them as you drove in."

Walter didn't respond. The silence curdled. Resnick, pretending to ignore the CID agents, rustled some onion skins. Finally, he rose.

"Well, if you will excuse me, I guess I have to see to the displaced persons," he said.

"Of course, Mr. Resnick," Walter agreed. "The displaced persons."

Resnick walked to the steps, stopping at the top to say, "I, I don't know anything about child prostitutes in town," without turning around.

Fred and Walter exchanged glances. Walter struggled to squelch a smile.

Resnick paused a moment longer before starting down the wooden stairs.

Walter broke the silence in the office. "He don't know nothing. Right. Hey Fred, you think this Rosen fellow killed the old guy?"

EPILOGUE

Mediterranean Sea, South of Cyprus, 1946

Passed Midshipman Douglas Lewellyn-Hoag of the Royal Navy cursed the bloody blockade duty off the coast of Palestine and the bloody Jews who made it so bloody necessary.

"Shall it be the port side then, sir?" Petty Officer Ramson inquired.

"Quite," Douglas said. Ramson was a good sort, if a dullard.

He silently cursed the bright sun and calm blue Mediterranean Sea. They were all in Royal Navy tropical white uniforms, the men in square-neck short sleeve pullovers and shorts and Douglas wearing an officer's short-sleeved, button-down blouse.

Ramson, as coxswain, directed the rowing of the whitewashed whaleboat toward a fine white motor yacht with a plumb bow and champagne-glass stern, hove-to under the three-inch naval guns of HMS Aubry, a Captain-class frigate late of anti-submarine duty in the North Atlantic.

Late was quite the fashionable word, thought Douglas. He had been late in birth, making him tardy to the family succession. His brother Tiggy had beaten him to be the firstborn son *and* had survived the bloody Commandos. Rotten luck.

The timing of his birth made him late for the war as well: the meaningful combat had ended before he had finished training. He had even been unpunctual for bad weather. Since he reported aboard the Aubry, his first assignment in the fleet, the Med had presented a raging two-foot, gently spaced swell.

Oh, but he could be quite on time to search this bloody yacht for bloody Jews, even if this boarding would cause them to miss dinner. That, on top of his having dawdled coming off morning watch and missing breakfast.

Douglas's stomach rumbled. His sailors snickered.

Ramson, of the broad shoulders and narrow waist, brought them smartly alongside. Douglas pulled his own childish shoulders and pimply face up onto the yacht's weather deck. Ramson came up next and the balance of the whaleboat's men came up after them.

The yacht's crew, a smart short man in whites and a captain's cap flanked by two elderly hands, lined up to the right. The passengers were loosely grouped on the fantail. The closest passenger, a trim man of average height, wore a lightweight white suit, black tie and Panama hat. A woman in a modest crème linen dress and matching broad-brimmed hat sat on a settee that stretched the full width of the yacht. Next to her sat a boy in a white shirt and khaki shorts. A pitcher of lemonade and a number of glasses were on a low table. The man in the suit came forward.

"Good morning, Lieutenant," he said, sounding American. "Welcome aboard."

"It's 'Passed Midshipman,' guv," one of his sailors offered.

Anger rushed through Douglas like a hideous infection. He choked back his urge to yell at the man. It was entirely fair that he be mistaken for a Lieutenant.

"Good morning," Douglas said to the man in the white suit. "Do apologize for the inconvenience, but we will need to see papers. Please wait while I speak to the captain."

The man waved companionably and faded back. Douglas dealt with the captain and crew, bloody frogs all. None of his sailors were present and he found them gathered at the small table drinking lemonade. The woman served them, smiling with her lips closed.

"*Mister* Ramson, shall we not search this vessel?" Douglas tried for a severe tone and started well, but his voice cracked on the word "vessel."

"Very well, sir. Stem to stern now, lads."

The men put down their glasses, winked at the woman, and spread out across the deck.

Bloody ratings.

"Don't be too hard on them, Lieutenant," the male passenger said, walking forward. "My wife did so want to entertain."

This time, there were hints of Canada in his speech. Bloody colonials. He wished they would get their own damnable accents right.

"Ian Mackenzie." The man shoved his hand out, probably wanting a "shake."

Horrid colonial habit, Douglas thought. He ignored the outstretched hand.

"Is this your vessel?" Douglas asked, with as much gravity and maturity as he could muster, clasping his hands behind his back in the manner of his father, the marquess.

"No. I've engaged it for a trip from Marseilles to Palestine."

Mackenzie did not strike Douglas as a Mackenzie. He thought this man presented more like a bloody Mediterranean type. Greek, Italian or, heaven forbid, a bloody Jew.

"I see. What would be the purpose of your visit?"

"My wife is a Jewess, and she would like to see the sights before we take a liner to Canada."

"Very well. Your papers?" Douglas stuck out his own hand with the complete expectation of compliance.

Mackenzie smiled. He reached into his upper left suit pocket and produced them. He had a Canadian passport. Douglas checked the picture and squinted at his face, noticing the scar along his jaw line. Douglas forced his eyes from the scar to the other papers.

"You and your wife are Canadian and your son isn't?"

"My wife and her brother, Lieutenant. They are both displaced persons —Hebrews, you know—at the hands of the Nazis, eh? My wife is Canadian by virtue of our marriage, and we are waiting for her brother's passport to come through."

Douglas could not get his mind off the scar. It was bleached white. He wondered how Mackenzie had gotten it. Had he been in the war?

"Lieutenant?" Mackenzie prompted.

"What! Ah, yes?"

"Care for a drink?"

The two men crossed to the small table. The man with the scar poured from the pitcher Douglas's sailors had significantly depleted. Realizing he had become thirsty under the biting sun, he drank deeply.

"Tasty." He drank again, gulping the sweet cool liquid and soon felt a pleasant warmth spread out from his stomach.

"If I may," Douglas asked, surprising himself, "where did you get that scar?"

"A gift from the krauts," Mackenzie said, worrying a silver holder of some kind.

"What's that?" He heard his own speech slurring.

"Cigar. Want one?"

He thought he very much wanted one. He would enjoy a cigar on the quarterdeck in the hot sun while the men searched.

Mackenzie handed him the silver item. A *Reichsadler*, the imperial eagle with a swastika, had been etched across three connected oblong chambers. Douglas pulled off the cap and removed a cigar.

"Wait." Mackenzie deftly clipped the tip from the rounded end.

Douglas felt happy. He giggled.

"Light?" His host chuckled companionably and ignited a shiny Zippo.

Douglas put the cigar in his mouth and leaned into the flame. A few puffs later, he managed to produce a respectable fragrant cloud.

"What happened to that middle tube, if I may?"

"Stabbed a kraut in the chest. It caught him right there." Mackenzie pointed to the damaged center cylinder. "Lucky bastard, eh?"

Douglas thought for a minute. That couldn't be correct. The deck lurched and he fell into his host.

"Easy sailor."

"But if you have it," Douglas said, returning the case, "the German could not have been lucky, could he?"

"Not in the end, no."

This man had killed someone, not from a ship, behind steel plate, but face-to-face! Just like Tiggy! Douglas puffed on his cigar. His sailors began to cluster on the fantail with the meaningless purposefulness of the lower ranks.

He started to feel queasy. Funny, the weather didn't seem to be deteriorating. The men—gobbing off as usual—suddenly annoyed him. He opened his mouth to speak sharply, but instead, the lemonade came shooting up from his stomach. He barely made it to the rail before vomiting a stream of liquid over the side, his cigar riding it to the brine.

He felt most demeaned and wiped his lips on his forearm. The sailors studiously ignored him, shocked expressions on some of their faces. Ramson smiled, as always. Bloody idiot.

One of the men snickered. Another giggled and then the whole gaggle burst into laughter. Douglas burned with embarrassment.

"As you were!" Mackenzie shouted.

The loud command, issued in a manner brooking no disobedience, silenced the sailors.

"This man is your officer," the Canadian continued. "You owe at least his rank respect. If this were my regiment, I'd smack the snot out of all of you. Get off my boat."

Ramson hurried the crew over the side.

Douglas felt some measure of relief as they filed into the whaleboat. As he followed, he shot a grateful glance at Mackenzie, who, puffing on his cigar, nodded in return.

"Shove off!" Ramson ordered.

The men pulled across the bright blue sea for the Aubry. Douglas risked a last, over-the-shoulder observation from his perch on the rear bench. The yacht had started to move, motoring slowly for the Holy Land. The passenger in his white suit and Panama hat watched them from the fantail.

Douglas waved.

The scarred man he knew as Mackenzie did not.

AUTHOR'S NOTE

The American organized crime juggernaut that became *La Cosa Nostra* (LCN) is well-documented and studied, as is its absorption or elimination of other ethnic criminal enterprises coming out of the thirties. Richard "The Boot" Boiardo and Abner "Longy" Zwillman were real gangsters who worked to spread the LCN in Newark, New Jersey and the Meyer-Meyer Gang can be seen as surviving as an independent criminal enterprise in their neighborhood just a little bit longer than the others (see *Tough Jews: Fathers, Sons, And Gangster Dreams,* by Rich Cohen [Vintage 1998] and *But - He Was Good to His Mother: The Lives and Crimes of Jewish Gangsters*, by Robert A. Rockaway [Gefen 1993]).

The First Special Service Force (FSSF) was a real unit in World War Two and existed as described. Its battle history includes documented operations in the Pacific-Asian, Mediterranean and European Theaters of War. Today, many Canadian and American special operations units officially trace their linage to the FSSF. The credibility of Barry's claims regarding his service therein is left to the reader to evaluate.

Strongly held disparate views on all issues is a common trait within the Jewish community, then and now.

Poland was a country beset by enemies, and Poles were under great pressure from 1939 on. Poland moved from freedom to Nazi tyranny to

Soviet tyranny in six years, and the aftermath of World War Two brought no relief—Soviet subjugation lasted until 1989. While there was cooperation with both Nazi and Soviet exploiters, and the murder of returning Jews did occur in the immediate postwar period, there were instances of impressive Polish heroism in the face of the horrors afflicting Polish society, including women such as Irena Sendler (see https://collections.yadvashem.org/en/righteous/4017433), and Rivka alludes to another such righteous person in SHADOW TRADES. Yad Vashem, the World Holocaust Remembrance Center in Jerusalem, Israel, lists 3,866 Polish citizens recognized Righteous Among Nations for their work helping Jews during the Holocaust.

It is not hard to find equally impressive examples of Polish patriotism and dedication to the rule of law and universal human rights from the war and postwar periods. A notable example is Captain Witold Pilecki of the Polish Cavalry, who, among his many operational achievements, infiltrated the Auschwitz Concentration Camp to collect intelligence and organize resistance and then escaped in 1943 to report his findings. He continued his exemplary service to Poland throughout and after the war, until caught by forces under Soviet control and executed in 1948 (see *A Captain's Portrait: Witold Pilecki - Martyr For Truth*, by Adam J. Koch [Freedom 2018]).

Ernst Hoffman becomes one of the estimated 18 million Germans and ethnic Germans on the move after World War Two. Most were expelled civilian ethnic Germans, citizens of countries other than Germany. Prisoners of war under Soviet control found it difficult to unilaterally return home. It is estimated that three million Germans and ethnic Germans died of non-natural causes before they could arrive in Germany between 1945 and 1950 (see, for example, *Orderly and Humane: The Expulsion of the Germans after the Second World War*, by RM Douglas [Yale University Press 2012]).

From the effective end of the ancient Jewish independent nation-state in 70 AD, the territory between the Jordan River and the Mediterranean Sea, south of what would become Lebanon and north of the Sinai Peninsula, was under the control of the Eastern Roman Empire, the Byzantine Empire, the Ottoman Empire, and from 1917 AD, the British Empire. During the post-World War Two period, The British Government had a difficult time adjudicating the demands of the many constituencies involved, and one of the outcomes was heavily restricted Jewish immigration into the area the Romans and British called Palestine. Barry uses an innovative and expensive tactic to evade immigration controls (see *One Palestine, Complete: Jews and Arabs Under the British Mandate*, by Tom Segev [Metropolitan 2000]).

ACKNOWLEDGMENTS

I am forever grateful to my first reader and editor, champion, and wife, Susie.

GLOSSARY

(E) English, (G) German, (H) Hebrew, (I) Italian, (P) Polish, (R) Russian, (Y) Yiddish

Ashrei (H): An important prayer in the Jewish daily, sabbath, and holiday services, made up of mostly Psalm 145.
Bar mitzvah (H): Lit. "son of commandment," meaning a Jewish boy's passage, automatically on his thirteenth birthday, whether recognized by others or not, from the status of being a minor to his majority in the eyes of Jewish law. Commonly used to refer to the practice of publicly demonstrating religious competence in the prayer service, followed by a celebration.
Beis (H): House, as in "House of..."
Boychick (Y): American Yiddish, from the English "boy" and Yiddish diminutive ending "—*tshik*."
Bubbeh (Y): Grandmother
Burgermeister (G): Lit. "master of citizens," the city manager
Capiche (I): American Italian slang for "you understand," from the Italian *capisci*, meaning the same thing.
Cheder (Y, H): Lit. "room," a traditional Jewish elementary school teaching students until bar mitzvah.

Dybbuk (Y): An evil spirit that possesses a person.

Einsatzgruppen (G): Lit. "deployment groups, " circa WWII. Mass execution units of the Nazi regime sent into Eastern Europe and Russia behind the army to kill communities deemed enemies of Nazi Germany, staffed primarily by *Schutzstaffel* (SS) and Security Police personnel.

Farshsteyn (Y): Understand

Feldgrau (G): The green-gray color of German *Heer* uniforms and material in World War II

Frau Perchta (G): A winter goddess in Germanic and alpine paganism.

Gemara (H): The Talmud is a compendium of Jewish oral law, so called because the devout believe this body of regulations was transmitted directly to Moses by God on Mount Sinai and not recorded; it was passed on orally until it became historically expedient to write it down. It is made up of two separate works published together. The Mishna is the older of the two, stating the law, and the Gemara follows, explaining and expanding ideas present in the Mishna.

Geschäftsinhaber (G): Business owner

Gonif (Y): Thief, grifter, person of low or no moral character (masculine)

Hashem (H): Lit. "The Name," a useful euphemism for God, used by the Jewish devout.

Heer (G): Army

Minyan (H): Quorum of ten Jewish men necessary for prayer services, according to Jewish law, with gender at issue in some congregations today.

Mishnah (H): See Gemara, above

Mitzvah (H): Commandment

Niftar (H and Y): Dead, with a connotation similar to "having passed away."

Nu (Y): Lit. "so," but a word of universal usage, meaning whatever the speaker intends, from "so" itself to "where have you been?" to "let's get going," to anything else in context.

Nudnik (Y): A pest, nag or bore

Papasha (R): Lit "daddy," common slang for the Soviet PPSh submachine gun, routinely loaded with a 71 round drum magazine, and so used here.

Parashas Kedoshim (H): Jews read from the Torah every sabbath of the year. Each individual portion is called a *parsha* and has a name. *Parshas Kedoshim* begins at Leviticus 19:2.

Rashi: (H): acronym identifying Shlomo Yitzchaki, a medieval French rabbi of great renown.
Rathaus (G): Town Hall
Rav (H): Rabbi
Reb (Y): Equivalent of "mister"
Rosh (H): First, head or chief
Selektion (G): Selection. Used here as used by staff at the Nazi death camps to refer to the process of choosing inmates for forced labor or mass murder.
Shaygets (Y): Unbeliever (masculine)
Shabbos (Y): The Sabbath, an important, biblically mandated holiday that, for Jews, occurs weekly on Saturday.
Schutzstaffel (G): Lit. "protection squadron," circa WWII, a paramilitary formation with personal protection, security and direct combat missions, including the administration and operations of concentration and death camps and related activities. Often referred to as the "SS."
Siddur (H): From the Hebrew root for "order," a *siddur* is a Jewish book of prayer and supporting materials.
Shul (Y): Lit. "school," synagogue, a Jewish house of worship
Smicha (H): Ordination
SNAFU (E): American slang acronym, originating with soldiers, standing for "Situation Normal, All Fouled Up." The "F" is editable to indicate higher levels of frustration or for personal preference.
Tak (P): Yes, agreement
Treyf (Y): Unkosher food, therefore food not proper for Jews to consume.
Tsoris (Y): bother, trouble
Tzedakah (H): Lit. "righteousness," also commonly meaning charity, and so used herein.
Wehrmacht (G): Lit. "Defense Force," the term for the German military, circa 1935-45. (*Bundeswehr*, lit. "Federal Defense," today).
Yeshiva (H): Lit. "sitting," a school, traditionally for men, between bar mitzvah and marriageable age.
Zaydeh (Y): Grandfather

ABOUT THE AUTHOR

Mitch Stern is an attorney and consultant, and has served as an FBI Special Agent, a police officer and investigator, and in the Marine Corps. He lives in Maryland with his family.

To find out more about Mitch's books, visit:
severnriverbooks.com/collections/mitch-stern